THE
SECURITY

SCOTT BUTLER

For Vader, the lord of calm,
loyalty and a family's best friend.
Gone, but not forgotten.

PROLOGUE

'Don't lie to me!' she screamed, backing into a chair as she fought off his advance.

The chair's skinny rear legs slid across the floor before it tipped sideways. She landed in a heap on the floor, her head hitting the timber boards.

'I ain't lyin', he shouted back.

She sat up, rubbing her head where she'd struck it. Blood was smeared across her hand. 'Then you're stupid.'

'Fuck knows I musta been to 'ave married you!' he spat back.

'Say what you want, but I know you're lying,' she said from the floor, pulling matted strings of hair away from her face. 'Sh-she was there – wasn't she?'

'Who's she?'

'That girl. Lana, or whatever her goddamn name is!' She got to her feet.

He took a step back. 'Don't know what you're talkin' about. Pile o' shit, as usual.'

'You say it in your sleep ya know. You talk about her.'

'Stop talkin' 'bout nuthin', he replied, wiping a sleeve across his mouth.

She took a step towards him. 'Sayin' how good it all feels. Goin' on about what you're gonna do to her. How do you think that makes me feel?'

'Who fuckin' knows? It's like living with a goddamn fridge!'

He stood over her now, the tendons in his arms and neck standing out, his stomach bloated, strained against his stained light-blue shirt.

He was drunk. The child could smell him from where she sat. Her head was pulled down, turtle-like, eyes peeping out from almost-closed fingers, as she sat peering between the wooden banisters. It must be Thursday. Pa always got paid on Thursdays. He'd celebrate as he always did – by drinking.

Her mother was crying now, tears mingling with blood, saliva running from the corner of her mouth.

Her lower lip wobbled itself into speech. 'You slept with her, didn't you?' She stared at the floor as she spoke.

'Why do you care?'

'Because you did the same to me, before you left your wife.'

He struck her. Her head hit the floor, harder this time. A dish fell from the table above her and smashed into pieces that flew to each corner of the kitchen.

The child cried out. Both faces turned towards her.

'Now look what ya gone and done,' he said, his face screwed up like cloth. 'Ya happy now?' He crossed the room. 'Clean this shit up. I'm goin' ta bed. Don't wake me when ya come up.'

He walked up the stairs, clipping the child over the head. 'Stop pokin' ya nose inta things what got nuthin' to do with ya. Now get ta bed!' He carried on past, then slammed his bedroom door.

The child watched her mother crying on the floor, hiding her face. Finally she got unsteadily to her feet. She folded her pale green robe across her chest and began to clean up, collecting pieces of the broken plate from the floor. She stood in front of the rubbish bin, crying as she emptied the pieces into it. Her body shook, and blood ran freely down the side of her face now. The rubbish bin lid flopped shut as she turned away from it, removing her foot from its pedal, a large jagged piece of white porcelain clenched in her right hand.

Her mother looked like a robot now, placing one foot in front of the other as she headed for the stairs.

The child ran for her bedroom, pulling the door almost shut, peeping through the gap. Her mother paused on the landing outside her room. She caught a glimpse of the porcelain's sharp edge, the pale hand holding it now covered in blood as she pulled the door closed with the other.

The child lay down on her bed, listening in the darkness. She pulled the pillow down hard over her head as the screaming started.

1.

'Why are you here?' said a voice above me.

My eyes opened slowly, reluctantly, letting in a slither of the dawn light coming through the wooden shades behind her. My head was fuzzy from sleep.

'I'm here because I need to be,' I replied, rubbing tired eyes. My mind had kept me up again.

'For what purpose?'

I drew breath in and pushed it out slowly, ran fingers through hair cut short. 'To rebuild and strengthen, to grow my mind … and body.'

She was standing still in the pale light, a silhouette that didn't move when she spoke.

'To what end?'

I hesitated, hearing myself breathing, feeling my lungs rising and falling, the muscles in my stomach aching from yesterday's exertions. My heart beat steadily in its chest. My throat was dry, raw, as it usually was when I woke.

'For a future.'

'What does it look like?'

I pushed myself up. 'Something safe, stable … present and clear.'

She moved closer towards me. 'What doesn't it have?'

'A past.'

Madam Rai placed a cool wet cloth over my face, blotted the side of my temples where sweat had been running.

'Good. Keep your mind clear. Only then can we fill it with things that matter. Things that make a difference for who you need to be. They're right in front of you, not behind. Start with water today.'

I nodded, stood, then bowed to her as she left.

I dressed quickly, pulling on the white robes I wore every day. Two wooden pales had been strung onto a brace that sat across my shoulders.

At the top of a ladder of stone stairs was a waterfall with a pool at its base. There were one hundred and fifteen steps. I counted them on the way up, scooped up water and stepped them out back down. I'd bathe today, though only once the wooden tub was full and heated.

Thirty-one, thirty-two, three … four. My cold legs gradually warmed to the task as I climbed. My feet were naked, frozen, though hardened from the hundreds of thousands of steps I had taken. Ninety-eight, ninety-nine, one hundred … one, two.

I could always hear it before my face felt its spray. Water tumbled over the cliff above me into the deep freshwater pool at its base. How many times had I done this? I pushed the thought away, took the wooden brace from my shoulders and filled each bucket.

The water was cold today. My reflection rippled on its surface. I was thinner than I'd ever been. I stretched my arms, rolled my wrists and felt my shoulders snap back into position.

It was gray overhead as I made my descent. Daylight was coming, though there would be no golden morning shafts or blue sky today. I did my best to keep the buckets steady. The steps became harder to navigate with water on them. I could see a column of gray smoke below me. She had lit a fire inside. I ignored thoughts of a hot shower, the modern kitchen, the television, the satellite dish on the roof below. *None of it matters, it's not for you. Clear your mind. Forget. Do what you're asked to do. Be present.*

It was midday by the time I'd emptied the last of the buckets into the tub Madame Rai had prepared for me. It was full to the brim. Stones had been placed in a circle beneath it, and kindling had been stacked in a small pyramid in its center. I looked at the wood pile; it was getting low.

'Eat this before you chop wood,' she said, handing me a bowl of rice.

I took my time, eager to eat, though disciplined to ensure it happened slowly. I had lost meals before. I chewed the rice until it became paste, siphoned the flavor from each grain before I swallowed.

Once it was gone, I made my way to the wood shed, ran my hands over the wheel-shaped slice of wood I had sawn from a tree. A chainsaw hung on the wall. No such luxury was afforded to me. I took up the axe, tested its edge, found it blunt and spent the next hour sharpening it with a heavy file that had been placed next to it.

It was almost dark by the time I'd chopped and stacked the wood. My hands felt rough to the touch, skin raw, cut up across the palms of my hands.

'Come with me. Light the fire,' said Madame Rai.

She placed a box of long Big Red matches on the table in front of me, but pointed at the sticks beside the tub. I took wood shavings from the small box of kindling, added splinters of wood and worked the sticks hard until they sparked, willing the box of matches to disappear, ignoring the thought of how easy it would be to just open them.

I'd been punished before. Patience is a virtue. The wood shavings caught. I added the wood splinters, then carried the flame to the small pyramid of wood beneath the tub. I carefully added larger pieces to the pile, watched carefully as they too gave up their energy.

'Now we train.'

The sun was long gone by the time she'd finished with me. My arms hung in loose ribbons, my back ached and my feet were sore. I took the robe off and lowered myself carefully into the tub, the water now steaming. I cupped my hands and poured it over my head, down my neck, kneaded the pain from the parts of my body I could reach. I ran an index finger over the thin puckered scar that ran across the base of my stomach and stared into space. I pushed thoughts from my head, focused on the warmth, the feeling of now.

I was ushered out of the tub before it cooled. I dressed, tied back what little hair I had left and went to my small room, detached from the main house. I sat on the floor, legs folded under a small table and waited to be served. A platter of raw fish, steamed legumes and a bowl of rice. I watched the steam rise, waited for the door to close before starting. I ate slowly, as before.

Now clean and fed, I placed the tray outside my door. I knelt in front of a candle beside my bed, bent my head and whispered, 'to rebuild and strengthen, to grow my mind and body.'

I blew it out and lay in the dark, spent.

2.

The car came out of nowhere, though Hadley clocked it all the same. It was a large gray SUV, a Cherokee, or something close to it. He'd noticed it because the revs were high, the engine was screaming and the tires squealed as it approached his armored vehicle.

It swerved across two lanes to join them on the I-80 Scranton to New York highway. Toronto was a long way away. He knew how this worked. They'd attempt to stop him by targeting one of the rear tires with a shotgun, or use the car itself to take it out. The latter would be risky, so he checked his rearview to see if a gun appeared. No sign of one yet.

He was sitting alongside the driver, a new recruit he'd met a few months back who'd worked security for several years. He'd come highly recommended, though Hadley knew none of his sources, so he'd called around and cross referenced them all the same. He'd checked out fine.

His name was Paul. He'd been a bouncer, and while he was a little arrogant, he seemed fairly harmless. He could handle himself, which was the first thing to test in any recruit.

The safety deposit boxes were welded to the floor and the surrounding bodywork of the vehicle. Steel plates three-inches thick wouldn't yield their contents easily. Inside were diamonds, the pink variety the black market loved, and there were lots of them. A dealer in Toronto had secured them from a buyer in New York, who had repatriated them from an illicit deal through the courts.

Hadley had been warned by other teams that with all the publicity around the case, they would be targeted. He'd asked by whom, and was told he could probably take his pick.

He pulled on the cuffs of his leather gloves, tested the seatbelt to make sure it was firm.

He didn't ask Paul if he'd seen them. He took hold of the handle grip bolted to the truck's ceiling and leaned into the door, waiting for the shift he knew Paul would make. Evasive action would mean the opposite here. If you could see the move happening, you needed to disrupt it by forcing them into it earlier, to catch them off guard.

Paul spun the steering wheel to his right, and Hadley braced himself as they collided with the side of the SUV. He heard the screech of metal on metal. The SUV bounced into a sedan alongside it. The sedan was turned and forced into the following traffic.

The gun was out now and the shots started coming.

They drove on, Paul swinging the truck from side to side so they wouldn't be easy to pinpoint. Traffic peeled left and right, clearing the way for them.

'Get off the highway, Paul, we need to slow them down!' said Hadley.

Paul clung to the steering wheel, kept it straight and accelerated.

'No,' he said. 'We need to be in plain sight. Choppers will come in. They can't attack us in open space!'

'They can and they will. See the size of the fender on the blue van up ahead?'

Paul leaned to his right. 'Yeah?'

'That look natural to you?'

Paul took a closer look at the van, swerving the truck more to his left so he had a better view of it down his right-hand side.

'It's not very shiny,' continued Hadley, 'and it's twice as thick as most of them should be. That's because it's reinforced steel, not chrome. Look at the base of the car, the tires. They're low to the ground, not flat. That's because they're carrying a lot of weight. Chances are it's a block car, padded out with bricks and concrete. We hit that side on and it'll be us that lifts. Take the next exit, and do it quickly!'

But it was too late. The blue van turned sideways in the middle of the highway, and the driver jumped out, rolled free and sprinted for the safety of the shoulder.

The weight of their own truck meant there was no time to avoid it. 'Aim for the cab!'

Paul was pulling the steering wheel in the other direction. 'But the exit's on our right!'

Hadley grabbed the wheel and pulled it hard to the left. The right-hand side of their truck was torn open as it struck the body of the van. The rest of it smashed through the cab, its glass and framework shattering on impact. The van's fender ripped free and struck the front of the truck before it slid underneath them, puncturing two tires.

Their truck was smoking now, thick black plumes pouring out of the engine bay. The wheel rims sparked and screamed on the concrete as they kept going.

Hadley heard the sound of the Cherokee's engine behind them.

'Arvin? Have you got a visual?' he said into his phone, still gripping the handle on the side of the truck.

'I'm quarter of a mile behind you.'

'Great. The Cherokee?'

'A few cars in front of me.'

'Any others?'

'Black Mustang, further back. That'll be their pace car.'

'Anything else?'

'Nothing I can see.'

'Good. Take out the Mustang. We'll pull over another mile on, we won't make it much further. The exit's just ahead. We'll hold them off until you get there. Use the shoulder and circle wide, collect us on the right. We'll be in a stand-off position.'

Arvin accelerated. The Mustang was a car in front now, all low fat tires and jet black. He could hear the engine purr as he approached. It was far from a standard machine. There wasn't much time. He could hear shots being fired up ahead and saw the truck swaying to the left and right.

They hadn't seen him. Arvin was in a nondescript white sedan. It looked pretty normal, though it too had been custom built. The exhaust had been silenced, though the engine was more than capable of keeping up with the Mustang.

Arvin removed a gun from his vest. Like the car, it had been muzzled for minimal sound. He moved up behind the Mustang, focused on the front-right tire and squeezed a shot off, then hit the brakes. The tire blew and the Mustang pulled violently right, narrowly missing the car beside it. Arvin flew past it on the left-hand side. He could see the driver still fighting the wheel and looking for traffic to avoid as he was dragged toward the shoulder.

Smoke covered three of the four lanes. A wrecked van blocked the center. He was following the Cherokee. He saw it pull up in front of the truck, which sat in the right lane closest to the shoulder, further down. Three men were on this side of it, firing round after round at the truck now stopped in front of them.

The truck was a mess. Most of this side was missing, and what remained was pocked with bullet holes. He could see inside it, the safe box clearly on display. He breathed deeply. If he'd had anything to guard, that's where he would have been sitting.

Cars were veering to the left as they passed, desperate to avoid the carnage that was taking place. Arvin peeled right, firing as he drifted by. The assailants turned and ducked, one falling as he was struck in the legs. The SUV's front tires exploded as bullets found their mark.

Arvin swung the car around the Cherokee, along the right shoulder and in behind the truck. The truck doors flew open, and Hadley and Paul dove in the back of the sedan as Arvin pulled away. The rev counter rose as shots sounded; tires squealed as they drove onto the exit ramp. Arvin saw two of the men running for the truck before the turn obscured them.

'The safe?' said Paul. 'The diamonds, what are we–'

Hadley raised a hand. 'Toni?' he said, his phone already back in his hand, switched to speaker.

'Yeah?'

'I can see you're travelling well. You look to be thirty minutes ahead. Where are you now?'

They heard the sound of a motorbike engine rising and falling as she changed through the gears. 'Just blew through Scranton.'

'Good, good. We're following, the truck's down, though they'll go to work on the safe until they can free it. We should be–' *Chirp*. 'Did you–' *Chirp*.

'You there?' she asked.

'Sorry, we keep – damn it!' said Hadley, looking up. A drone was flying fifty feet above them. It hovered, before accelerating at high speed away from them.

A motorbike flew past in the opposite direction. Its driver was dressed head-to-toe in black, with white stripes running down the sides of a leather jacket, a daypack strapped to his back. He veered onto the highway, as they tore past the on ramp.

'Toni? You there.'

'Yes. What happened?'

'A drone caught our signal. There's a bike following it … following you. Its got your phone's signal. We'll give chase, though the next on ramp is miles away and traffic is piled up below us. The chaser made the on ramp, you'll be on your own.'

'Okay.'

'Keep going. Don't stop unless you have too. I don't want them to think we know what's happened, otherwise things will change rapidly. They'll call in for support, or more of it, if they haven't already. Leave the phone on. You've got a good lead. Keep pressing, there's a long way to go. At your next fuel stop, transfer the phone to your backpack. Place the goods on your person, your backpack under a truck. Make sure it's heading north. North-west would be ideal. We'll meet at the agreed place. And Toni?'

'Yeah?'

'If the drone sees you, shoot it down.'

'Right. The rider?'

'Medium height, black leather jacket with white stripes down its sides, black pants. Undoubtedly carrying. He'll probably know from the drone's signal that you're on a bike.'

'Roger that.'

'Good luck.'

Toni knew she wouldn't make it to the petrol station. The sky was blue and the air clear, which would no doubt make the drone's passage that much faster. She'd calculated the timing in her mind as soon as Hadley called. The highway was as straight as she needed it to be, though that meant the drone was unobstructed. Even with her head start and driving well beyond a legal seventy miles an hour, she had no chance.

She removed the diamonds from her pack and left her phone inside. Stashing the bike in a stand of trees off the side of the highway, she climbed a hill behind it. She balanced the semi-automatic on hard-packed dirt, added a sight-scope and focused on the backpack across the highway. The line of sight was clear.

She'd been right to pull off – she heard the drone before it came into view. It was flying in a straight line towards the other side of the valley. It stopped abruptly, hovering above the backpack before dropping slowly above it. It paused as if in thought, before it exploded. Metal and lights flew everywhere as it hit the ground.

Toni unscrewed the scope of her gun, broke it down, tucked it into the back of her jacket and ran for her bike. The guy following her would have been told the drone was defunct, and that he should approach it with caution. She had at least fifteen minutes on him, though he'd be pushing hard.

She jumped on her bike, kicked the stand free and skidded onto the road, her rev counter screaming as she changed through the gears.

At her stop, she refilled her tank, then headed back in the opposite direction. She counted off the time, checking the other side of the highway as she tore along the inside lane, riding as fast as she was able.

She saw his helmet glinting in the sun. He was tucked down, close to the tank, keeping his speed high and resistance low.

He saw her at the same time. Pulled a gun from his jacket, leveled it at her as she approached. Toni slammed on her brakes, dragged the bike behind a large silver jeep, obscuring his view. His head snapped around. A concrete median barrier prevented him from crossing. She saw his white-striped arms working the clutch and throttle.

Now she flew, ignoring the speed limit as she weaved through cars. She could hear him coming. He was on the other side of the strip, zig-zagging at high speed through the honking oncoming cars. She sped under an overpass. He took the on ramp, turning it into an exit, then he was flying above her, crossing to the ramp on the other side.

Now he was closing, his engine screaming behind her. She kept weaving in and out of the traffic. He was driving down the shoulder, his gun in one hand.

She saw Arvin's white sedan coming the other way. Hadley was in the passenger seat and the new guy was in the back. They saw her fly past.

She tore up the next exit. He was right behind her. She crossed over and headed north once again. He was the better rider, no question. Bullets thudded into the concrete behind her. She swerved in and out of traffic, then she was past Arvin, cutting in front of him and accelerating. Her assailant dropped another gear and roared after her.

Ahead were two trucks, their low speed forcing her to drive through the middle. She checked over her shoulder. His face shield was black, revealing nothing. He raised himself off his seat to a standing position – they were doing one hundred and twenty miles an hour. His gun was pointed at her head. This was it.

Arvin's engine roared to life. The gunman heard it and whipped his head round, before the sedan collided with his back wheel, sending him sideways under the twelve-wheeler to his left.

Toni sagged in her seat, breathing hard, before pulling to the side of the road.

It was done.

3 .

The questions began again with the dawn light. I answered in kind, preparing myself for my day. I felt stronger than I had for weeks. Were they weeks? Months? Time had left me long ago, as it had once before.

I rose quickly and dressed. Today I would be collecting. This season's wood pile was getting low. We were almost through winter, though it needed to be replenished for the next.

I had to find the wood first. I was given an oversized backpack. I placed some food, water and a file inside it, then strapped an axe and large handsaw to the outside.

A box of old newspapers sat in the corner of the woodshed. I'd been told to leave them alone, to cut myself off from the things that didn't matter. Things that could cloud the mind I was trying so hard to free.

A face on the corner of the front cover drew me in. I reached for it, slowly pulling it out so as not to tear the faded yellow paper.

Four faces were shown beneath a story of a jewelery heist foiled by a security team. I knew one of them. It had been years, though it was him. He looked a little older, heavier from what I could make out in the picture, but there was no mistaking his face. He was part of the reason I was here, in recovery.

I ran a finger across their faces, felt the crumpled yellow paper, rough beneath my fingertips, before Madame Rai appeared.

'What are you doing?' she asked. She strode over to me and took the paper from my hand.

'I was getting my things.'

Her face told mine it was lying. She studied the story, me, then folded the paper and returned it to the box. 'The sun is rising, get going.'

I bowed, picked up the things I needed and ran for the driveway, my head full of thoughts I couldn't suppress.

The forest was an easy five miles away, down a series of gravel roads. I had to run there, choose a tree to cut down, then saw the trunk into large wheels of wood. The trees were balsam firs, huge things that stood at least sixty feet tall and were almost two feet thick. I'd done it before, more than once.

It would take me all day. I'd have to stack the wood in a pile, wait for Madame Rai to come, then fill my backpack with the remainder and carry that home. The orange pick-up would be there, waiting for me to unload it when I eventually returned.

I listened to my feet strike the gravel, felt it crunch as I pushed forward, the backpack swinging with the weight of the saw and the axe on either side of it.

So he was doing okay. Did he deserve to be? Ignore it, Kat. Focus on where you are, what you're doing. Which is what, exactly?

I drew fresh air into my lungs, inhaled to capacity then emptied them as slowly as I could, which isn't easy when you're running. I was deep in the forest now. I looked left and right, searched the long dark corridors between tree trunks for a sign of anything. This wasn't our forest. It was owned by the province. They'd be logging it eventually, though I'd never seen a truck or anyone here for as long as I'd been around. Which was how long?

I had to choose carefully. The tree needed to be mature; its bark would be rough, a scaly red-brown, the wood hardened so it wouldn't take long to cure, once cut. We had enough wood for winter. They'd burn this next year.

How many times had I been here?

The gravel road ended in a wide crescent. I walked to my left, found a clearing deeper in, placed my pack on the forest floor and set about sharpening the axe with the long file. I hadn't been this far in before. I had to be selective about where I took the wood from. Random places spread throughout the forest, on the edge of where it wouldn't be missed.

In no time at all the blade caught the ridges of my fingertips as I ran it gently over them. I put the file away, braced myself with a solid stance and struck the tree at its base. It didn't budge. It would be some time before it moved at all. The clearing would give it plenty of room to fall once it did. When the sun was above me, it would be near midday. I wanted the tree down with a third of it cut before then.

His face appeared in my head as I struck the tree. I ignored it. Bark flew to the left of me as I swung. I worked harder, swung the blade faster, eager to forget where my mind was trying to take me.

The top cut had grown. I was just shy of a quarter of the way through the trunk. I went to work on the undercut, being careful to make sure I had the felling direction right, as Madame Rai had taught me. I was sweating now, my body having adjusted to the cool temperature. I went to the opposite side of the trunk, used the offcuts as felling notches, then carved thin slices out of it to line up the tree's path.

I studied the forest floor. Listened as birds sung in the trees overhead. Watched as a light wind caressed the treetops, absorbed what I could before I swung my axe a final time and silenced all of it. I hit it hard. The fir stuttered at first, a death knell to an audience of one. It stood straight a final time, then plunged earthward, crashing to the floor, scaring away what little company I had.

I swapped the axe for the saw and went to work on the trunk. The sun was climbing now; it had reached the bottom corner of the clearing. I was almost halfway through it, well ahead of where I wanted to be. I sat down on the fallen trunk and drank deeply from a bottle of water I had packed.

I took out a small bowl of rice, using two fingers to spoon it into my mouth, when I heard something. Probably just a rotten branch falling. No, it was something else. Car tires on gravel. I grabbed my axe, let it hang loosely at my side as I strode quickly between trees, back toward the road, hunched over as I moved.

It couldn't be her, she was too early.

There were two voices. Through the trees I could see a red truck parked in the cul-de-sac. Someone screamed. I ran faster. A bearded guy in a blue and black checkered shirt was fighting with a girl. He held her hair tight, half of it wrapped around his hand as he pulled her toward him.

Now she was screaming; he was yelling back. He'd forced her against the side of the truck. Her pants had been ripped open, they slid down her legs. He had her arms pinned behind her with his left hand, his right hand unbuckling his belt. He was still grinning when he looked back and saw me. His smile disappeared when he took in the axe. He stepped back, let her arms drop to her sides.

'Who the fuck are you?'

'Me?' I asked, stepping clear of the trees. 'I'm Kat. What are you doing?'

'Well come here, kitty-kat. I've got something for you. Put your axe down. There's plenty to go around.'

What he was doing, what he was trying to do, had half done … it stole all thought from me. The face from the faded yellow paper appeared on his shoulders. It was an ignorant face, unconcerned about who or what I was. What I should have meant to him. It looked through me, like I had already been condemned to the past.

I ran at him. I was strong – stronger than the woman. She turned, her blues eyes meeting mine. She found her voice as I swung the axe past his forearm and took him in the right side of the head. He crumpled. I dropped the axe, stared at the blood that ran between my fingers, down my hands, that covered my white robe. His blood. I stumbled to the nearest tree and threw up, strings of vomit flecking the simple shoes I wore.

When I could breath again, short sharp gasps of air that somehow made their way out, I gave her water and the keys from his pocket and told her to drive, far from here. I watched her go. The tires spat chunks of gravel as the engine gunned for the gap in the trees. I could just make out her tears in the rearview as she drove away.

I dragged his body to the base of the tree I'd chopped down. I used the axe to dig a hole in the soft earth and hid my mistake deep inside it. I gagged again as I covered his face, then looked up. The sun had disappeared below the trees of the clearing I stood in. Madame Rai would be here in a few hours. I washed what blood I could from my robe with the water I had left, before turning it inside out.

I set about sawing the rest of the tree and my pile of round tree trunks grew. I rolled each of them to the gravel cul-de-sac, ensuring there would be no need for her to venture in. I split the few she would make me carry home, and placed them in my pack.

It was dark by the time I arrived back. The orange pick-up with its full tray of wood sat in the drive. It was another hour before it was empty. The tub had been heated, and I climbed into it still wearing my robe. I set about cleansing the robe, and my head, of the day.

I screamed. They'd come for me. I was being pulled down a vast corridor by a thick black rope tied around my waist. Blood trailed behind me as I tried to break away, to roll over, to find a handhold on the floor or the wall I was being thrown against, anything to tear myself free. But I couldn't. There was no escape. I couldn't hear them at first, though their voices got louder as I was being drawn closer, a dull chatter, now their silhouettes were clear, I could almost make out their faces, they were shouting, then screaming at me. I screamed back. Shadows with elongated hands that clawed and scratched at me. They reached for my arms, grabbed my legs and pulled me in.

'Why are you here?' said a voice above me.

My eyes flicked open to the dawn light.

It had been a long time since I hadn't answered.

I was done. I couldn't stay.

4.

Hadley switched from his right arm to his left, but kept the pushups going. Sweat dripped off him, though he smiled to himself. He was halfway through the morning routine he followed religiously, six days a week: sit-ups, squats, weights, crunches, box jumps – all of which followed a five mile run.

Dawn was his favorite hour. His mind was fresh, ready for whatever the day might throw at him. Being out there, in the cold crisp air, the darkness of the trees in High Park as the light began to creep in, making the most of it before the city woke up and started to pollute the day.

And today would be a good one. He'd been called by a guy named Chris Finch last night. A local artist who had found international fame. The coverage they'd gotten from the foiled diamond heist had done exactly what he'd hoped – put them on the radar of high-profile clients.

Hadley finished his work out and checked his watch: seven fifteen. The meeting wasn't until eight. Chris wanted to come and meet the team, which was fine, nothing wrong with being eyeballed. That gave him plenty of time to cool down and shower.

He toweled himself, grabbed a blender from the kitchen, threw in a combination of dried apricots, blueberries, his protein supplement, coconut water and a few broccoli stalks he found in the back of the fridge. He rolled up the front door, grabbed the paper from the pavement and sat on a chair facing the street.

His office wasn't much, but he loved it all the same. A gym, a boxing ring, and a few spaces to hang out in – that was all he needed. The place near Spadina & Bloor West had been his uncle's. A brother his father had never really cared for.

He ignored the paper, sipping his morning drink and thinking about his own brother. It seemed like a lifetime ago.

The deep blue color of the sky had faded, like a thin sheet of white plastic had been drawn across its face, pronouncing the day dead. Clouds appeared as Hadley straightened his hat. They began to coalesce as he made his way to the podium through the rows of white chairs lined up precisely in front of him.

Graduation day. It was one of those autumn days that on first impression looked to be cool and friendly. Hadley had been an active sergeant in the military, and his kid brother was now following in his footsteps.

Hadley's decision to drop out of school early hadn't pleased his parents. After several years of trying to find himself, drinking and fighting his way toward no real destination, his parents had decided for him. They had called a friend to fast-track his application into the military.

Hadley hadn't argued, he'd agreed. And he'd thrived. He understood structure; the military's precision, instruction and competition. Most importantly, he loved the physical aspect. He'd grown stronger, and had learned to temper his thought instead of acting on impulse, which he'd always done in the past. The recognition had come. First in deference from colleagues, then in promotion.

He caught sight of his parents to his left, but they didn't turn toward him. They'd made it clear – what they'd wanted for Hadley wasn't what they wanted for his younger brother James.

Hadley stood behind the microphone staring at the sea of well-dressed people. He chose to look at one, his brother. He did his best to present a formal face as his pride threatened to break through. Pride in seeing someone he loved wanting to do what Hadley did, to throw the college education he'd been handed right back in the faces of the parents who should have loved them both. For who they were, not for what they had or hadn't done.

Hadley spoke briefly before turning to face the graduates. He shook the hand of each soldier before cheers erupted from the gathered crowds as hats and protocol were cast aside. He wrapped his brother in a bear hug, rubbing his skinned-head and smiling like nothing else mattered, before the rain began to fall.

'Hadley?'

He'd been a million miles away. 'Yeah.'

'It's seven forty-five, the guys are on their way and you're dreaming and stinking up the place,' said Toni.

'Yeah, right. I'll grab a shower.'

'Good. You do that. I'll get some coffees. Any idea what he drinks?'

He looked blank.

'Silly question. He's an artist. I'll get five of something different.'

'Right.'

Hadley moved quickly, pushing all thoughts of his brother aside. His shower lasted all of two minutes, then he was drying himself and pulling on a pair of freshly ironed jeans, a shirt and a pair of shoes he hated wearing. First impressions last, he told himself.

Chris arrived a few minutes after Arvin and Paul. He was short, about five foot six and chubby. He had bright red hair and pale freckly white skin that clashed with the purple suit and yellow cravat he was wearing. Probably Irish. He'd brought a girl with him, Trixie, a personal assistant by the looks of things.

Toni handed Trixie the coffees which she scanned, choosing two, then Toni directed Paul to the fridge for a bottle of water.

'Nice place you have here, Hadley.'

Hadley smiled, took his time before he answered. Despite the late call he'd done some reading. Chris was renowned for his work, though was almost better-known for his acerbic tongue.

'It isn't really, though it works for us.'

He introduced his team, then asked them to take a seat. Chris took the end of the couch and Trixie sat on the arm beside him.

'I'm assuming you all know who I am,' said Chris, looking at Hadley. The team nodded.

'Good. I'm a painter, photographer, sculpturist, and some might say arrogant bastard, which I'm good with.'

Hadley chuckled for the group. The rest of them only managed to smile.

'Occasionally I'll travel to promote my works. Quite often I'll be asked to speak at various events, or to meet with clients internationally where my work may be commissioned, though typically I'll need someone on the ground here to manage my own local exhibitions. What would security at one of my events look like to you?'

Hadley cleared his throat. 'Depending on the exhibition's size, the location and the event itself, you'd have two staff. One who'd manage point, the other in support until we had a good feel for how they run. There would only be one entry and exit. I'd have CCTV cameras in all rooms, whether locked or unlocked. Doors would be coded with a minimum of six digits and would also require a digital key that would be changed weekly. We would have a pre-registered event list, which would be cross-checked at the door. Phones would be switched off upon entry, depending on your own policy, bagged and held at the front desk. Ideally your place is elevated, with concrete steps at its front, or steel bars if it's street level. The same would go for the back door.'

'Sounds good,' said Chris nodding. 'Would we get you as point, or one of your team?'

Again Hadley took his time, watched Chris's eyes glide over his team. They passed by Paul, stopped at Toni, rose and fell, before they moved on then back to Toni, having dismissed Arvin.

'I'm afraid I'm spoken for. I work with Christie Fallon.'

'The fashion designer?' he replied, with a slight grin.

Hadley nodded, knowing he had him. 'I have every confidence in each and every one of my team. It comes down to what suits you best, the type of security you need and what we both agree best fits the profile.'

Chris stood up, extended his hand to Toni. 'See you at my office on Monday,' he said, then walked out through the roller door. Trixie trailed him, her coffee and an oversized phone balanced in one hand, the other holding the keys to the car. Toni had the good grace to smile.

5.

Arvin stepped off a street car on the corner of College St and Manning Ave in Little Italy. The Green Grind was a small cafe Toni had chosen. It wasn't far from their usual base, just a few blocks further west. It was a Saturday morning, so he doubted they'd bump into any of the team.

He'd meant to run, knowing Toni definitely would have, though he wasn't feeling great after a bad night's sleep. His immunity felt low and his throat was raw. The cafe was in a red-brick building above a Drug Mart. He'd grab a few things once they were done.

The place was busy. A series of yellow cables with naked bulbs on the ends hung from the ceiling. Menus were written on chalkboards within picture frames, placed on a white-brick center wall. Toni was seated in a corner next to a cabinet that was straight out of the seventies. She was dressed in her running gear and was halfway through a coffee.

She signaled him. 'How you doing?' she asked, standing and turning a cheek to receive a kiss. 'Or shouldn't I ask? You're looking a little peaky.'

Arvin coughed into a sleeve.

'Doesn't sound good. Were you out last night?'

'I wish I had been. Might've gotten more sleep that way. How's the coffee?'

'Great. Grab some juice as well, they're really good here.'

'Right. I might get something with ginger in it,' he said, calling a waiter over. 'We eating?'

'We'd better be. I'm ravenous.'

Arvin had always liked Toni. She was black and white about everything. Pulled no punches and gave everything one hundred percent. She'd been Hadley's first recruit. He wasn't sure how'd they'd met, though he knew they were close.

Arvin surveyed the room. They had the best view of the street and the cafe, which was no surprise. Where you sat was important for anyone working in security.

He caught a few other patrons staring at them. Arvin was Asian, tall and pale, while Toni was darker skinned and Mexican. They were an unusual combination.

They ordered, and settled into easy conversation. Their food arrived just as Toni started talking about what he guessed they'd come here for.

'So what do you think of the new recruit?' she asked, plunging a fork into her pumpkin pie.

'Paul? I don't know.'

'Come on Arvin, it's you and me. You can't sit on the fence. I think he's bit of a dick,' she said, smiling.

Arvin sprayed juice all over himself. He grabbed a few napkins, held one to his nose and used another to pat himself down.

Toni laughed at him. 'What? You don't agree?'

Arvin nodded, reaching for water, gulping it down. 'He's slightly out of sync with the rest of us.'

'Out of sync? You heard Hadley bitching about the truck. It was over a month ago, and he's still banging on about the fact that Paul ignored him.'

'It was one of his first assignments. It was a pretty hectic one at that. He didn't do too badly.'

Toni moped up the last of her pie, dropped a folded napkin onto a soft mound of untouched cream and leaned back in her chair. 'That's fair. Do you know what his background is?'

Arvin took a sip of his juice. The ginger was much stronger at the bottom. Between that and the coffee, his throat felt much better.

'Hadley mentioned he was a bouncer, worked the door for a few local bars. He's done various jobs with a few agencies. Other than that, I hear he's got a few links to music events and the like. Some sort of security event co-ordinator. He knows the lead singer from that local band. What's their name? They're massive … The Ceiling?'

Toni rolled her eyes. 'The Vaulted Ceiling. That'll be Jordan Franks. I had a girlfriend whose older sister went to school with him in Burlington. I hear he was a great guy back then. They've been around forever. He's barely hanging on to reality these days, apparently. I give him less than five years before it's all a memory.'

'Well let's hope it's a little longer. Sounds like Paul might be signing on with him as his Head of Security.'

The place was full now. They had to talk a little louder to be heard.

'Really? Good for him. How about you?' said Toni.

'I've got a friend who's in a production for the acting academy. He's hooked me up with a guy who came through there and is on the rise.'

'Would I know him?' asked Toni.

'I doubt it. His name's Leroy James. His family are African-American. They moved here from New Orleans, years ago. He grew up in Etobicoke.'

A waiter asked if they'd needed anything else, but both were done.

'Is he getting many roles?'

'Quite a few. He's a really nice guy. A bit of a comedian, though a bit rogue. Still, I've got my fingers crossed. How are things going with Chris?'

'All a bit early in the piece really. So far so good.'

Arvin laughed. 'He didn't like me much when I met him.'

'Don't worry. He's like that with everyone. He's talented, arrogant and a pain in the ass, which probably describes our entire client base.'

'At least we're getting one.'

'Too true. Are you happy with all of this?' asked Toni, pushing her plate and cup to one side. I mean, with what we've signed up for here? It just feels like it's on a trajectory to who knows where.'

Arvin took his time answering. 'There are worse things to do. We're all here to make some money. Hopefully we can do that and have a bit of fun while we're at it. We all just need to focus on keeping a clear head and holding it together. That way we might have a chance of coming out the other side in one piece.'

'Amen. You done?'

Arvin nodded. 'I'll get this one.'

Toni gave him a hug and left. Arvin paid with a card. His hands were steady. He could feel the juice and his breakfast threatening to rise in his stomach. He waited for her to walk around the corner, then headed downstairs to the drug mart to fill a prescription.

6.

Present day, three years later ...

I can see the lights of the city dotted through a dark gray night. The CN Tower looms large above it like some sort of color conductor waving its wand at the night sky.

Red brake lights switch to green as our train moves between rails, bumping and clanging its way into the city. Montreal is only five hours behind me, though it feels like a lifetime already. It had been a place just south of Labrador City she'd taken me to. Hidden me away in a remote corner of Canada, for which I was thankful.

I thought about how we'd parted, amicably, with a polite hug. Though that was her way. I could see what my leaving meant to her. She'd done her best to mask the disappointment, but I'd spent too much time with her not to see it.

I wiped the glass windows free of the mist, then stared at my own reflection and the city beyond it. What can you say to a woman like that? Someone who takes a broken person, a complete stranger, and sets about rebuilding her. I knew something equally bad had happened to her, though she'd never said as much. It was in the way she carried herself – strong, leaning in to whatever came next, overcompensating for what she'd chosen to leave behind.

I hadn't shared my story. She'd never asked me to. She'd accepted the situation and insisted I dealt with it too. In hindsight, it wouldn't have been difficult to guess. My face had carried plenty of words, written in cuts and the bruises, buried in the hollows beneath my eyes, in the jagged text that traced the shape of my broken limbs, covered the body I dragged with me to meet her.

My view disappeared as the temperature adjusted. I wiped fresh circles in the window pane with a woolen-gloved hand, revealing silhouettes of a place I'd told myself never to return to.

I thought about the money she'd given me. I'd found it wrapped in brown paper and folded carefully into my white robe. She'd found the garment, covered in blood, and had cleaned and pressed it without saying a word. She knew what I'd done. The box of old papers never reappeared in the woodshed.

Montreal had been a promise I'd made to myself, something I'd shared with her. I'd visited the places I'd dreamed about, finally free to experience something I hoped would allow me to lose myself, even if it was only for a few years. They had been mine.

I'd taken a job that traded on the only aptitude I'd shown any real interest in: writing. It was a small bilingual paper. They'd been patient as I'd gotten to grips with Quebecois, one of the few basic skills I'd learned inside. I'd enjoyed this city, the outlier in the center of the vast expanse that is Canada. A bit like me, really. Yet here I was.

The train came to a halt at Union station. I searched the seats around me as the lights came on. It was a Friday night, so the train had been half empty until we hit the city's outskirts. From there, teenagers had piled in at every stop for a night on the town.

I waited until my carriage was empty, stared at the open doors and the concrete platform beyond it, in two minds as to whether or not I should get out. A speaker offered assistance, advising me that we had arrived at our destination, Toronto – the super city.

'So, Ms. Reid,' said Thom.'

'Yes,' I replied, leaning forward in my chair.

'What brings you to Toronto?'

'It's the city I grew up in.' I smiled as wide as my mouth would let me.

'Ayuh? Whereabouts?'

'Around, I guess. We moved quite a bit, though we were never far from the city. Near the Danforth mostly.'

'Born here?' he said reclining.

Clearly I'd been sitting too far forward. He looked a bit preppy. Like one of those guys who'd led the student body. He wore a striped woolen vest, had a beard, and his teeth were yellow, probably from smoking hand-rolled cigarettes as he punched out three hundred words a night on his IBM Selectric, watched over by a black and white poster of Hunter S. Thompson. I knew the type. There were plenty of them further north. Harmless, which suited me.

'No, Winnipeg, actually.'

He sat up. 'Well, don't worry. You're here now.'

I don't know how many times I'd heard that.

'Listen, you come highly recommended from one of our, ah ... smaller Montreal papers. I understand you're a blogger?'

'That's what I do.'

'Have a chat to HR. Steve tells me you'll be writing lifestyle and entertainment. Let us know what you need to get started. I'm excited to have you here, so welcome aboard, Jo.'

He stood, offered his hand. 'You mind if I call you that?'

I took it. It was chalky, limp. I smiled back at him.

'Is that short for Joanna?'

'No,' I replied.

'Good. Alrighty then. Let me introduce you to the team.'

There were rows of cubicles, each with grey fluffy sides. A lighter gray plastic casing held them all together, ready to be undone and reconfigured should things not go according to plan. They were crammed in. Teams were assembled in tight groups, some seated around a single desk instead. We were sharing floors, journos in one area, copywriters and sales beside them.

My desk was perched in a windowless corner a few feet back from the washrooms. It didn't matter. I had space, and plenty to think about.

7.

The large steel doors were fastened to iron rings on either side of the art gallery entrance. Snow flurries had piled up against the base of a stone wall to its left. It was cold up here in Montreal.

Two large heaters glowed brightly above the doors to welcome guests in. Underneath them stood two tall dark-haired girls, their hair piled delicately upon their heads. They wore sheer black dresses that criss-crossed their chests and wrapped tightly around their necks, collar-like. They held white trays with black flutes of champagne. The girls were gorgeous, except for the scarred and puckered bullet holes that bled from opposite cheeks.

'Really?' said Chris, taking a flute from the girl on the left. 'Tell me the subject matter isn't going to look like your face, or I'll turn around and take this with me.'

She just smiled down at him and greeted another guest.

'I mean – honestly,' he said, turning to look at Toni standing a few steps behind him. 'You know what I'm talking about, don't you, honey? Didn't he roll this same mistake out last year?'

Toni smiled. 'Let's just get in there before we both freeze.'

'The voice of reason – as always,' said Chris, shrugging his shoulders.

The space was huge. Church-like, with colored glass that glowed gently under the candles set in front. Staff in deep-gray cowls waited on the gathering crowd, giving the whole place a dark-gothic feel.

'Should we have brought torches?' said Chris to no one in particular.

Lights appeared in front of them as a camera crew made their way over. Toni stepped quickly in behind, preferring not to be seen.

'Chris Finch! Peter Halstead, CTV,' said a slender, clean-looking presenter dressed in a thick blue suit and white shirt, the obligatory black woolen scarf double looped and knotted around his neck. 'Lovely to have you here in Montreal. Are you excited about seeing Henry's work?'

'Oh, absolutely. It's always so nice to catch up with a friend, to view a fresh body of work,' he said, smiling at the camera.

'What do you think we can expect to see?'

'Well, I hate to speculate, but by the looks of things, something a little dark, perhaps?' he said, being uncharacteristically coy.

The presenter laughed with him. 'We've enjoyed your work to date. Anything in the pipeline you can share with our viewers?'

'Plenty. Though as good as it is, tonight's probably not the night to do that. I'll keep you posted.'

'I'm sure it is, and we look forward to that. Thank you, Chris.'

He nodded and walked past the presenter, heading toward the crowd beyond.

Staff collected coats and directed them to a large marbled wall with a self-portrait of Henry Mason set into a heavy golden frame. A bearded photographer in a vintage tuxedo stood behind an old camera box and gestured for Chris to stand to the left of the portrait for a photo.

Toni stifled a laugh as Chris stuck three fingers down his throat. The camera seemed to explode and the smoke cleared.

'Let me guess,' he said. 'A digital camera with a smoke machine attached, hidden beneath cloth.' He finished his flute.

'A photographer never reveals his tricks, Mr. Finch.'

'That would be a magician,' he replied, handing him his glass. 'Where's the bar?'

Toni followed him in, searching the room for any people Chris had upset before. There were several, who turned away or whispered to a friend as he passed. His shock of red hair was easy to spot. Chris ignored them all, as he was prone to do. If he hadn't been so talented, the invitations would have dried up pretty quickly.

Chris sipped steadily from a tall vodka tonic, the lime bobbing beneath the ice as he walked. He shook hands with a few guests, stepped past the majority, refusing photographs.

The crowd had gathered in a large area surrounded by tall men dressed as sentinels silhouetted by a blue-grey cityscape behind.

The Grim Reaper stood at the podium, a sickle held high, his face hidden within a deep black cowl. The spotlight found his head, the cowl was pushed back. A grotesque, large and misshapen face appeared.

The crowd gasped, while Chris laughed – a little too loudly, drawing stares from the people around him.

The mask came off and Henry smiled from beneath it. 'Thanks for joining me tonight, to celebrate my latest work – Purgatory.'

The crowd applauded. Chris whispered into Toni's ear. 'What was it last year? Sanctum? It should have been called Rectum, total bunch of ass. Am I right, honey?'

Toni covered her mouth and looked at the floor, trying to keep it together.

'Purgatory began as a story of heartbreak. Developed by the feeling of deep resonance and disgruntlement. This was felt by …'

Toni looked around the room. She searched the exits, the toilets and everybody's faces. Nothing to be cautious of. She turned back to see an empty spot where Chris had been, before seeing his mop of red hair working its way back toward the bar.

She'd have to tell him to pace himself, or this could end up like the dinner and turkey fiasco of late last year. The host hadn't enjoyed it at all when the evening's oversized turkey had appeared on Chris's head, before it swan-dived into his pool, ruining dinner.

She knew he wouldn't listen. *Just watch him, Toni.*

The paintings, as Chris had predicted, were awful. He walked once around the room, barely stopping to look at anything, before sitting down on a couch, apparently done.

A few socialites had tethered themselves to him and were now seated alongside, making light conversation. Toni stood quietly behind him, waiting.

Henry appeared, his cowl now hanging down his back, a drink in hand. His own guard trailed behind.

'Chris,' he said, approaching with his hand out. 'Thanks for coming by. How did you find it?'

Chris didn't get up or shake his hand.

Here we go.

'Ordinary, if I'm being honest with you, Henry.'

Henry stood still. He took his time drinking from his flute. He laughed. 'What? Not enough colour? No eye-popping heroics with dicks and testicles floating above the patron saint for a wedge of PR?'

'None of that, really. I just thought it was crap. A solid follow-on from last year's disaster. I'm surprised anyone's back. Don't worry, I'm sure you'll get some coverage with that costume you brought from your closet. Does Mimi love it?'

Henry cleared his throat. 'We're no longer,' he said looking away.

God, Chris could be a prick, she thought. He was slurring now too. Dangerous.

'Sorry. I'd heard that. My mistake.'

'Why don't you … just go.'

'But I came all this way.'

'Only because I paid for it. You heard me – fuck off.'

Henry's security guard moved in. He was a shortish guy in a loose suit that didn't give much away. With a polished head, dark skin, leather gloves and a bluetooth receiver clipped to his left ear, he looked a little flash to Toni. She could tell he was pissed off.

Chris stood to leave, a little wobbly. 'If you insist. You've just given me my night back,' he said, finishing his drink. 'Any recommendations?'

Henry's fist appeared from beneath his robe and flew in Chris's direction. Toni caught it before it landed and pushed it past him, twisting his arm and forcing him to the ground. His security guard lunged at her before she stretched a leg out and buried it in his crotch, sending him gasping against the base of a near wall. She put the heel of her shoe to the back of Henry's head and twisted his arm further the wrong way. He yelled as she did so, before the old-time photographer reappeared in an explosion of light.

Fuck. Now she'd be on the cover of *The Star*.

The guard stared at her, his hand pressed against his crotch, still in pain.

'Stay where you are, or I'll break it,' she said.

Chris was grinning, clearly loving it.

'Chris. Get your coat – we're leaving.'

'Sorry, ladies,' he intoned, patting one of them on the shoulder. 'Looks like I'm off.'

8.

Casino Du Quebec looked like a giant golden spinning top, nestled on the banks of the Saint Lawrence River. Its base was lit up in neon-purple, softening its exterior. By day the vertical strips of concrete above looked like teeth, perpetually hungry, having been fed twenty-four-seven since 1993. The driver opened the back door for Toni. She stepped onto the concrete steps, surveyed the area before Chris followed her out.

Chris looked up at the huge glass façade. 'Come on then, honey, let's go and see if this town wants to drop its panties, eh?'

Toni shook her head, checking her watch. 'It's getting late, Chris. I should be calling it a night.'

'Lucky you're with me then, sweetheart. I've got money in my pocket that needs to be burnt. You're still on the clock,' he added, smiling as he placed a hand on her shoulder. 'Relax a little – you deserve it. I only wish I'd taken my own picture of Henry's face wrinkled up under your boot.' He laughed.

'Not really that funny, Chris. You were a bit of a prick back there.'

'In this business honey, you have to be.'

The space inside was huge. The atrium was a drawn-out carpeted affair, before it collided brutally with two thousand slot machines. They looked like caged animals discreetly tethered to the floor, talking to each another through flashing lights and sirens. Their digital screens rotated between fruit, kings, mermaids, and monkeys.

Toni followed Chris through a maze of tables and machines. Leering punters moved their eyes slowly from her feet to her tits, glancing up quickly at her face before returning to her tits once more. She ignored them and pressed on.

Toni knew the layout only too well. It was psychological architecture at its best. Time was a key factor. No one knew what it was. There were no windows or clocks; no wristwatches on any staff.

The bar, and the counter to cash-out your chips, were buried deep in the back of the building, forcing you further from a potential exit should you want to leave. Row after row of machines, each the same as the next, were set up to confuse you, to mask the way out. She'd spent more than her fair share of time in these places.

She followed Chris to a back room. A tall lean guy, immaculately dressed, looked at him and took a second glance at her. They were handed champagne and walked through to a private setting. The lights were lower, the music softer – the drinks stronger.

Toni chided herself for being there, though it was his money, not hers. She was still being paid. She took her place at the craps table alongside Chris. It wasn't her game. She played Texas and Blackjack. Games you could have some sort of control over, versus just throwing your money away on dice or spinning wheels.

'Winner Seven!' said the stickman, pointing at the dice in the middle of the table. Toni watched from beside Chris's shoulder, as the stickman raked in the four and three shown on the dice, then pushed it back toward her. Chris was happy. She watched the boxman push chips into a slot, left of the table. They hadn't been Chris's.

Toni shook the dice again, being careful not to drop any or throw more than one in the air at a time.

'Yo-Leven!' sounded around the table as the boxman siphoned off another pool of chips. A punter finished his drink, got up and left, his chips now spent.

Chris squeezed her shoulder and took a drink with his free hand, having shifted his chips to the Don't Pass Bar – he was betting against her. Toni rolled once more, her eyes focused on the part of the table she wanted them to land on.

'Snake-eyes!' the stickman shouted.

Chris hoisted her in the air with a bear hug. Toni let out a yelp as she laughed with him. The boxman remained impassive, collected more than three thousand in chips and pushed them towards Chris.

It was getting late. He had drunk a lot. She'd watched him go to the washroom several times, returning with a kerchief plastered around his nose. Subtlety seemed to be deserting him. Each time, Toni waited and walked him back to the table to watch him lose even more. She'd tried to steer him toward the door, but a button-nose blond with her ass and tits poured into a turquoise dress, held his attention.

Sadly, she was his type – which they knew. Probably a prostitute employed by the casino to keep him here. Just another trick they'd gotten wise too.

Toni watched as Chris's chips dwindled. Stone castles that had turned to sand before his eyes. He surveyed the table, threw a large roll of Ben Franklins and a black card onto it, ordering fifty-grand's-worth of chips. He asked for them in ten thousands, then told the blonde to push all five chips on to a mix of horn bets.

Toni shook her head. They paid big, if they ever paid at all.

The table held its breath as the blond was given the dice to throw. Toni stared at the chips placed across a network of white squares on the green felt. They were simple white chips with broken yellow strips around the rim, *Casino Du Quebec* written in an elegant copperplate hand beneath *$10000* in a larger, bolder font.

She watched the dice fall and thought of an earlier time.

It had been hot in Matamoros when they'd come. She'd been just over ten years old. Her mother had run screaming into their little stone house, the oranges she held spilling, then rolling in different directions around the brick floor of the small kitchen.

The smell of the salt air coming in off the Gulf reached her through the open door, then the sound of the jeep pulling up outside. She stared up into her mother's eyes, saw the thin stream of tears coursing down her face, felt their warmth on her left shoulder as she picked her up, unsteadily, from the floor.

The dirty-brown stuffed rabbit she'd been playing with watched her go, as she was carried quickly towards her small bedroom at the back of the house. There was a cavity under its floor, beneath a panel hidden by a small chest of drawers.

She put her down then pushed the drawers aside and raised the floor panel, gently pushing Toni down through the hatch. Mommy was sobbing now, holding a finger to her lips as she slid the panel back into place.

Toni could hear the drawers being pushed back over the top of her. It was dark. The air beneath her room was still, cold. Then she heard the voices, yelling as heavy boots ran into the house. Gunfire. The pleas of her father, begging for forgiveness. '*Por favor! Por favor!* No!' Her mother screaming with him.

Then nothing.

She had no idea of the time. How long she'd been trapped under her bedroom. She was hungry. The cold had woken her. She was shivering. Then she heard a voice. Her friend Mayte was calling for her. Toni slapped the boards above her head, and heard footsteps coming closer. Now she was screaming. Screaming for life, for air, for the loss she knew she was about to face.

Torchlight appeared above her as the panel was lifted. Toni was crying now. She recognized the two faces – Mayte, who lived a few doors down, and Maria, Mayte's mother. Maria lifted her from the dark hole and into soft warm arms that squeezed, then held her. She felt Mayte holding her hand as Toni buried her face in Maria's shoulder.

Maria carried her out of the house. Toni closed her eyes as they passed a body lying at the front door, though not before she recognized her father. She only opened them again when the door was closed, hiding the horrors that lay behind it.

An American banknote had been attached to the door with a knife, the word *pagado* – paid – written across it in blood. The face on the note, with its receding hairline, its eyes haunted and wise, had scared her.

She'd come to love and hate Ben Franklin and the poverty her family had endured, what it had done to them.

The dice rolled gently to a stop at the end of the table, revealing their numbers.

'Little Jo from Kokomo!' yelled the stickman, as a four and one stared back into the faces around the table.

'Fuck!' said Chris slapping the side of it.

'Sir?' said the boxman.

'Sorry, I'm done. I need the john,' said Chris, waving him away and walking off unsteadily.

Toni stood in silence as she watched the five white and yellow chips being swept up, then pushed to the side of the table. The boxman flushed them down the slot, snapping her back to the present.

Chris emerged from the washrooms with the blond in tow, checking his nose as he walked. Toni followed him out to the car.

'Thanks, honey,' he said to her. 'You okay to get home tonight?'

She nodded.

'You did good tonight,' he added, flipping her a chip which she plucked easily out of the air.

She felt the embossed numbers on its side and stared at the $500 written on its surface, thinking of the money she owed to Faris in Toronto as she flipped the chip end over end. She pushed the tall skinny figure from her mind. He could wait.

'Be good now,' Chris said as the window shut itself and his car pulled away.

Toni stared at the brake lights heading down the road, then back at the doors to the casino. Despite the hour, she couldn't walk away.

9 .

I'd met Christie at a press function months before. It felt strange to be in a room with her, with all these lights and cameras. Just knowing she was one of their clients. My peers with their microphones held aloft, waiting on her every word. To be honest, I'd heard it all before. She'd answered several of my questions, even allowed for a few follow ups, much to the annoyance of everyone around me.

I'd enjoyed the attention. She'd invited me to walk for her at her next show, to give me the whole experience of what it meant to be in the industry. I'd been reluctant, but I agreed, as my editor had been excited about the prospect.

It had been an eye opener. To get in front of the girls, to see and experience everything first hand.

She'd kissed me at the after party. Discreetly, the squeeze of her hand letting me know there would be more to come. It had felt familiar, a reminder of times past. I gave into it, not knowing where it would lead, though I figured, neither did she.

My head spun in slow arcs. The weight of gravity pulled me in one direction. My arms ached as I felt the cuffs tighten from each side of a slowly spinning wheel. It was a circular frame with two struts forming an X through its center. I could see myself in a wall of mirrors toward the back of the room. My hair fell in front of my face each time I was turned upside down.

I tried to look at the rest of my body, but couldn't. I was facing the other way. My legs were splayed wide apart, strapped to x-shaped struts. Flashes of white appeared in the mirror between the strands of hair I was sweating through. I was covered head to toe in white latex. All of the wrong parts of me were naked, on display.

I braced myself as I saw her approach. Flashes of skin and red lipstick stretched back to reveal white teeth. I grunted as the leather whip found its mark on my ass. The gag in my mouth prevented me from saying anything.

She was sick. Had to be. Did she recognize something in me?

'Arrrggh.'

That whip again.

'Fggen twstd btch.'

'What did you say?' Christie asked.

'Nthg … I dnd sy anythgg. I … Arrgghh!'

'You like that, don't you? You shouldn't. Maybe it just needs to be a little harder. What do you think?'

I could see her approaching again.

'Arrrgggghh!'

'Better?'

She circled me. I could hear her boots striking the dark wooden floor. She stopped me spinning. Held me upside down. The floor became the ceiling as blood rushed to my head. I could hear her breathing above me. Her boots were level with my face. She'd chosen black latex. Her top, pants and boots were one. I felt the leather strings of her whip graze against my nipples, felt the handle stop beneath my chin, poke me as I struggled to remain conscious.

'You want to wear my clothes?'

'Mmmggh.'

'Do you think you deserve to? I'm not sure you're pretty enough to be a model.'

My vision began to blur; things became fuzzy as my head began to spin.

'You're kind of cute though, in a funny, lost kind of way …'

She kept on talking, though I could no longer process the words.

'Ahhhgggh.'

The whip again. More pain, then darkness.

— ✸ —

I had found him at a local club. He was a few years older now, though I liked what I saw. In hindsight, it had been his confidence I'd liked – something I was lacking.

He hadn't recognized me. He had been on the door, bouncing those who tried to talk their way in, or throwing out those who'd made it in but couldn't cope once they'd gotten there.

He wouldn't let me pay for drinks. There were guys who would do that for me, though after a while, no one was allowed to. The bartender had told me it was on the house. My man on the door had said so. If you'd approached me, chances were you wouldn't have been there long.

I'd loved it. The attention, the knowing. The privilege of not needing to worry about anything. Of just being a silent witness to everything happening around me, not needing to watch my back or think twice about anything. Just being.

He'd been handsome, funny, and eager to please. We had met years earlier, though I hadn't forgotten his face. It had kept me going for so long. A girl from a chaotic past who'd wanted nothing more than a fairy-tale future. I'd been sure he could give it to me.

We'd begun dating. Slowly at first. I was cautious, which he respected. He liked that I wasn't known. Someone new, from somewhere different. All mystery, an enigma was what he'd call me. Untainted.

Though he would get to know me. I'd tell him, eventually. There was time to let things play out, to not overthink everything that was now. Just once, Kat. Just once.

— ✖ —

I was tied to a bed face-down when I came to. The gag had been taken away as I drew in lungfuls of air. Mirrored tiles were on the floor and the walls in front of me. She was on top and inside me. I could feel hard ribbed rubber forcing its way in.

'What the fuck are you–'

She slapped me hard on the side of my face, reigniting the memory of a broken tooth.

'You bitch. Christ, I–'

'Shut up and take it!' she said, thrusting harder.

'Let me loose, honey … and I'll reciprocate.'

'Shut up. I … I'm … I'm–'

I started laughing.

'Fuck you!' she screamed.

Tears were running down my face.

'That's right you little bitch, cry your heart out!'

'They're not tears, sweetheart. I'm laughing at you.'

She stopped fucking me. I could see lipstick smeared across her face in the mirror.

'I'm laughing at this fucking charade you're running here.'

She got off me.

'Ohh. Did you cum already? Or could you see yourself in the same mirror I'm looking at?' I asked.

'You're fucked in the head. You know that, don't you?' she spat.

'Really? I'm not seeing it. This is your playhouse – isn't it? Run out of dolls? Is that why I'm here? I'll play, honey.'

She was watching me closely now.

'Hand me the keys and we'll play.'

I could see her face clearly now. She was frozen, like she was seeing me for the first time. I was scaring her. Good. I wanted her to be scared.

'Come here, Christie. Don't be shy. I thought we were just getting started. Are you okay, honey?'

I could see her boots retreating.

'What? Are you kidding me? You're going to leave me here?'

I rolled onto one arm, my wrist still tied to the headboard, turned my face and laughed. Laughed at a bully who knew nothing, but who might have just learned something.

She was gone. Several minutes later, the sound of her boots was replaced by one of heavier shoes and deliberate steps. My hands were unlocked and a soft fur blanket was draped over me. My clothes had been folded and placed in a square beside my head.

He was a tall good-looking man, several years older than me, who somehow managed to look both hard and soft at the same time.

'Are you okay?'

I nodded.

'Christie's left. Would you like something to drink? Tea, water?'

'Please, that'd be nice. Who are you?'

'My name's Hadley. And you?'

'Just a friend.'

He smiled. 'Well, I'm sorry about that. She can get a little carried away. Take your time. Grab a shower. I'll drive you wherever you need to go.'

I gave him a smile as I pulled the fur closer.

She was exactly how I thought she'd be. I knew what I had to do.

1 0 .

Jordan Franks stepped out of the darkness and into the light at Toronto's Scotiabank Centre, to rapturous applause. Applause that moved from cheering to howling as he returned for the second part of The Vaulted Ceiling's set, holding an electric guitar and wearing nothing other than a cock ring.

He launched into the opening chords of 'Blood Fills Me,' soaking up the rising noise of the covered theater and the twenty thousand souls there to listen – to him. His heart began to hammer as the powder he'd inhaled nested in the back of his throat. He cleared it with the scream that had opened doors and legs around the world.

His fingers ran the length of his guitar as thin veins of sweat trickled down the sides of his head under the heat of the spotlights. He was killing it. He had nothing left to give. This was him, naked, as God intended him to be.

Something connected with the side of his head. He shook it off and leaned forward, his closely cropped head of blond hair held beneath the microphone as he belted out the first chorus, his arms taunt, body lean, strong. The crowd surged with the familiar rhythm.

> 'The hills are dark, they're black and gray,
> There's light above them,
> people listening, people twisting – hear them say,

They'll come a-running when they know,
My world's a stage, feel its flow,
Take its pulse and you will see,
The air, the earth, its blood fills me.'

Paul Samuels, aka The Hammer, watched in dismay from his place beside the door, as his client ran across the stage with his shaved, flaccid penis slapping the sides of an electric guitar he recognized, but couldn't hear. Jordan had forgotten to plug it in.

Someone threw a bottle of water at his head to try and get his attention. It connected, but failed to stop him. The band kept playing. Who knew what Jordan was on? At least the mic was working. Then again, it might have sounded better if it wasn't. He was wasted. Slurring through the lyrics, eyes wild, and sweating like he'd just inhaled an ounce of coke chased down with a quarter bottle of Crown Royal. It had become a comedy show.

The crowd booed and hissed at him. Jordan was nodding his head, like he was Angus Young, willing them on, listening to them from a different planet, not hearing anything. They were beginning to leave now, early. Turning their backs on a band that had been great in its day, with a lead singer who wasn't tonight. Paul searched the faces of the rest of the band. He could tell they weren't happy.

Some of the crowd were pushing forward, wanting to watch the spectacle that Jordan had become. Paul stayed where he was. This was where he needed to be. The crowd would be angry, he'd make sure they dispersed quietly.

Jordan had really fucked it this time. Fucker looked out of control on stage. Any more of this shit and Paul would be looking elsewhere for employment. He'd seen first-hand how ugly this shit could get. Which was why he was by the door, trying to gauge how the crowd was reacting.

This was where you got a first look at any sign of trouble. You could see it in their faces. Disgruntled, pissed off. Ripped off was always the starter. But they were mostly kids. Young pimply things who could barely string a sentence together, let alone take a run at some sort of security breach. But there only had to be one. Usually a little older. A fan with a bit more confidence, maybe with some sort of obsession, might just have a go.

Paul watched as a trickle of faces bitched, laughed, or drooled at each other as they began to leave for gate three, which led outside to Bay Street. Maybe they'd be okay. Half of the crowd look as wasted as Jordan. They had their cigarettes at the ready, their jackets wrapped around themselves, girls hanging off boys showing each other pictures on their phones, no doubt of Jordan's cock.

Paul shook his head. Jordan would be fined for that fiasco. Add it to the ever-growing list. Fucker was running out of time, that was for sure. Hadley wouldn't be impressed. Then again, when was he?

A pale white kid with headphones around his neck, shoulder-length black hair, wearing a bright blue jumper and a leather jacket sauntered past. He stared back at Paul like he wanted to say something to him. Paul could see the hate in his face. Whether it was reserved for him or the show he'd just walked out of, he didn't know.

It was the kind of face he wanted to punch, just to sit him down on his ass. They always thought they knew it all. *Go ahead son, please.*

The kid walked away, buttoning himself up as he headed for the main entrance. It was cold out, late October and there were already flurries on the ground. They'd all go home, and he might just get to fuck that cute little redhead or one of her mates he'd seen hanging around the side stage.

He checked the auditorium. Jordan was still staggering from one end of the stage to the other, playing the last on their set list. Paul called for one of the center's security staff to take his place at the door, and headed backstage.

'Hammer, ya fucker!' said Jordan from where he was sitting in the back room, now with no guitar, still in a cock ring.

A group of girls were lined up in the corridor out front screaming for autographs, half of them carrying knickers in their hands. Tommy, a stage hand had probably paid them to be there.

Paul closed the door behind him.

'Ya fuckin' hear it man! Lovin' it yeah,' Jordan said, cutting up another line and inhaling it with a note handed to him by that fucking dealer Riley, who was seated beside him, smoking a joint.

'Get some clothes on, Jords. Best we pack this shit up and get going.'

'Fuck man, really?' he said, his face barely holding itself together.

'Really, Jord. The rest of the band's already gone.'

'Bullshit?' He shook his head, inhaled another line. 'Cunts.'

Paul got Jordan to his feet, wrapped him in his robe and belted it. He forced boots onto his feet and a large black hat onto his head. He threw an arm around him as he walked him past the screaming girls and down the corridor.

Jordan was grinning like an idiot and whispering in Pauls' ear, 'Don't worry, buddy, we've got several back at the ranch.'

The cold was biting. A wind had blown up and was coming in cool off the top of Lake Ontario. A small crowd was gathered on the other side of York St, held back by staff and a cluster of orange barriers set up across the road. Paul scanned the crowd for faces, then spoke into a mic clipped to his ear, asking for the car to be brought round.

A few minutes passed before the lights appeared from Lakeshore Blvd. He opened the back door and ushered Jordan out, just as he spotted the kid in the leather jacket. He was jumping over the barriers, screaming crazy at them as they passed.

'You're nothing, Jordan! You … you stupid fuck!' he spat.

'What?' said Jordan.

He was near them now. His pale face looked haunted under the streetlights, teeth bared, eyes wide as he launched himself, clawing the robe from Jordan's body, forcing him to the ground. The coffee the kid held burst and covered them both as he fell.

'Fuuccck!' Jordan screamed as it scalded his skin.

'You're a disgrace!' said the kid, forcing a hand around his neck.

Jordan kicked himself free and tried to stand. The kid was already on his feet, pulling a knife from his side pocket, but Paul's fist found his face first.

The kid fell, sack-like, to the ground. Paul booted him hard in the side of his back before he gathered up Jordan's robe and pushed him into the car. Around them, cameras popped, flashed or silently filmed.

11.

Any good journalist will tell you that while writing a piece from your own perspective might sound great, seem funny or be ironic, it'll likely be read as one dimensional. Black and white, missing colour, depth.

Experiences bring that colour. You need to get inside their heads to really understand what you're seeing. To appreciate their view.

I made my way into the diner on St Clair Ave West and took the free seat beside him at the counter. He was perfect. His online description of himself had been pretty accurate, which was rare.

He was short, skinny and lanky, with long brown hair. He wore a dark green German-issue army jacket, and his cheeks were brushed lightly with acne. He was a fan of the Vaulted Ceiling. He'd told me as much online, gushed about it. Well, I would be too. I was dressed head to toe in black, wearing a tour shirt from yesteryear.

His eyes took me in.

'I'm Jo.'

He took my hand. 'Tyler.'

I signaled the waitress for coffee. She poured it from a glass jug that boiled on a hot plate in the corner. It was a cold night out and as bad as the coffee looked, I knew I'd feel all the better for it.

'So, you're looking forward to the show?' I asked.

'Oh yeah. The Ceiling are old school, but they know their material.

Jordan Franks is a legend, man. They've been doing it forever, but he's still got it, eh?'

I smiled back at him. 'You got a favorite track?'

'That's a tough one. I've got a few. "Blood Fills Me", "Still Water Black", "It Was Never Yours." They're all great. I'm a fan of their first couple of albums, though, back when they were pushing it out on vinyl. You?'

I doubted it. The kid looked like he was a touch less than twenty. Vinyl had been relegated to specialty stores since the time he'd have been starting school.

'"To Somebody Lost,"' I replied, having picked out an obscure early track online.

'Really? Damn! I haven't listened to that track in a long time.' His face looked puzzled. 'Was that off their third album? I'm trying to place it.'

'No, it was the third track on their first EP, *This Trip Is Yours*. It came out a year before they blew up with "Magnified."'

He nodded to himself, clearly loving it.

'You want a drink?' I asked. 'This coffee is shit house.'

'Yeah, why not?'

'Couple of beers, please,' I said to the waitress.

The drinks arrived, and I listened as he waxed lyrical about Jordan Franks. How he'd grown up in the same neighborhood. How he felt connected to him in some way that others weren't. That he could now play half a dozen tunes from a few of their albums on guitar. What his bedroom looked like with its sea of posters pinned to every surface, many of them signed. How he'd dyed his hair blond before being sent home from prep school.

'Have you heard what they're saying on social media?' I asked cutting him off.

His face changed, began to screw itself up. 'What, Facebook? Or on the fan forums?'

'The latter. "The Ceiling is Falling."'

'I hate that fucking site. They're bitches. There's no loyalty at all. Just a bunch of jealous trolls with nothing better to do than make something good, bad.'

'I hear you. He hasn't lost it.'

'No fucking way, man! He's got plenty to give.'

'That said, Seattle wasn't pretty.'

His eyes began to water. He looked unsure of himself, of me, then laughed. 'It's Rock 'n' roll, man. He came out shit-faced. He's entitled to once in a while, eh? He apologized, didn't he?'

I agreed. 'I've got to be honest and say that I'd love him to reel it in a little, you know? Turn it on for the fans. Deliver a show that kicks ass and sends these trolls packing.'

'Fuckin-A. This is his hometown, man. He hasn't been back here for a while and I reckon that's exactly what he's going to do. Another beer?'

'Sure.'

We were a few drinks down by the time we were due to go. I'd read enough to know Jordan would arrived shit-faced. His shows since Seattle had been a little more subdued, a desperate attempt at good behavior, 'for the fans,' though the man was a train wreck. He was crawling from West to East. No further help had been required. Montreal and Ottawa had been lackluster. They were halfway through the tour and this was his hometown. What does anyone do when they get home? Try harder, or go harder?

We finished our drinks and headed for the TTC, jumping on the Yonge-University line down to Union. Most people hate public transport. They're missing out. You can read people and situations that much better when you're part of it.

The doors opened as we pulled up beneath the Scotiabank Centre at Union. Fans were everywhere now, pouring out of doors, gates, walkways, pooling in the center of the station and heading for the stairs. I left Tyler and headed for the washrooms. I had to change.

I'd made it backstage, like any girl dressed in clothes a few sizes too small is able to. He was there, in front of me. Scanning the crowd, pacing back and forth like some sort of caged lion, looking for fresh meat to evict from the seething mass that filled the center.

He had no hair and looked quite a bit bigger. His T-shirt was black and predictably tight. It had been years since I'd seen him. They hadn't been good ones. I wasn't sure how I felt, looking at this man. This thing that had caused me so much damage. I caught his eye, flashed a smile from beneath a red wig. He smiled back. That stupid smile that told me his cock was doing his thinking for him.

He hadn't recognized me. I focused on his face.

He hadn't been easy to live with. We'd started well, as most couples do. Fucking more than thinking. Sex aside, he'd seemed gentle. Bringing me gifts, taking me out, small things that had mattered. And I'd felt good for it. Felt good to be stable, to be able to enjoy the moment without a care or a consequence.

Then the drinking had started. One cold beer a night had turned into two, then three, followed closely by nights out with the boys. Before the two seemed to find each other and he was gone most nights. We fought. Constantly.

Maybe I was destined to seek out this kind of a guy? Was this as good as it was going to get? I worked hard to bring him back, and he had followed. He listened, agreed to temper things and I knew then that he could be good.

Until he hit me. Hard enough in the face to break a tooth. I studied my cheek in the mirror for far too long. Watched it rise like a cake in an oven as my body iced it with a black and blue brush.

And I thought of a much earlier time. When my father had done this. Attacked my mother without a thought for anything. Incapable of killing the rage that had gotten him there.

Well, I wouldn't do it. I wouldn't – couldn't let that happen to me.

But he brought me back, pleaded for forgiveness, promised me all would be well. He asked me to hit him. I did. Hard enough to burst the blood vessels in his left eye for a month. Things quietened down. He came back.

— ✖ —

I lay underneath him in the penthouse Jordan had rented at the Four Seasons in Yorkville. He grunted and sweated as he fucked me.

This was the guy I'd cared so much for.

I thought of the blade I'd buried in the bottom of my clutch. How easy would it be to pull that out and drive it deep between these shoulder blades? Or into this thick, sweaty neck that had managed to turn away from things that should have mattered.

He hadn't recognized me. I wasn't surprised; he hadn't before. Then why fuck him? *Be done with it and kill him.* It would have been easy, though he deserved much worse. I wanted to know, to try and understand. *Well, now you do.*

I'd never hated him more.

There it is then, do it.

Not until his world collapses. When he's desperate, when there's no other way. Then.

I felt him groan, then cum hard. He rolled off me, presented me with his back, mumbled something and fell asleep.

I lay there for hours, thinking of another time. About a different person. How things might have been. I heard him wake, felt him rise, then heard the basin running. I could feel him staring at me, then not much more than a pause before the door closed.

1 2 .

Paul licked the inside of his mouth. His tongue searched for any sign of hydration, but failed to find any. His head was thumping. He kept his eyes closed and rolled onto his back, dropping a forearm across his face to prevent any light from finding its way in.

Where the fuck was he? He could feel someone next to him, breathing gently. He opened an eye, saw a few strands of red hair before smiling to himself. *That's right.* He rolled himself toward the edge of the bed, trying to limit movement while gently pushing himself out of it, using his right hand, which throbbed.

His knuckles were reddened.

The kid.

He was pissed at that fucker getting through the center's security lines. Fuckwits. But he was pleased he'd seen him early enough to stop him in his tracks. A knife, of all things. The little shit.

Jordan had hit it hard. The drugs had kept coming, courtesy of Riley, and so had the girls.

Paul had been patient, watching over his charge and the people around him until the party had begun to fade. He'd made polite conversation with the redhead, but had kept an eye on her all the same. She'd teased him throughout the night – something he'd learned was a likely sign he'd get lucky.

He'd gotten that, and then some.

He slid onto his hands and knees, searching for his clothes, which were spread across the thick-carpeted floor. This was the last place he wanted to be when Jordan woke up, no doubt needing everything to help sooth his battered ego. By midday it would have well and truly landed. Not to mention getting away from this chick. What was her name? Gina? Jerry? Whatever. The groupies were always so needy; texting, messaging, trying to work their way back in and all that shit. It was a show, for Christ's sake! Did they think they'd take them along with the band?

No. Best left behind. Leaving as little detail as you could manage, which Paul had gotten down to an art form. Hadley would be watching him closely. There was bound to be some shit in the press, which he'd hate, and that would be all he needed. His relationship with Hadley was far from steady. That was understandable. The old dog needed to learn some new tricks – his bag was empty, and Paul knew it. The team and their client base was established, though no one seemed to have any idea about what should happen next.

He slipped into a bathroom, filled the basin with cold water and buried his face in it. He splashed water under his arms and pressed a warm towel to his body. The wall was a mirror, showing him every detail he wasn't quite ready for. He flexed a bicep, studied the vein that snaked across the top of it, before donning his shirt and pants. He gently opened the bathroom door, searched the darkness of the room before making his way toward the door on the other side of it. He clicked it quietly shut, then headed for his car in the basement.

The gym always smelled great. All concrete and steel, clean, hard, just the way he liked it. He loved it when they toured at home. Toronto was always great at this time of year. The crowds were a little more manageable. Fewer tourists, with autumn having well and truly run its course. No one cared about what shape they were in, wrapped up in jackets, toques and shit.

But Paul did. The body always needed to be fed, to be worked. Otherwise it got lazy. Fuck that! Not for this guy.

He straightened himself, arms back, pecks out, and headed for the desk, smiling as he walked. That blond chick was on reception today. Good. Love her – what was her name? Kylie? Kate?

Paul gave her his best look, direct, head on.

'Hi Kate' he said, leaning on the polished steel countertop. 'How you doin'?'

'It's Kylie.'

Fuck!

'And I'm good, thank you. Towel?'

'Yeah … uh, please,' he replied, taking it.

'Rough night, eh?'

Cheeky bitch.

'Late one. Working, ya know?' He smiled.

She gave him an expression that implied she did know.

He turned away, scanning his membership card as he passed through the turnstile. He'd run cardio a few days before, so he'd hit the weights and the bag today. Purge himself of some of that shit he'd inhaled last night. Plenty of time to wrap it all up in the sauna. With any luck that yoga instructor, Carmen, or whatever her name was, might come down and–'

'Paul,' said a woman's voice behind him.

Oh, fuck. Just what I don't need.

'Toni,' he replied, turning and smiling.

'Another hard night by the looks of things,' she said.

'Well, you know … not all of us get to wander through art galleries, museums and shit. Must be pretty exciting though, eh?'

She shook her long black hair. Today it was tied back in a ponytail. She wore a purple and black Lycra suit that showed the strength of her body. Her black T was pulled back from the tops of her arms, cut short above her midriff, showing off the dark colour of her skin and her abs.

She was a powerful woman, not bad looking, either. He'd been tempted several times, though a lack of interest on her part convinced him she was probably a dyke. He hated Mexicans, anyway.

'Depends … if your idea of excitement is fucking groupies – last – then so be it,' she replied.

'Fuck you.'

'Not in this lifetime. Have you looked at yourself this morning?'

Paul rubbed a hand over his head, felt it bristle under the palm of his hand. 'Wished you'd woken up to it, eh?'

'What do you think?'

'Probably,' he grinned, winking at her.

Toni rolled her eyes. 'Well, you looked pretty good online last night. Really took it to the kid with his penknife.' She smiled.

'What? It … it was a fucking switchblade. Little prick was going to–'

'Yeah, genius, sure. Just another great showpiece for the company. Have you heard from Hadley?'

Paul looked away, stared at the weights and oversized mirrors in the distance. 'No. Should I have?'

'He's in town next week. Thought he might have called you ahead to meet.'

'Well … he hasn't. I'll call him.'

'Why don't you straighten yourself out first.'

'I'm straight, just mind your own shit.'

Bitch. He left her there, towel wrapped around her neck, thinking about what he could do if he grabbed either side of it.

1 3 .

Contagious – Jo Reid

I confess, I was there. If you have any sense, you wouldn't have been. I'd like to explore the issue of talent versus entitlement. Jordan Franks is a superstar currently trading on yesteryear.

There it is. I've said it.

What goes through the mind of a superstar? All the hard work they put in. The hard times they endure ahead of getting any semblance of recognition. The fear of failure, of putting yourself out there. Not knowing if what you're doing is something that people want to see, read, listen to, eat, or just choose to ignore.

And then suddenly, they've heard what you've said; tasted what you've made; seen what you wanted them to. They love what you've done. Gray skies part, become transparent, then blue shines through, followed finally by a perfect golden light. You're up. People are calling, wanting to speak to you, then pleading, begging for your ear. You're noticed. You're on top. You're talking on shows, scribbling signatures, if you've got the time. The people around you want people to know, that they know – you.

What then? Your ego tank is now pleasantly full. Overflowing, in fact, with friends, family, distant relatives, ex-girlfriends, boyfriends, one-night stands now calling. Well, it's easy. You indulge them. Give them a glimpse of what you have. What they don't. You make a proverbial pig of yourself. You roll in it.

Then, caked in mud, you might find yourself in front of a mirror, reflecting on what you've done or, in fact, what you haven't. Your manager's in your ear; the label, shareholders, business partners are starting to talk. You can hear their whispers. Chances are you ignore them. You keep going.

That's what you do when what you've done so far has been so so right. The lines are blurred. You don't need opinions, this is who you are. The world can deal with it. And it does.

The bad behavior is noted. You're now tabloid fodder for the world's press. You become a categorical display of the cycle of life: of nothing, to something, to anything they want you to be.

With his cock ring and splintered vocals, Jordan Franks is being turned into something right now. And it's not pretty. Get out, Jordan, while the going is good. Take some time off. Walk away. Get some air into those much-damaged, water-deprived, air-starved lungs of yours. Take your security with you. Punching a kid, no doubt a die-hard fan barely out of his teens, while you're carried to your limousine – all caught on film. Not a good look. Wouldn't you agree?

My take on the Vaulted Ceiling's show? One I wish I'd recorded on TV that fell off my PVR schedule because the rest of it became full.

Comments:

(This is a forum for feedback, please be courteous, not abusive with your responses.)

Anon: Hi Jo. You are full of shit. Were we at the same show? Jordan rocked. I think you're probably just a sad, lonely woman – are you a woman? With nothing better to do than put someone with talent, unlike yourself, down.

Jo: Hi Anon. Glad you're willing to step out of the shadows and put a name to your comments. I could be a woman. What do you prefer? Sounds to me like men, so let's go with that.

Si: @Anon – You're a dickhead. I was there and he sucked.

Anon / KJ: @Jo – F*!K YOU DYKE!

Jo: @Anon / KJ – Two more letters, you're so brave! Stick with the doll you keep in the closet buddy. I'm sure she (he?) loves listening to Jordan as much as you do.

Sal: @Jo – Hi Jo. I think your article is a great one. You paint a clear, simple picture about the realities of stardom. We often give celebrities the benefit of everything. They get away with a lot of things they shouldn't and as a result, their sense of entitlement grows at a rapid rate alongside their egos. Your point about the security does seem a little misguided to me. Yes, the guy hit the kid and I don't condone that at all. But the fact is, the kid had a knife and intent. That's bad news and talks to a troubled teen. I think he got what he deserved, what the security guy is paid to do – protect.

Jo: @Sal – Did he protect Jordan? Or did he just attack someone? If he'd just wrapped his arm around the kid's neck and dragged him away, no problem. He didn't. He slammed his fist into his face. The kid's probably sitting in a dentist's chair as we write. What's that going to do for the kid's future? For his mindset on what is right or wrong? That fist has probably ignited a hatred for more than celebrities, and chances are, you and I will be reading about him in the future. Not in a good way I might add.

Anon / KJ: @Jo – C@#T.

Jo: @Anon / KJ – Cock.

This thread has been frozen and will be screened. No further comment can or will be posted.

1 4 .

The small black roller door was up. It was off a small alleyway at the far west end of Bloor St; closer to Chinatown than downtown, though it suited them well. Several weeks had gone by since they'd last met, and with all the fuss in the media around Chris's visit to Montreal and Jordan's show, they had plenty to discuss.

Paul was circling Toni inside the ring. Sweat mingled with blood from a small cut above his right eye. He was grinning at her, like he was pleased he'd been hit. His right hand was raised beneath his chin, his left was held slightly below the other, guarding his chest as he pressed forward.

Toni skipped lightly around him, comfortably away from the ropes in case he decided to charge. She'd been scoring easily off him with body shots for the last two rounds before catching his head gear at the start of this one. He hadn't been ready for it.

Paul shook his head; spots of blood spattered the blue canvas floor. He watched them fall and dot themselves between the S and T of the Everlast logo before he lunged forward. An elbow found her right breast, while his left glove drove hard into her stomach, forcing wind from it. She stumbled backwards before throwing herself to his left, almost losing her footing, but managed to duck the right-hand roundhouse he'd sent at her face.

Paul's grin stretched a little wider. He'd enjoyed that. Their eyes followed one another cautiously around the ring. They could hear the others arriving, though couldn't afford to look. Paul was pushing harder now, forcing her toward the ropes.

Toni held her ground, stepped into, then around him before he switched feet to southpaw, steadying himself. Paul focused on her chin. He watched sweat run down the sides of her face, collecting at her jawline. He'd love to break it. Then he saw his chance, a patterned move that would take her right into his left hand.

He launched himself at her, knowing the clock was almost done. Toni held her ground again, put her head down to avoid his glove and led with her knee, stepping into his body instead of away from it.

He felt the hardness of her Lyrcaed knee connecting with his balls. They spread to either side of it, before he collapsed in the fetal position on the floor, gasping for air.

'Ahhh. Bit … you, fuc … ohhh …'

Toni stood above him. He was curled up on the canvas, his gloves trying ineffectually to massage his crotch.

'You put your elbow in either one of my tits again and you'll be going commando for more than a few days, shithead.'

The bell sounded, along with some light applause from around the ring. Toni stepped through the ropes, grabbed a towel from a corner post and made her way over to the water cooler. It was balanced on a wooden stool beneath a large black and white poster of Robert De Niro in *Raging Bull*, his left eye cut, swollen; blood running freely as he stands over his fallen opponent.

She took her time filling a bottle.

Hadley called them in. 'Alright, party's over. Get some air into your lungs, Paul, and join us at the breakfast bar.'

A few minutes later they were gathered. Paul was stretched out on an old couch in the corner, his legs wide apart, a cold unopened can of coke balanced between them. Arvin was crouched in a corner watching silently, his back pressed against the wall. Toni was standing, breathing lightly, leaning against a concrete pillar. Hadley was circling the floor, dressed in his usual off-duty kit: gray and white camo pants with a black T.

'How are we all doing?' he asked.

A few non-committal mumbles came back.

'Its been a bit like that, hasn't it? On the whole we're doing alright. Can't say the media coverage these last few weeks has been great. Any reason why?'

There were a few blank stares.

Toni spoke. 'What are we supposed to do, Hadley? We're there to protect, to react as quickly as we can. It's not our fault cameras are on site. They're events, for Christ's sake.'

'Exactly. Which is why we need to be a little more discreet about what we do.'

'I'd have thought a little publicity isn't a bad thing,' said Paul, from his position on the couch.

'Usually no. Depends upon perspective, and unfortunately for us, this bit of coverage doesn't paint us or our clients in a favorable light,' said Hadley, throwing a copy of the *Globe and Mail* at Paul.

It had been folded to the 'Arts' section. He took a quick look at it, then threw it across his lap. 'Nobody reads this shit, anyway. It's for snobs. I'd pick up the *Star* or the *Sun*.'

'Well, as much we all know that more pictures and bigger headlines make it easier for you to read,' replied Hadley, 'a lot of people with a lot more money than you and I would ever see, might disagree.'

Paul carefully unfolded the article and began to read it.

'What it tells me is that we need to be more careful about the way we go about things. Our clients, and I mean all of them, are high profile. They crave the limelight and relish any coverage they get. If we're not careful, we get sucked into it. Launching yourself at a kid with knife in full view of multiple cameras isn't going to do our business any favors. Discretion is key. Toni, you're equally guilty of being dragged into something. Think smarter. Do your job, but try to anticipate a situation that would be best avoided.'

'I'm sorry, Hadley,' said Toni. 'If I have a client who's being attacked, even if it is in response to their own stupid behavior, I'm going to step in. I'm paid to.'

A few grunts around the room signaled agreement.

Hadley nodded. 'I hear you. But let's imagine that the bodyguard you took down got to you first. On camera, perhaps. Then what?'

'Well that's obvious. He couldn't, and I look great on camera.'

He smiled. 'I agree, though if he had, where would we as a company be? I'm just asking if it could have been avoided. Was Chris drunk? How was he behaving? Could you have removed him from the event before things went pear-shaped?'

'What the fuck!' said Paul, slapping the inside of the paper. 'Who is this? This article is bullshit! This isn't a review, it's a fucking take down.'

'Of who, Paul? That's my point. You offered yourself up by leaping into the light with a kid you could have tackled and dragged away into the crowd, versus leading with your fist. Think about what you're doing. About the future we're trying to build here. All of you need to think.'

Paul's cellphone rang. 'Sorry, Hadley,' he said, checking the screen. 'It's Riley. Fucker only ever calls me when the shit hits the fan. I'd better take this.' He levered himself gently off the couch, keeping his legs wide apart. 'Yeah, Riley. I can't really, I'm in a meeting. What's the problem?' He shuffled toward a far wall, out of earshot.

'My point is,' said Hadley, 'think about how we're going about things. We have four solid clients – make that three and half – in our portfolio.' He winked. 'We can't afford to lose any of them. We need to think about how we can recruit, and–'

'What the fuck!' said Paul. 'Which hospital? Why? Forget it. I'm on my way.'

The others turned to look at Paul. He was sweating as he forced himself to walk, bowlegged, toward the door.

He surveyed their faces as he passed. 'It's Jordan, he's in hospital. He just tried to kill himself.'

1 5 .

The party kept on going. Jordan had been up here for three days solid, choosing to stay on at the Four Seasons to wallow in his post-concert misery.

My review, which had just hit the newsstands, had no doubt driven him deeper into whatever depressive coma he'd fashioned around him. I watched from a corner of the room, drink in hand, as a plethora of girls vied for his attention. But I knew it was me who had it tonight.

Things would really begin right here, right now – with me.

The insistent ring of the phone had finally stopped, replaced by a knock at the door. The manager of the Four Seasons opened it and surveyed the room. He looked like a hotel manager should – thin and pasty – and was made all the thinner and pastier by the large dark-skinned security guard standing to his right, who must have been six-and-a-half feet tall and half that wide.

The manager spotted Jordan lying on a corner of an oversized couch. He pulled the plug out of the wall before 2-D from Gorillaz could talk to us about future pixels and his rhinestone eyes.

The girls filed out, one by one. I stayed where I was, watching as they collected handbags and half-drunk bottles; whatever they could carry out with them. I ignored the giant who was grunting and pointing at the door from above me.

Jordan used his free hand to signal that I was staying. Half his face was hidden inside an almost empty glass. I smiled back at the giant, who the manager told us was named Corey, and watched as he retreated through a closing door.

Jordan picked up a bottle of Jack, then me, and took us both toward his bedroom. His robe fell down the side of one arm as he laughed, his eyes rolling around in his head. I'd managed to get myself in the door dressed to the nines, confident I'd be what he wanted.

He threw me onto the bed. He looked nothing like the front man of the Vaulted Ceiling, the hero of the underclass, born and bred in the poorer pockets of Hamilton. The local boy done good. User of a thousand women. The boss of the person I hated. Well, I'd use him.

Careful, you might have to hurt him to do that.

With distance came suspicion. He was cheating on me. The signs were there; the late nights were nothing new, though clean shirts and flowers suggested nothing good. I started checking his phone, while reminding myself what he did for a living. I'd find nothing there.

So one night I followed him, from the club he'd been working at to a little speak easy a few blocks north of Yorkville. There was almost no one in it. No one, except for her.

I stood in shadows, watching from behind a large tree across the road. The window panes were small and square, framing their faces perfectly. She looked like I had a year or so earlier – smitten. Happy to be where she was in that moment in time, a moment I should have been enjoying.

How long had he been doing this? I couldn't tell him anything now. You have to walk away. But I couldn't. I stood transfixed, watching from behind my oversized tree for as long as they were inside. He looked relaxed, charming. Everything I'd known and had somehow lost along the way.

To her. To this girl. But why? How does anyone make that change?

Do they suddenly decide that what they were into one day no longer matters the next? I turned my back as they rose to leave, slipped into the shadows and walked away, doing my best to harness the hatred for the girl I'd seen with flowers in her hair.

— ✸ —

His bedroom was predictably large. Huge mirrored-glass walls complemented the oversized windows. Low lights tucked under nightstands kept the room in view.

He made love to me like something that had come in from the cold: slow, paralyzed, with little to no thought as to how things might progress. The exact opposite of how you'd envisage a rock star going about it. Then again, would they even care?

I climbed out of bed and took a small plastic bag filled with a flakey white powder out of my clutch. He smiled on seeing it float into his field of vision. I tapped out a large line and chopped it up, adding his own coke to what I had. I kept a second line clean of the ketamine, gently held a rolled note to my nostril and inhaled the contents.

The coke slid down the back of my throat like liquid toffee, stretching itself slowly on gentle fingers. Jordan got to his knees and inhaled, no half measures there, as expected.

Ketamine is an anesthetic. Its effects are more pronounced when added to alcohol, because both are respiratory depressants. When it's combined with coke, then acid – well, your guess is as good as mine. You've probably got less than five minutes before things take a really bad turn.

I lay him on his back, slid on top of him, and fucked him hard. That was personal, because I could. My life and its disasters have been dictated by too many men. It felt good to take some semblance of control.

Madame Rai had taught me constraint. A temporary gift of acceptance. I'd had enough. This is what I could do. What I was capable of. I pushed care aside and thought of what I needed to get done.

His eyes strayed from me to the wall, then seemed to move of their own free will.

I ran a bath, filling it high, though not so deep that he'd drown in it. I led him into the bathroom, turned the lights down and helped him into it. His head was lolling from side to side now. He was burbling. He wore a stupid smile that told me he was done.

I went back to the bedroom, pulled on gloves and cleaned up everything I could, wiping the surfaces down with a damp cloth. It's amazing how focused you can be on coke when something needs to be done. I tucked what was left of the ketamine and the acid into my clutch and made my way to the suite's small kitchen. I found a good-sized knife, stainless steel with a sharp blade, in the top drawer.

The knife felt light in my gloved hand. I let my fingers crawl up its handle until I could feel the ridges beneath the base of the blade through the soft leather. Light danced down the tip of polished steel.

I found his cellphone and took it with me to the bathroom.

He was almost asleep. He looked liked any aging man who'd been given too much too soon. Lost.

I took his left hand. 'I'm sorry, Jordan. Really. You're an asshole, though you haven't done anything wrong to me. But you have to many, many others.'

His blue eyes found mine. He looked sad, confused, anything but focused.

'You're a means to end. And this,' I said, holding up the knife, 'might just give you something to think about.'

The blade sunk its serrated teeth deeply into his wrist. I ran it from one side to the other, separating skin and veins as I went. Blood began to pool, to run down the side of his arm.

His face began to sag upon itself. His mouth drooped and his chin began to wobble. Then he was moaning.

I took his other wrist. He flinched, but couldn't move as I did the same to his right hand. He was screaming now, madness interspersed with laughter. I washed the knife then placed it in one of his bloodied hands, let it slip from his grip and fall to the floor. He pulled his hand back and slid it into the tub.

Blood blended with water; pink became crimson then deep red as it ran quickly from his veins. I dried his left hand, used his thumb to unlock his iPhone. The screen blinked on. I dialed 911 and handed it back to him as I heard it connect.

He stared dumbly at what he held. A woman's voice on the other end of the phone began speaking. He screamed back at it, then laughed hysterically. He stared at me, looked at his arms and dropped his phone to the tiled floor. I could hear her voice asking him what was wrong.

I heard him screaming 'blood!' as I pulled the hoodie of my jacket over my head and ran for the door.

We were under way.

1 6 .

'Paul, isn't it?'

Paul turned to face a tall pale-skinned doctor with dark eyes pulled down by the heavy bags beneath them. They darted between Paul's own and a clipboard he carried.

'That's me, doc ...'

'Anderson. Doctor Peter Anderson. You're here to see Jordan. I understand you're with his security team?'

'I am. Is he alright?'

'He's okay.'

'Oh, thank god,' said Paul, running a hand over his head. 'Is he through–'

The doc touched his arm. 'Before you go in, I want you to know he's in a fragile state.'

Paul chewed his bottom lip, shrugged the hand off his arm and straightened himself up, not liking the height he was giving away. The doctor was at least six-four.

'Okay ... I mean, what kind of state?'

'Aside from the cuts to each wrist, nothing else physically, beyond being tired and needing rest. Just go easy on him. He's being watched twenty-four-seven by the staff here, which is normal practice when someone attempts suicide.'

'Do you think that's what this was? I mean ... I heard the reports, though it's not Jordan. It's not what he does. He's touring, for Christ's sake!'

'I doubt he'll be doing much of that.'

'Fuck!' Paul said, slamming his fist against the wall. Sorry, Doc … I, I didn't mean to–'

'It's alright, Paul. I understand your frustration. But I need you to be calm when you go in there. He's swallowed a cocktail of drugs, which we've seen in plenty of musicians before, though there were traces of things that shouldn't have been present. They point to something beyond the norm of some kind of high.'

'So he made a mistake, grabbed the wrong thing or something.'

'At this stage we can only speculate. All I'm asking is that you go in gently. Be positive. Don't let him feel like he's let anyone down.'

'Loud and clear,' Paul said, taking a step back. 'Can I see him now?'

The doctor motioned Paul through the door. Paul pushed it open and made his way into the room. It stank of the usual chemicals – bleach for the floors, and who knew what else. Behind curtains, Jordan lay on his back staring at the ceiling, a drip connected to his arm. Clear fluid ran through it while monitors tracked his progress on small screens around him.

Riley sat in a chair at the foot of the bed, flicking through the latest edition of *Cottage Life*.

'You mind if I have a bit of one-on-one, here?'

'Nah, not at all, man. *Mi casa es su casa bra.*'

Fucking tool.

'Great.' Paul smiled as wide as his mouth would allow.

He waited for Riley to close the door behind him. Jordan hadn't said a thing. He just lay there, staring into space.

'Hey, buddy,' said Paul, taking a seat beside him. 'How you doin'?'

Jordan's eyes rolled to his left to look at him. 'Alright I guess … thanks, mate. Could be worse, right?'

'It could be, buddy,' he said, nodding in agreement. 'We're here, though, aren't we? Can I get you anything?'

'Sure. Couple of grams of blow and a few hot chicks would be nice,' he said, coughing himself into laughter.

'Well I'm glad there's a sense of humor in there, though I think that's the last thing you need, man. What's going on, eh?'

'Dude, I … I don't know. One minute I'm partying, all's good, then the next I'm out … ya know?'

Paul moved in a little closer. 'You sure it isn't a little more than that, Jord? I mean, I'm here, mate. We're all here to make sure things are going to be okay.'

'I've heard them talking.' He sighed. 'I don't think I tried to kill myself, Hammer, if that's where you're going. I mean, I was fuckin' bummed about the last show an all. I was crap, man. There's shit I need to figure out for sure.'

'We all have off days. Shit happens, man.'

'It's more than that, dude. My head and where I'm going doesn't seem altogether clear.'

'What do you mean?'

'I just need a bit of time.'

Paul watched as Jordan's eyes traveled around the room.

'I read that article, you know.'

'The *Contagious* one?' said Paul. 'You mean that bitch … Jo Reid? That was fucking bullshit! Cunt didn't know what she was talking about.'

'Was it a chick? I don't know. Either way, there was plenty of truth in what was written, man.'

'That's just one person's opinion. You can't let that shit get inside your head,' said Paul, tapping the side of his own.

Jordan raised a hand. 'Dude, I've had a great run at it.'

Paul started to open his mouth before Jordan cut him off. 'Now I'm not saying I'm done, by any stretch. I just need to take some time out. Give up the bullshit for a while and rethink what the fuck it is that I want to do with myself.'

'You want to sing, Jords. That's what you do.' Paul looked closely at him. At thirty-nine, he looked drawn and pallid. Hard living had indeed taken its toll.

'Do I? I look like shit, don't I?'

Paul smiled back at him. 'You're in a blue gown, on your back, hooked up to all kinds of shit. It ain't a shoot, man.'

Jordan pushed himself up in his bed. 'I'm suspending the tour, Hammer.'

'What? No you can't, man. We're not even halfway through it!'

'Sorry, buddy. If I keep going, I probably won't make it to the other end.'

'You'll be okay … we'll just need to … to–'

'Stop, Hammer. Please. I've already spoken to the guys. There's a press release going out through the label this morning. I'm in here for a few days and then I'm heading down to Mexico for a little time out.'

'What about me? What do I–'

'Sorry, dude. You're not needed right now. I'll make sure you're sorted for the month and some. I'll let you know as soon as we're back on.'

Paul bit his tongue, looked sideways at the wall beside him.

'When do you think that might be?'

'At this stage I'm not sure.'

'Okay, Jord. Do what you need to, to get better. I'll wait to hear from you.'

'Hammer?'

'Yeah.'

'I'm sorry, man. It's for the best, though. We'll come back stronger.'

Paul nodded, grabbed his hand and pressed his elbow against Jordan's, then walked out of the door, closing it behind him.

'Everything okay, bra?' said Riley.

'Fuck off.'

'Whoa. Calm down, man.'

Paul grabbed Riley's face in his right hand and squeezed his cheeks together.

'Fuck you,' he said under his breath. 'You're the reason things are so fucked. Cunt. You feed him more shit like this again and you'll be in here looking a lot worse. Know what I'm saying?'

Paul looked to his left and saw the doctor staring at him from a distance. He released Riley, ran his hand over his head and pushed Riley into the wall, then headed in the other direction, searching for an exit.

17.

Bulbs flashed and red phone lights glowed from behind barriers, as the media and fans captured images of the actors they knew and loved. The public, held a row behind the press by thick steel barriers, did their best to push forward into the bright lights just up ahead.

Security at the Princess of Wales Theatre called for calm; pointing fingers at faces and appealing to the crowd on King Street to take a step back. They did the opposite as Tom Francis appeared. His hair was slicked back in straight furrows, the sides of his head shaved clean, his bright smile almost as wide as the red carpet he stood on. The limousine sped away as Tom was intercepted by a television crew at the top of the stairs, much to the delight of the onlooking crowd.

Tom turned and waved at the fans, who responded in kind with more screaming. He finished the interview before walking his latest girlfriend into the theater.

Leroy watched the pandemonium of Tom's arrival, then told his driver to circle the block one last time.

'Are you kidding me?' he said, a tumbler of whisky in his hand. 'Look at this shit. That motherfucker was awful. You saw it, didn't you, Keanu?'

Arvin Reeves nodded, saying nothing.

'And what d'you think? Can he act or not?' Leroy pushed.

'He sucked,' Arvin replied.

'That's my man!' said Leroy slapping his thigh and draining the last of the whisky. 'Pull over, Terry. We're going in.'

Fans jostled for position as the door was opened. Leroy jumped out, his hands held high, with Arvin close behind him. A mild cheer sounded and a single bulb flashed as he walked past. Leroy turned it on with a jig down the carpet as he made his way to the stairs. He shook hands with fans while delivering the megawatt smile his parents had spent a small fortune on.

Leroy could see the camera crew eyeballing him. Lindsey Pacquor, the anchor, turned away to adjust some cords and spoke to the crew behind her.

She's going to ignore me, that blonde bitch. She probably fucked Tom the night before at the Four Seasons.

He'd seen her. She'd had her hands all over him.

His face lit up as the lights behind the camera flashed on.

'Leroy, how are you?' asked Lindsey, her blue eyes wide beneath lashes heavy with mascara.

'Hi, Lindsey! I'm good thank you, darling. Really pleased to be here.'

'Are you loving Toronto?'

'What's not to love? This festival is what film's all about. Real people, enjoying great films. My family's here, so I spend quite a bit of time Canuck-side, you know?' he added, smiling big.

'Really? I had no idea. Now the film. Rumor has it there was a bit of tension on set between you and Will. Any truth in that?'

'No, not at all. The only tension was in the drama Will pulled together.'

'So he was good to work with?'

'Great. A visionary – you know. One of those gifted people we look to for direction and really, just enjoy being on set with.'

'Good to hear. So your part in the film, Leroy,' she said, checking her clipboard. 'You play the tortured brother.'

'Well, I don't know if he's tortured, though he does come with a lot of baggage,' he said, laughing.

'Sounds perfect.'

I hate you.

'So, not much screen time in this one?'

Her neck was slender, he could probably break it.

'Well … it's never about the minutes. It's more about the quality of-'

'Veronica! Ronnie, darling!' she said, turning. 'Sorry, Leroy, we'll have to leave it there.'

You bitch.

'No problem, Lindsey. Thanks for the time.'

He didn't need her, anyway. They'd see what he'd done on screen. Let the work do the talking. If she was lucky, she might get a chance to speak to him on the way out, though he doubted it.

Leroy made his way to the bar, grabbed a drink and made small talk before the bell chimed for the showing. He headed into the auditorium, with Arvin following. He walked straight to the front row, shook a few hands on the way in, before walking past Tom, who turned his head to one side as he passed. Leroy sucked in air – the front row was full. There was a single seat with his name printed on it in the second row. He recognized some of the extras and camera crew alongside it.

This is bullshit.

He called over an usher.

'Yes, sir?' said a kid with a mop of dark hair and pimples all over his face.

Leroy whispered in his ear. 'You've got me seated in behind with the crew here. I'm not happy with that. You need to move me to the front row.'

'Sir, I can't. The film is about to start.'

'Then you better get this shit done, if you know what I'm saying. 'Cause I'm not sitting there. Get the manager.'

Leroy stood to one side. A murmur broke out among the seated cast and crew. A few eyes caught the room's side lights as they looked up, then away from him in unison.

Leroy stood still. A large woman with a pen light and a clipboard approached.

'What seems to be the problem here, sir?' she whispered.

'My name is Leroy James,' he said through the side of his mouth. 'I'm in this film. In fact, I'm on stage for the Q&A session after it. Yet you've got me seated in behind here with the camera crew. Why?'

She raised a palm and flattened it out for calm. 'Mr. James, I apologize if there's been some sort of mix up. I can assure you that the seats have been allocated according to the director's wishes. The film is about to start.'

Will Rogers, that fucker. I knew he hated me.

'Well, I don't see why he'd wish for me to sit back here.'

She shifted her weight to her other leg. 'That's not for us to know, that's for the director—'

'Whose festival is it?'

She looked confused.

The spotlight came on as Will Rogers took to the stage to loud applause. He bowed deeply before spotting Leroy.

'Good evening all. Thanks for coming out. Good to see you Leroy, grab a seat,' he added smiling.

The crowd laughed as a second spotlight found Leroy's face. He smiled and waved at the director before taking his second row seat, seething inside. Arvin followed and stood to the right of the stairs beside him.

The credits began to roll to rapturous applause. It wasn't quite a standing ovation, though it was well on its way. Leroy was pleased. He shook a few hands around him before staff took him backstage. Arvin followed through the side curtains and stood to the left, as the cast sat down and were handed microphones.

Leroy looked up at the crowd before him, then sideways at the cast, only to see the large woman he'd argued with earlier sitting in the MC's chair.

Great. Just what I need.

They were midway through the session before Leroy was asked a question. She had to repeat it before he heard her, having drifted away.

'Leroy, I was asking how you found playing the brother. His relationship with his father and the majority of the cast was dysfunctional, and it's probably fair to say he was estranged. How did you prepare for the role?'

A gentle murmur sounded from the second row, where the crew sat.

'I thought the script was a good one. I've always admired Will's work so I jumped at the chance to work with him. I come from a family of six–'

Someone in the crowd coughed while saying 'bullshit'.

Leroy ignored it. 'So I understand what it's like, not being able to get along with everyone. I took that energy, those thoughts, and did what I could to bring Harlo to life.'

'And I thought you did that resoundingly. Wouldn't you agree?' she said to the audience.

Another round of applause.

'Your role in this film was a short if not intense one. I personally felt that you opened up all sorts of possibilities for Harlo. Would you have liked him to have had a chance to say more?'

'What actor wouldn't?' He smiled. 'Though you judge the merits of each script and what you might be able to bring to it before you sign on. But yeah, I agree. I think there was plenty of scope for Harlo to bring more to the piece.'

'Will, what do you think?'

'The character I wrote is what he is. I thought Leroy delivered a great character. It felt like he had been working on it for years.'

The crowd laughed. Arvin saw Leroy's shoulders rise and reset themselves. He felt his own grow tense.

'Thanks, Will. I aim to please.'

'And occasionally you did,' Will added, grinning.

Leroy felt the whisky rise inside of him. *Don't say anything Leroy, suck it up.*

But the words tumbled out before he could catch them. 'Maybe if we'd had better direction, the process might have been a little smoother.'

The crowd began to whisper.

'I'm sensing a bit of tension–'

'If you just acted and kept your mouth shut, you might've been given more to say.'

'Maybe if you'd directed, instead of spending your time banging Ronnie in your trailer, we might have been given more of an opportunity to add something to it.'

The crowd laughed with him, while Arvin shook his head slowly from side to side.

Will was on his feet. He lunged at Leroy, catching him on the side of the chin with his right fist. His microphone chirped with feedback as it thudded to the floor.

The place erupted as security stormed the stage. Leroy had Will in a headlock before he was ripped away by a hefty looking guy dressed in a white T-shirt and jacket. Arvin saw the rings on his fingers, saw Will nod to him before he leapt across the stage and caught the punch aimed at Leroy's head.

The guard looked up at Arvin, who began to twist and hold his arm, working him to the floor. He threw himself forward, breaking Arvin's hold, but his legs were swept from under him as Arvin spun again, his leg pivoting, hitting the guard squarely in the face. Blood burst from his nose, covering Ronnie, who was sitting in the seat next to Will's, dressed in white. She screamed.

'See, Will,' said Leroy, brushing himself down. 'Much more drama than the shit you're producing.' He turned to the crowd. 'Evening all. Hope you enjoyed it,' he said, dipping his head. 'Mrs. Rogers,' he said into the microphone before handing it over.

Will's wife gave him the fingers. The crowd began yelling at each other, desperate for their phones, which had been left secured in plastic bags at the front of the theater.

1 8 .

'Keanu! Keanu?' said Leroy from the far side of the bar.

Arvin raised his glass of soda water as he approached. He hated the nickname.

'That's the shit I'm talking about,' Leroy said, pointing at the two girls on stage. They were now completely naked, leaning against the brass pole, before sliding to its base. 'You need whisky, son! We gotta get that carrot removed from your ass!' he laughed.

One of the girls was Asian. She looked so familiar it was hard to look away. Leroy knew it.

'You missing that shit, aren't ya? Well, look around, there's plenty here.'

Arvin shook his head.

'Not while you're working, huh? Well, I gotta admire that. What if I told you you're off the clock?'

'Thanks, Leroy,' he said, placing his glass on the bar, turning to leave.

'Hold on Keanu, I said 'if'.'

Arvin turned to face him.

Leroy hesitated, before laughing. 'Nah, I'm just playing with ya.' He took some notes out of his jacket. 'Terry's here, he'll get me home. You did good tonight.'

'Promise me home's not far away,' said Arvin.

'I promise. Though I'm taking one of those fine-looking girls with me.'

'I'd search them, even though they look clean.'

'Damn right!' Leroy said, laughing, his white teeth stretching the sides of his face. He waved Arvin away and signaled for another drink.

Arvin left the noise behind him, closing the door and passing the bouncers as he stepped onto the street. It had been raining lightly. The road glistened under the bright neon lights of Yonge St. He watched them change from one ad to another and thought of another life.

Tokyo's Hachiko Square was playing host to an afternoon of the usual crowded chaos. Aoto ogled the masses scrambling from one side of the street to the next on one of the world's busiest pedestrian crossings. Teen girls poured out of the steel column that was Shibuya 109, dressed in a riot of colour. Ganguro- and Yamanba-styled girls wearing platform sandals, bleached-blonde hair clipped to one side. Their faces were deeply tanned, and they wore white lipstick and eyeliner, like inversions of Marcel Marceau.

Aoto was pleased his girlfriend had left all that behind. They made their way to one of the many sake bars beyond Shibuya station. Several rounds later his head was buzzing. They took the Ginza line to Kyobashi, to a friend's party. It was in a large basement flat packed with faces he hadn't seen for some time. Jars of lager were poured from a stack of mini Asahi kegs, no doubt supplied by someone who worked there.

The lager was cold. It washed away the sweet taste of the sake. His head cleared. Myoki looked beautiful tonight. Her heavy white-furred jacket now hung on a coat rack near the door. A sheer blue dress with red and white flowers hovered gently above her pale skin.

They had spent time with her family earlier that morning. He could tell they didn't like him, though in time they might accept him.

A heavy hand landed on his shoulder as Ren greeted him. A long-time friend and the worst of influences. They walked through a projector's light. Son Goku flew across the white-washed wall, his blue laser lights destroying enemies to his left and right in the bright animated colors of a classic Manga movie. Aota smiled. He'd always had a soft spot for him.

He followed Ren through a side door. Myoki caught his eye as he passed through it. Ren closed the door behind them. It was a small bedroom with a single bed and a desk with a green light. Ren pulled a long wooden pipe from a duffle bag he carried. Ren had an uncle of Chinese decent who loved opium. These days it was harder and harder to come by, though somehow, he still managed.

Aota had regular cravings for the opiate, though he knew what it represented. He was careful in the way he used it. Enjoyment had to come in small doses. He was wary of what it could do. His friend loved the descent and was always only too willing to chase it.

Ren packed the pipe and raised it over flame to vaporize and inhale its contents. He reclined and lay back on a pillow before barely managing to pass the pipe to Aota. Ren rolled onto a cushion on the floor before Aota repacked and held the pipe to his own lips. He could taste the ash mixed in with the Chandu.

Myoki appeared at the door as he was inhaling. He tried to wave her away, though she was already closing the door as she stepped inside. She took the pipe, despite his fading protests. He passed out watching as she held the pipe to her lips.

It hadn't worked out between them. He'd watched her change over several months, then cling to Ren more and more, before he caught her. In bed with his best friend – naked, comatose, the pipe on the floor beside them. He'd stood over her, touched the gentle curve of her face, felt the once soft and supple skin, drawn tighter than he'd ever remembered it being.

Aota had beaten his friend badly soon after. They hadn't spoken since. He'd watched them at parties from a distance, and he'd tried to stop her. To speak, to do anything he could, to free her. Her parents had slammed the door in his face when he attempted to speak to them, telling him she'd disappeared. They lay her ruin squarely at his feet.

Ren had called him a few months after, his voice barely recognizable through the sobs echoing down the line Aota held gently to his ear. He hadn't heard properly, though he'd understood. Myoki was dead.

Her funeral had been a simple one. A pale wooden casket lowered gently into a family plot beneath twin cherry blossom trees on the outskirts of Kyoto. He'd tried to apologize to her parents. Their faces, her mother's in particular, had said more than words ever could. She'd slapped him, hard, which he'd accepted, bowing deeply as he departed.

Several of her cousins had found him drunk at a bar nearby. They'd punished him. Beaten him hard until he bled from every orifice. He'd been carried into a local hospital with broken arms and legs, saying nothing to the NPA when questioned.

He'd left Japan as soon as he could walk.

Arvin opened the door to a generous apartment in a high-rise jutting above the canopy of the Annex. Leroy had the suite above him. He stowed his jacket away, washed his face with a basin of warm water and switched on a lamp fixed to a small desk in the corner.

He slid a window open, peered through the black mesh that covered the outside. Rain fell softly through the streetlight below him. He sat down, slid the desk drawer open and pulled a glass pipe out from a hidden slot beneath it. It wasn't opium, but it would straighten him out.

1 9.

'Hey, Joe,' said Thom.

Jo stared at him from behind her desk in its quiet corner.

'See what I did there?'

She nodded. 'Can't say I'm a big Hendrix fan.'

Thom stood still, his mouth open. 'Really? He's the foundation for what guitar is today. "Foxy Lady", "Little Wing", "The Star Spangled Banner"? I mean, think of what he did before he died.'

Jo pushed her keyboard to one side and placed both elbows on her desk.

'Don't get me wrong, I like some of his classics. "Purple Haze", "All Along the Watch Tower", "Voodoo Child", "The Wind Cries Mary", all killer tracks. I just hate how he died.'

'Well surely you can't judge someone on how they checked out?'

Jo sat back in her chair. 'It's hard not to, really. I mean, he choked on his own excess. He pretty much pioneered the twenty-eight club, which so many others have since joined. Joplin, Morrison, and Cobain in more recent times.'

'Come on! You can't hang that on Jimmy. I mean, where's the control on his part? The guy doesn't know what followed him.' Thom's face was squeezing itself now, his brow forcing its way toward his nose. 'And besides Cobain, none of them were intentional.'

'I'm not saying they were. Though it's the lifestyle they're all chasing.

They get idolized. It becomes a vicious circle.'

He took a seat.

'That is a long bow you're drawing there, Ms. Reid. And besides, there are still plenty of theories around Hendrix being murdered.'

'True, though the fact that those aren't popularly believed, points directly back to the world's acceptance of his lifestyle and what seems to be his inevitable death.'

Thom picked up a pen from Jo's desk and started spinning it between thumb and forefinger as he spoke. 'Well, I see you're no fan of Jordan Franks,' he said.

Jo made a face. 'They were okay in their day. I just think his is done.'

'I get it. Great piece, by the way. They loved it upstairs. Bit confrontational in the thread that followed, but the views on it, the numbers around the whole section, really were quite impressive. So well done.'

'Thank you, Thom.'

'What are you doing after work?'

'Sorry?

He looked confused. 'Oh, I mean, a few of us are heading out for a drink. Come along. It would be great for all of us to get to know you a little better. That is, unless of course, you have plans?'

Jo scanned the room behind him. A few of the faces she knew were grabbing jackets, getting ready to go.

Thom tapped his watch. 'C'mon on, it's home time. Join us. Just a few drinks, totally casual.'

Jo gave him a non-committal face, but powered down her computer.

'There you go,' said Thom.

The bar was a large one. It was filled wall to wall with suits, and girls who looked like they'd be there for the long haul, their faces freshly retouched, lipstick reapplied, mascaraed eyes bright.

She'd lost the thread of conversation as she watched these people spilling drinks over one another, laughing and just being themselves.

She'd missed out on all of this, her youth having been stolen from her in the worst possible way.

Had it been the fifth or sixth family that had finally given up and turned her in? Did it even matter? It had been downhill from there.

'Jo?'

Someone tapped her shoulder.

'Jo. You okay?'

It was Mickey. One of the tech guys.

'You're a million miles away. Get you another drink?'

She stared down at her pint; it was still half full.

'Thanks, Mickey, I'm good,' she replied, a brief smile making it to her face.

She watched Thom. He was leaning against a wall to the left of the three tables they had joined together. A few of the younger girls clutched G&Ts and looked to be hanging off his every word. He was clearly in his element.

'Loved your blog, by the way,' said Mickey, returning with a drink and taking the seat next to her.

'Thanks.'

'I hear you've come to us from Montreal.'

'I have. From a smaller paper, though a good one.'

'I'm sure it is. I love it up there. You live there long?'

'About three years.'

'Before then?'

'Bounced around a bit, checking out this oversized country of ours.'

'And what did you like the most? Actually, don't tell me. You're hard to read, though I'll give it a go.'

'Are they usually easy?'

'Ouch. I'm going to go out on a limb here and say skier. You look kind of sporty. Maybe a boarder. So, I'm picking time in BC, probably Vancouver. The go-to would be Whistler, yet you ended up out here. I'll play it safe and go for something in the middle. Banff, Lake Louise.'

She'd seen pictures of the Springs hotel. Its massive buttresses, and hundreds of windowed rooms nestled among a forest of snow-capped trees, an ice-blue lake in front of it. She had probably trained passed it when she left Winnipeg, though she'd never see in it with her own eyes.

'Not quite. Can't say I've made it onto skis yet. Are skates close enough?'

'Ottawa then. Ahh … the coffeed banks of the Rideau Canal.'

She smiled. 'They are a bit of fun.'

'What do you like to do when you're not working? Or skating, for that matter?'

'Reader, writer. You know, some of the simple things.'

She liked Mickey. He was relaxed and seemed normal enough. 'And you?'

'The usual: S&M, heavy drugs and LARP battles.'

'What?' She found herself smiling. 'I'm going to ignore the first two because I know you're teasing me. What the hell are LARP battles?'

'Live Action Role Play.'

'What? Like some sort of movie scene?'

'Kinda. Think of an open field, fake swords with people charging at each other and shit.'

'Braveheart?'

'Braveh–,' he choked, spraying his beer on the floor, nodding to her as he recovered and smiled. 'More pointing and charging than monologuing, though.'

'Villain or hero?'

'What do you think?' he asked, finishing his drink.

'Remains to be seen. It's hard to pick a hero. I find it's easier to start with villain.'

'That's a little dark, don't you think?'

Jo just shrugged her shoulders. 'With the things I've seen over the years, not really.'

'I'm intrigued.'

'You shouldn't be.' Jo took another sip of her drink.

'Sounds like we might be going clubbing afterwards. You coming?'

'I can't. Sorry, Mickey, There's something I have to do.' She stood and grabbed her jacket from a stool nearby.

'That's a shame. Another time then, Ms. Reid,' he said, offering his hand.

'Another time, Mickey,' she replied, shaking it.

She slipped out, unseen by the others, her pint still half full.

2 0 .

'Hadley?' said a voice slightly louder than a whisper.

He could hear her sobbing. 'Christie? Are you okay? What's happening?'

'Sorry to call … I, I know it's your night off, though I … I need your help.'

'Where are you? What can I do?'

'There's someone, maybe police-' She started crying. 'I'm fucked, Hadley. I need you to … to come.'

He could hear her wiping tears from her nose as she spoke. 'Now. Please.'

'Alright, I'm leaving. Are you showing at the Exhibition Center?' he asked, grabbing a jacket and his keys, then reaching for the door.

'Yes. I'm … I'm out the back in the washrooms.'

'Are you carrying anything?'

'A little … I-'

'Get rid of it, Christie. All of it. Not down the toilet, they've probably got catchment bags on the outlets or something tonight. Are you in a room or a cubicle?' he asked, striding into the car park. The lights of his SUV blinked a bright orange from all four corners as he unlocked it.

'It's a room with a … a catch on it.'

'Good. I need you to focus and to move quickly. Don't answer the door. Say nothing until I tell you to. Can you reach any of your staff?'

'No. I can't. There are men outside I'm … I'm fucking trapped.'

Hadley tore open the door to his SUV, jumped behind the wheel and drove up the exit ramp. His phone was now paired and locked in its hands-free position. His tires squealed on the concrete as he left the building

'Is the roof a sealed one? Or is it square-tiled?'

'I'm not sure I understand.'

'That's okay. Just breathe, deeply. One in, one out. Is the underside of the ceiling, the side you can see, solid? Or is it one of those white-tiled, removable square ceilings?'

'I think it's the removable tiled one.'

'Great. Do you think you can reach it?'

'I'm not sure.'

'Are you wearing heels?'

'Off course I'm wearing fucking heels!'

Hadley braked hard, then indicated as he turned. His Chevy gripped the road, making the corner. No flashing lights in his rearview.

'Breathe, Christie. Slow it down … and breathe. Now pull the toilet seat down, and stand on it.'

He could hear her moving, the lid snapping shut and her feet clacking as they stood on top of it.

'I can't reach it.'

'Are you carrying scissors?'

'A small set on a necklace,' she said.

'Good. Take it off. Open them up and pry the side of a ceiling tile open.'

'I can't.'

'Stay focused, you can do this,' he said. 'Are they still calling out to you?'

'Yes,' she hissed down the line.

'Whatever you do, don't acknowledge them.'

'I'm not … I mean, I won't. How far away are you?'

'Five minutes,' he said, sighting the lights of Metro Hall. He'd had a clean run through the city. He would hit the cordons shortly, but his pass would carry him through quickly.

'How's that tile coming along?'

'I can't get it. It's too high.'

'What else can you see in the room? Is there anything that might help us distract them in order to get you out?'

'I can't see … I mean, there's nothing.'

'Look again. If you can't reach that tile, you're in trouble, Christie.'

She was crying now, an angry sobbing coming down the phone.

'Push yourself.'

'Shut the fuck up, Hadley!' she said through clenched teeth.

'Okay. I'm just … just breathe. You can do it.'

'I got it. The tile, I managed to shift it, just a little.'

'There you go. Good. Keep at it. Now get that gear up there, throw it through the gap if you can manage that.'

Hadley pulled hard on the steering wheel, dodging traffic on his way to David Pecaut Square on John St. The fashion show was happening inside the Hall.

'It's gone.'

'There you go. Now, do your best to pull that tile back into position. You need it to look like it's never been touched.'

'How the hell am I supposed to do that when I could barely reach it the first time?'

'Delicately. With the scissors. Just breathe. You don't want it crumbling all over the floor, otherwise it'll be the first place they'll look.'

'So what, I move the tile back into place and welcome them in? Is that the fucking plan?' she said, spitting into the phone.

Hadley turned the corner. Now he could see the Exhibition Center. 'Just try, Christie. They're coming in, unless I can get you out.'

'Alright already. I'm trying,' she hissed.

Hadley flashed his security credentials to a valet at the main entrance, then left his vehicle in a staff park.

'Fuck! It's no good, the scissors are too small. I can't get it! They're banging on the door. What do I do? Hadley?'

'Is there a smoke alarm attached to the roof of the room you're in?'

'Yes.'

'Good. Have you got a lighter?'

'Yes.'

'Great. Can you get close to it?'

'It's next to the tile I moved. I could stand on the edge of the seat if I balance carefully. Fuck! They're forcing the door!'

'Set it off, Christie. Set it off now.'

Hadley ran down the corridor, flashing his pass to staff as he crashed from one room to the next. An alarm squealed, and he heard staff beginning to direct patrons to the fire exits.

Hadley smiled to himself. 'Good work.'

He found a storage cupboard with *EMERGENCY* plastered in red and white across its face. He pulled out a heavy jacket, gloves, a helmet and a gas mask from the hooks nearby. He grabbed a fire extinguisher and smashed a glass panel to get the small axe in the space behind it.

'Which washrooms are you in?'

'To the left, in behind the stage.'

A stream of people had filled the corridors. Hadley worked his way past them, directing traffic toward the exits. He was beside the stage now. The place was almost empty. He kept going. The alarms were pulsing, screaming.

Two men were stationed around a collection of doors. One was staff security, short, solid and bald. The other wore a black waistcoat over a long black-sleeved shirt with a silver name badge pinned to his chest.

Hadley approached them. 'I need you both to leave the building now and head for the assembly area.'

'There's someone in there. We think she's locked herself in. She's–'

'Not your concern,' said Hadley, trying the door, then reaching for his axe. 'You both need to leave.'

They stared at him, then back at the door.

Hadley unhooked his axe from his belt. 'Now!'

They left. He gave them space, waited until they were gone. He lifted his mask up and raised the phone to his mouth.

'You there?'

'I am.'

'Stand back.'

'What?'

Hadley pocketed the phone, pulled his mask into place and swung the axe. He could hear Christie screaming inside. He was smiling to himself as he swung, watching as metal buckled and wood splintered. The lock broke and the door flew open. Christie stood there in a light-green dress trimmed with black leather. She somehow looked stage-ready, like she always did. She was smiling.

'Little dramatic, isn't it?'

Hadley hugged her, before pushing her to one side.

'Not that believable, if I somehow managed to coax you out when they couldn't.'

He jumped on the toilet seat and pulled the panel back into place.

'The gear, can't we–'

He picked her up, draped her over his right shoulder.

'Really?'

Hadley walked out of the room and down the corridor, past a few other fireman who gave him the thumbs up as he went by. The public had left the building now. He lowered Christie to the ground and dumped the gear he'd been wearing behind a side door. She brushed herself down, then followed him quickly toward the entrance, then past groups of people in the courtyard out front.

Hadley surveyed the crowd for any familiar faces. No sign of Christie's friends.

The place was awash with the color of fire trucks and police cars. Hadley stepped out into an otherwise still night, before a tall lanky girl dressed to the nines in a blue and black dress slapped Christie hard across the face.

'What the fuck?' Christie said.

Hadley recognized a girl Christie had been with. From memory, she'd stayed over.

'That was for your fun and games. I'm not your fucking rag-doll bitch. I don't care who you are.'

'Funny.' Christie smiled. 'And there I was thinking how much you loved it!'

'Fuck you.'

'Me? Oh, you should have said,' Christie replied, laughing.

Hadley took her hand and walked her quickly toward his SUV. 'Do something that stupid again and I might not be there to save you.'

'I'm sorry, Hadley, I won't. I promise,' she said, kissing him on the cheek.

'Good. Though I'm not sure I believe you.'

Christie just smiled and slumped into the darkness of the passenger seat. In seconds they'd turned the corner, leaving the flashing lights of the fire service behind them.

21.

I can see her clearly from where I stand, secreted quietly in a corner managing the entry and exit points to and from the runway's stage floor. She ignores everyone beyond the people and things she needs.

Scissors dangle from a thin chain around a neck that I have kissed. Between breasts I have known. I know what she is. She pretends she isn't. The face that she presents to the world is one of several she chooses to wear. Today's face? The up and coming fashion designer.

The fact that she's a bitch surprises nobody, apart perhaps from the unsuspecting public, who are routinely duped by the media. I guess that's me. I can tell she's good at what she does. I can see her working from where I'm hidden. Her turquoise-manicured nails flying, cutting, sewing, occasionally slapping and pinching. Her smile seems a little too big whenever she does the latter.

She has an appetite. Everybody does. You just need to follow them and they'll eventually reveal it to you. Don't expect to see anything pretty. It never is. Christie likes coke. No revelation there. It's the foundation of dieting in this industry. Though what she really loves is S&M. She's a control freak. She's controlled me; well, she thinks she has.

I see her leaving now, slipping quietly out the back. No doubt for a few lines of the white stuff. I follow her from a safe distance, walking down the concrete and steel corridor toward the washrooms behind the back stage. I pull my cap down as staff and others pass by.

I won't be noticed. I'm one of a hundred staff dressed in black doing all sorts of things around people who specialize in being seen. She takes a sharp left and disappears behind a closing door as I walk by. I check the hallway and double back, take the turn and press an ear against the steel door in front of me.

I can hear her rapidly chopping, cutting, sliding what can only be a plastic card across glass, then inhaling. No discretion here, Christie. It'll be a road to ruin for you, honey! It's a disabled stall so the door opens outward. I brace it with a white-rubbered doorstop left against a side wall. Bitch won't be going anywhere fast.

I take a walkie-talkie from my pocket and call it in. 'Pat? Yeah, it's Claire,' I say, rechecking my name badge. 'I'm by the washrooms, door 121 off the left stage corridor. There's a suspect in there who I believe is doing drugs. You might want to check it out. Over.'

'Roger that, Claire. On my way. Out.'

I walk to the other side of the building in behind the back stage. I find a free cubicle in a larger washroom and get out of the uniform I've stolen, changing back into the blue-black dress I'd chosen to wear for the evening.

I take my seat in the gallery and catch the last of a show, featuring men in beautifully tailored brown and black tweed suits. Shotguns and pheasants dangle over their backs as they walk the runway. Applause rings out as the last model closes the show with a large smile, his face made up to look beaten and bruised, his footprints leaving a bloody trail as he exits the stage.

An alarm sounds, and a voice calls for calm as patrons are asked to leave the building calmly and quietly. I watch the ensuing chaos of the audience's departure, and remember.

The sky had been purple and gray, rain threatening as I'd left the supermarket. A rolling thunder announced its arrival as the heavens opened up. In no time at all I was soaked through. My fingers were white and red from the weight of the plastic bags I carried. I was heading home to cook my guy a meal, though the item I carried, the one that played heaviest on my mind, was also the lightest in the bag.

I'd felt nauseous for the best part of three days. I was late. Inside the bag was a testing kit. I needed to know. I was desperate for the washroom by the time I got through the door. I dropped everything and headed straight in.

Positive.

Tears ran down my face. I was a young girl, happy. Things finally seemed to be clicking into place, the nightmare of my youth now being swept aside with something good. I'd show my child the love and care any child on this fickle planet deserved.

But that's when it happened. My happiness was short-lived. A six-week secret would remain one. His face. A face I'd loved, wanted to be with, wasn't present.

And I knew, right then, in that moment, that he didn't love me. Had never loved me. Didn't really care. The boy I'd put so much stock in, the idea I'd clung to for so long, was no more than that: an idea. Some sort of warped dream. And now this thing inside me would be lost. Unloved. My own youth, replicated. I couldn't do that. Wouldn't do that.

I couldn't tell him. What started as a gentle conversation rapidly turned into an argument. He left me; the boys had been calling.

It was after midnight when he returned, fumbling his way in with dropped keys, stinking of alcohol and fries. I was seated at the table in darkness, where he'd left me, my face stained with dry tears, not knowing what to do.

We began to fight. Words were eventually replaced with blows, the last of which came from a heavy boot planted firmly in the small of my back, forcing me to the ground. And then he was on top of me, crying with me, begging me for forgiveness I would never give.

— ✖ —

The night is clear as I leave the building. I stand outside on David Pecaut Square, looking back at the oversized shiny bottletop that is Metro Hall.

Fire engines bathe the square in light. There are three six-wheeled trucks, two of them with giant white cranes bolted to their roofs. Bitch has been smart enough to set off the alarm. They'll probably get her, anyway.

A side door bursts open. A tall silhouette of a man appears. His arm is wrapped tightly around her as they stride across the square. My heart beats a little faster. I need to get closer, to be sure. I walk quickly toward them, a small knife tucked into a handbag dropped loosely over my right shoulder, in case I need it.

Christie's makeup is streaked beneath her eyes though she's smiling as they move.

I slap her hard across the face.

'What the fuck?' she says.

I can see him studying me.

Does he recognize me? Yes, he does. This is just a warning, Hadley, a taste of what's to come.

He takes her hand and walks away. I watch them go. She laughs as she goes, but rubs her face as she crosses the car park, bathed in the light of the fire trucks.

2 2 .

It was nothing more complicated than a shoot, but Christie wanted Hadley there. She'd been rattled since the last show. They'd asked her to feature at a follow-up gala at the same venue a few weeks later. Begged her, offered her silly money, but she'd politely declined.

She'd opted for something simpler – a fashion spread shot in the subterranean walkways beneath the city. Now he stood at one end of it, blocking the way for any would-be onlookers, sending them up to the street at a nearby exit instead.

A young guy in jeans, with the obligatory washboard abs and vacant stare, stood with his legs apart in front of a graffitied roller door. He had a Tuke on his head and a red and black checkered shirt flapping at his sides, courtesy of a wind machine.

The loud clacking of steel on steel sounded in the subway down below. Hadley spun on his heel, shoulders tense as disc brakes squealed, straining against the rails, until he heard the train's arrival being called over the PA.

Wind pushed its way upward, tousling the blond model's hair, much to the chagrin of Christie and her photographer.

Hadley stared down the underground walkway, focused on its turning point and let his mind take him to an all too familiar place that refused to leave him.

— ✶ —

Sand and mud covered his fatigues. The sound of gunfire ripped through the air above and around him as buildings were set alight or collapsed. Huge holes had been punched through walls, through houses, through people who now lay screaming for help.

Helicopters swooped through the air over the dust-covered city of Kandahar, trying their best to push the Taliban back from the lines they were trying to forge. Bullets peppered the ground, lifted then dented it.

Hadley inched forward, staring at the limp form of a body lying half in and out of the shadows of a broken house fifty yards away. He shook his head, wiped the sweat from his eyes, then felt his lip tremble as he got closer. Now he could see the hands, one still clinging to an automatic rifle. He recognized the silver ring on the left middle finger. It wasn't; it couldn't be.

Before he knew it he was standing, then running amid the carnage taking place around him. He could hear people shouting; he wasn't sure if it was at him, or the people they were fighting. He didn't care. He kept running, stretching out now, diving as the ground in front of him exploded.

His ears were ringing. Dust fell gently on top of him as he lay still, his face to the sky. The giant belly of a Chinook flew overhead then disappeared beyond a wall. He tried to focus, to find the thing he had to have. The thing, the person he had to protect.

The dust cleared. The ringed finger lay still, the rifle now free of its grip. Blood had pooled beside it. He took the hand, pulled it close to study it, to see if this was the hand he thought he knew, was indeed the hand he didn't want to be holding.

Not here. Not now.

Tears pooled in his eyes. He leaned in and rolled him over. James stared through him. His gray eyes looked like white had been added to them. He was gone. Hadley could feel himself shaking, his whole body trembling as he clung to the lifeless brother who'd wanted nothing more than to be like him.

Gone.

He could hear them shouting. Could see them waving to him. Familiar faces with hard hats, pleading with him to move. To get away from his corner of the battlefield. Hadley tightened his grip, squeezed harder than anything he'd held onto in his life. Then they were on top of him, pulling his arms apart. Forcing him to let go. He started screaming.

The room was dark when his eyes snapped open. Sweat covered his skin. He felt the warmth of a body lying beneath his own naked one; could hear breathing, almost a panting before he pulled back. The model lay beneath him, eyes wide, terrified as Hadley's forearm was held rigid against his neck.

He pulled away, tension disappearing from his arm as he rolled onto his back. The model was coughing, gasping for air. He couldn't remember his name.

The light in the hall blinked on.

'What the hell are you screaming about?' said Christie, wrapped in a light blue robe. 'Let me guess, another tour of duty in your head? Oh, sorry, company. Didn't even see you there, honey. Oh, Hadley. You have been naughty, haven't you? I quite liked the look of that one,' she added pouting.

'Sorry Christie ... I–'

'Don't be. Maybe just look after your friend here. I'll punish you later.' She smiled, turned on her heel and padded down the hall. The room became dark once more.

'I'm sorry,' whispered Hadley.

The model just rolled over to face the opposite wall.

'Fuck,' Hadley said to no one.

2 3 .

Hadley pulled himself through the mud and into the trees as quickly as he could. His camo gear was filthy and it was getting dark as the sun began to dip behind the trees surrounding them. A soft rain began to fall. He loved being out among the elements.

He heard the quick release of an air gun. Yellow paint splattered on a tree trunk next to his head. He made himself long and rolled with his own gun into the safety of nearby scrub. He worked his way along the ground, whistling gently as he moved away from his previous position, alerting his team mates to the proximity of the opposition.

Jonas Strong wasn't a friend, he was the competition. A well-muscled, it had to be said, smart character who was well and truly full of himself. He was short, which didn't do his character any favors. He overcompensated in every possible way. A booming voice, an oversized jeep, and the need to let everybody around him know that he'd done it better, faster and smarter.

Jonas's security team was called the Gauntlet. They were a collection of five, one more than Hadley's team. Jonas originally hailed from LA, though with more and more films being made in Toronto, thanks to rebates and the city's ability to look like New York, it had become permanent.

Big brother had landed, or so Jonas liked to remind him. Well, not today. Hadley searched the trees for any sign of movement. Nothing.

He could feel his legs tightening, sense his muscles beginning to protest at having been out here for hours. Their scores were level, though the last set had been robbery. Jonas himself had been shot, but had raised the flag and fired his gun in victory.

No paint had been found on him, so he'd been awarded the win, despite a protest from Paul, who laid claim to the shot. Suffice to say, Paul hated Jonas.

Hadley fired at the sky twice from a concealed position, a practiced move to send his own team in the other direction, the assumption being that the opposition would veer toward the noise and a set play would be in motion.

Paul appeared near Hadley's flank.

'What are you doin' Paul?' Hadley whispered under his breath. 'Get to the left side of the run, you should be there with Arvin. Go now.'

'It's a bad play, they'll know,' he replied.

'It's my call and I'm in charge. Fall in.'

'Listen, Hadley, there's a few things–'

An air gun sounded. A pellet exploded on the side of Paul's shoulder, then another on the side of his head.

'Fuck!' he screamed.

Hadley ducked as a stream of pellets flew to his left. He could hear them closing, hear the sound of twigs and branches snapping as they approached. He tucked his gun into his stomach and dove into a shallow ravine. He could just make out the form of someone chasing him, movement through the trees. It looked like Jonas.

Think Hadley, think. That stupid fucker. Hadley began zig-zagging through the trees, diving through hoops of vines while searching to his left and right. There was more movement on both sides now, he was being squeezed. He saw a shallow creek on his left, the fortress was up ahead. His fortress. Paul was gone, there wouldn't be any support. No chance of holding off now.

There was a flash of clothing beside him – the taller character, Simmons. Hadley braced, stepped right, pushed off his foot and launched himself into the air and to the left. He crashed on top of his assailant, driving a shoulder then the gun hard into his back. Simmons collapsed with Hadley, though Hadley was on his feet first, his gun firing several rounds into his chest.

'Fucker!' screamed Simmons, a filthy look plastered across his face.

Hadley left him behind, carrying on toward the fortress. Leaves exploded from the forest floor as a figure appeared, gun raised, teeth bared. Hadley threw himself at him; pellets bounced in a line to his right, then at the sky as he fell backwards. They both scrambled to their feet, but it was too late. Hadley stared down the barrel and a full set of smiling teeth.

'Got you,' said the kid Hadley knew as Court.

Court's face screwed up as pellets riddled his back. Court turned around slowly to see Toni touching the side of her head from the first floor balcony of the wooden fortress above them.

It was short lived. Pellets covered her own body as a third assailant appeared, gun first, from out of the bushes alongside. Just as quickly, Jonas was beside Hadley, breathing hard, having chased him across three-quarters of the playing field. His gun was held steady to the side of Hadley's head.

'Too bad … Hadley … you had a bit of momentum going there. Stevens,' he said to the guy who'd just shot Toni – someone Hadley didn't recognize. 'Get up there … and grab the flag and let's be done with this. It's about time the West taught these Eastern turkeys how to play,' he added, grinning in Hadley's face.

Hadley could smell the tobacco of the Cuban cigars Jonas loved to smoke. Jonas fixed his position, not taking his eyes from the side of Hadley's head. He spat with his mouth twisted to his left. 'Seems you boys have had a bit of a rough time, what with one of your biggest clients wanting to kill himself an' all. That said, who wouldn't, with that fucker Paul looking after you? Like I said, Hadley, you should cut that shithead loose and jump on board with the Gauntlet. We'd be a good team. C'mon, Stevens, get your ass up there! We're still playing here.'

Hadley checked his watch. It was seconds away from five.

'Stevens! No good looking at that, son. You're do–'

A distant siren sounded.

'What the fuck?'

'Too bad, Jonas. That'll be Arvin,' Hadley said, looking at Stevens, reaching for the flag. 'You had some momentum going there.'

Jonas pulled the trigger, and pellets thudded into the side of Hadley's head.

He ignored the pain and laughed at him. 'You always were a sore loser, Jonas. Call me when you've got some class. We might consider taking you on.'

'Fuck you, Hadley.'

And he was gone.

The team laughed as they downed a second round of beers, leaning on the back of Hadley's SUV. Arvin sat on a nearby crate and Paul drank quietly, seated on top of a picnic table, yellow paint running down one side of his face. The Gauntlet had long since departed, with not much more than a cursory wave as they climbed into their cars. Hadley had expected nothing less.

'Great work, guys. Thought we'd blown it there when Toni got shot,' said Hadley, taking another gulp of cold beer. 'Well done, Arvin, really,' he added. The kid was a quiet one. An overachiever with a charming face. The most dangerous kind, Hadley thought to himself. There would be issues – everyone on the team had them, though Arvin's were much harder to see.

'Yeah, thanks for nothing, Paul, you silly prick,' said Toni, eyeballing him. 'I could hear you gabbing from halfway across the field. What the fuck was that? Let me guess, a change in strategy? Thank god they had the good sense to shoot you first.'

'Whatever, Toni. Whorebag,' Paul said, spitting at the ground.

'Pull your head in, Paul. Just do your damn job,' she said.

'C'mon guys. Cut it out,' said Hadley. 'Let's just enjoy the moment.

I brought us out here to show, once again, that despite our differences, we work well as a unit. Even when we're outnumbered or things aren't going our way, we're a team. We need to make sure we're acting like one, eh?'

Paul was the first to nod before the rest of the group agreed.

'These are challenging times, of that I'm well and truly aware. We just need to keep our heads and remain focused. Good things will come,' said Hadley.

'I hope so,' said Arvin, 'because it feels to me like someone has us in their sights.'

'Jonas?' Hadley replied. 'Don't worry about him, he's just a cocksure venture capitalist who thinks he knows more than the rest of the world. He doesn't.'

Arvin was thinking of somebody else, but said nothing.

2 4 .

'Well … wotchu think it looks like, man? He in there? The guy with the gun?'

Pat stood next to Ray, reading the lines on a TV monitor, saying nothing.

'What're we waitin' for? You think that coney-eyed mutha fucka goin' come outta there … like sum sorta … Muhammad-fuckin-Ali? Is that wotchu think?'

'No … I'm not saying that, Ray,' said Pat Sykes, a tall lanky white guy in a black leather jacket and jeans. He held a Glock in his right hand and was pressed up against a wall.

'What is you sayin', friend?' asked Ray, aka Leroy James.

'I'm saying that we need to think about our approach. Be cautious with our next step. The last thing we want to do is end up face down in this shithole.'

Leroy leaned up against the same brick wall. He wiped sweat from his brow as steam billowed out from a vented steel grating on the pavement beneath him. The camera rose above, then pulled away from them before panning to the right for a sweep shot. It spun around, then crept along the pavement to come back in.

'C'mon. Let's get up in there and kick some god-damn ass! That fat-ass muthafucka ain't nothin' to be scared of. He's probly sum kinda wide boy who trawls mall tiles for immobile pussy. He ain't even … I ain't …

'Oh fuck this! I am *not* reading this shit!' Leroy threw his arms in the air. 'I mean … are you fucking kidding me?'

'Cut!' screamed the director, from his vantage point behind the cameras.

A murmur spread across the set. Arvin rolled his eyes and took a step back, retreating into the safety of the shadows behind him. It was a rare perfect night, and the film crew had thanked their lucky stars for the light of the moon they had to work with.

'What the fuck are you doing, James?' said the director, now striding toward him.

Leroy kept on going. 'Who wrote this shit? Hasn't Eddie Murphy beaten our race up enough with this fucking, white guy, dumb-but-used-to-be-funny black guy stereotype?'

'You're paid to act, not fucking think. Dickhead.'

'Is that what I am?'

The director stepped into his space. 'It's what you're being right now. You've read the script. You signed on to the film. Now we're all being paid to make it.'

Leroy took a step closer. 'So you're quite happy to have your name attached to this shit? I mean, it's a turd, and we all know that you can't polish one of those.'

'Maybe not, though you can roll it in glitter. And believe it or not, an' I'm not saying I do, you're the glitter, son. So pull your fucking head in and do the film.' He began walking away.

Leroy started to follow him until Arvin placed a hand on his shoulder. Leroy stopped. Arvin squeezed it before he shrugged it off.

Leroy turned toward the crew. 'What the fuck are you all witnessing, here? Seriously? Would you honestly pay money to see this shit?'

Arvin tried to stop him again, but Leroy wasn't having any of it. Arvin's shoulders began to tense up as he braced himself for any sort of reaction, knowing there was no stopping Leroy now.

The director spun around. Arvin looked closely at him. He wasn't some flabby guy in a hat and a black jacket who drank coffee all day. He was the opposite. Young enough, despite his gray hair, to inflict damage. Leroy didn't see him approach; he was still pleading to the crew.

Arvin started in Leroy's direction, then found himself stopping. He watched as the director spun Leroy around and clobbered him hard on the side of his head. Leroy did his best to fight him off, but failed as the director landed blow after blow on Leroy's now bleeding face.

The crew cheered. Arvin dived in, took the director's arm and twisted it quickly behind his back. He screamed in agony as he was rendered powerless.

Leroy searched Arvin's face. He got to his feet, brushed himself down and shook his head before facing the director.

'You're fired, shithead,' said the director, spitting in Leroy's direction as Arvin let him go.

Leroy spun around, hitting the side of the director's head, sending him to the floor.

'I quit! You can have your piece of shit! Glitter out! Keanu, get Terry to bring the car around.'

'Fuck you, James. Good luck with your next shoot,' said the director, wiping blood from his lip. 'I'm guessing it'll be thirty seconds long and on foreign soil.'

Leroy gave him the fingers and turned on his heel.

'What was that back there? Look at my face, for Christ's sake.' Leroy removed a hip flask from the inside pocket of his jacket and took a large pull.

Arvin twisted around in his seat to face him as Terry drove away from the studio.

'I mean, what the fuck am I paying you for?' he added, taking another pull of what Arvin guessed was whisky.

He stayed quiet.

'I saw you, you know. I saw you stop before that cocksucker hit me.' He dabbed a cloth at the side of his face. 'You wanted him to, didn't you? I deserved it, didn't I? Is that it, Keanu?'

'That's not it at all, Leroy. I'm all for a fair fight, that's all. You antagonized the guy. Yeah, okay, I thought you deserved it. But I stopped him, didn't I?'

'I couldn't do the damn film if I wanted to. Look at the state of my motherfuckin' face.'

'Well you're lucky you're not doing it, then.'

Leroy stared at him. Arvin's heart started to beat a little faster. Leroy's face broke into a smile and he started to laugh. A thick deep laugh that Arvin joined in with.

'Stop, please, my face hurts. Jesus,' Leroy said, doing his best to hold it with his free hand. 'Let's go and get a drink.'

'Yes, sir.'

'And Keanu, pull that shit again and you're fired. Are we clear?'

Arvin nodded, as Terry put his foot down and pulled into the traffic.

2 5 .

The space on Scollard Street was vast, the light bright, making the white-painted walls sparkle brilliantly. There was no hiding in shadows here, though the invite-only crowd was a large one.

Toni had vetted the security on the door. Paul was one of them and wasn't happy about it, though Hadley had insisted. The company needed the money, and he wasn't bringing anything in with Jordan's self-imposed sabbatical.

So, what? was the name of Chris' latest exhibition. It was a combination of paintings and photographs focusing on people or things that flew in the face of convention. Toni surveyed the room, studying faces in the crowd and occasionally some of the images.

Here was a black and white photograph of a giant ninety-story block structure akin to a refrigerator, built next to what looked like a quaint, single-level heritage cottage. Beside that photo was another, of what looked to be a prostitute in heels picking up a cigarette butt from the pavement. She had no panties on, and there was a grin on her face.

Toni couldn't help smiling at the prostitute photo, though she wiped it from her face as she passed Paul, who chose to look the other way. He was such an asshole.

They were already an hour and half into it, and red dots had been placed on almost everything. Nothing cost less than twenty five thousand dollars. Toni stopped doing the math after she'd flown past five hundred thousand. No wonder Chris was such an arrogant prick.

Toni stepped to her left as he sashayed past, wearing a bright yellow suit with soft black feathers sewn into its shoulders. He looked every inch the canary – a good-looking canary, though a canary all the same. A gaggle of admirers followed him from one end of the gallery to the next.

She made another circuit through the throngs of people quaffing champagne and nibbling canapés. Trixie ignored her as she walked by. Blonde bitch. Skinny rake of a thing who did who-knew-what for Chris. That said, she knew how to put on a party and run his life, which couldn't be the easiest of tasks.

A face in the crowd caught her attention – because she couldn't see it. The head was covered by a black balaclava, which the man must have pulled on in the washrooms.

Toni launched herself at a group in front of her, knocking champagne flutes flying as she screamed at people to hit the floor. She saw Paul heading toward her from the front door. A huge chandelier exploded above them, glass shattering as a shotgun roared to life.

Now the crowd was panicking, crying and screaming for all it was worth. Toni scuttled from one side of the room to the next, forcing people to the floor. She looked over at Paul, who had a gun in one hand and his phone in the other. A second assailant cracked him across the head. Toni raced over, watching as Paul spun his attacker to the floor, snapping the guy's wrist in the process. Then she was beside him, her own gun out as she crashed into another assailant, forcing her elbow into the side of his neck before a voice behind her stopped everything.

'I wouldn't, if I were you.' His voice was rough, though steady. There was no hint of fear or panic in it at all. Just a calm command.

Toni looked up to see the shotgun pointed at her face. She raised her arms and stepped backwards. Paul had a Glock pointed at his head as he released the guy he'd pinned to the floor. The door was locked behind them by a fourth guy.

The guests were forced into a sitting position in the center of the room. Two guys, including the one with the broken wrist, stood over them. Toni chewed her bottom lip as her gun was taken and she was padded down in a search that bordered on groping. She closed her eyes and drew breath, smelling her assailant. He found a knife secreted in her left boot, and took it.

The man who'd spoken looked at his friend cradling his wrist, walked over and planted a boot in Paul's face, breaking his nose. Blood spurted all over the floor and onto the dress of a patron sobbing uncontrollably beside him. Paul too was padded down and his gun was taken.

'That's for being such hero – fucker,' said Paul's assailant.

He turned to the crowd. 'We're here for the artwork, not for you. It's insured, so don't be stupid. Let us take what we came for and you can get on with doing whatever it is you do. We already have the bag of phones you deposited on entry, but if any of you still have phones, hand them over. That includes any smart watches. Don't be stupid, you'll get them back. Any calls or texts go out, you die. It's that simple.'

One of the men opened a large plastic bag, as guests dropped their watches into it. Toni could only look on in silence with the rest of them as artworks were taken from the walls, placed on a chrome trolley and wheeled toward the back exit where she guessed a van was waiting.

'You,' said one of the men, pointing at Trixie. 'Get up! The key and code for the back door. Open it, now!'

They looked like they'd done their homework. It was over within ten minutes. The walls were empty. She heard the squeal of tires.

Toni ran to the back exit. The doors to the delivery bay had been left wide open. The bag of phones had been dumped near the exit gates. She ran to the gates, shook her head and took herself back to the main room, where the crowd were now standing and brushing themselves down.

Chris stood in the center of the room receiving hugs and kisses from the patrons floating around him. Their eyes met briefly as they surveyed the damage. He looked pissed.

2 6 .

Toni stretched herself across the blue felt of the pool table, left hand extended, index finger pointing at a yellow ball. Her black jeans tightened as she called it and launched into the shot, punching the ball hard into the back left corner.

'Ouch!' said a slim blonde girl in leather pants and a tight black T-shirt. A sleeve of tattoos ran up her right arm.

The Madison pub looked like a deluxe boutique frat house. It was spread across two large buildings tied together by an oversized balcony. A canopy of trees hovered above the complex, thanks to its location within the Annex, a hidden park-like suburb on the fringe of downtown. King's College wasn't far away, so a healthy blend of students and young professionals filled its spaces. It was getting late, but Toni had no intention of heading back to her apartment.

She drove the black ball from the top corner of the table to the bottom right-hand pocket. The white ball sped after it before backspin slowed, then gently tugged it back toward her.

'Another drink?' she asked.

'I'll get them,' replied Miche, collecting the empty glasses and heading for the bar.

Toni dropped another couple of loonies into the slot and racked up a triangle of balls. She was pissed about the night's disaster, though the Molson's were gradually easing the blow.

'So what do you think will happen?' asked Miche, placing two more beers on a side table.

'I guess we wait for the police report. Then my ass will be dragged in front of my client's lawyers, insurance agents, police etc. Then – who knows?'

She struck the white ball hard, splintering the triangle of balls around the table.

'Shit. Really?'

'Shit's fucking right. I could be on the street before the end of the week for all I know.'

'Well then, drink up, bitch. Let's go clubbing.'

'Yeah,' Toni said, nodding. She tossed the cue onto the table among the balls, grabbed her glass and drained it.

Lost and Found was a club on King St West. Brick walls, low lights, and purple and blue lounges hemmed in a crowd that loved to party. Toni's head was buzzing as she watched Miche spin in ever-decreasing circles through a dance floor that looked like there wasn't an inch of space on it.

Large groups hung out in booths drinking cocktails, or ran through shots of Grey Goose as a remix of Run DMC's 'Beats to the Rhyme' got the crowd going.

Toni had no idea of the time, though her head had long since let go of any serious thought – which had been her goal from the outset. Now she wasn't so sure if it was Miche who was spinning, or just her brain preferring to move, given she couldn't.

A set of thickly mascaraed eyes watching her from a distance helped her to stabilize. She searched the dance floor for Miche, but couldn't see her. She needed a drink; maybe water, and something alongside it.

The eyes were still there, focused on her. She made her way to the long bar down the left side of the room, doing her best to compose herself as she moved.

She found space and stepped into it, taking hold of the bar top to keep herself steady. She flagged the barman. A young face beneath a black fedora and a thick beard began speaking to her. She couldn't understand a thing he was saying, only managing to register the circle his mouth made around the word, no.

A light hand found her shoulder. Toni turned toward a pale face; the dark eyes were luminous. She was pretty, with thick red lips. Toni smiled. She knew that colour, it had to be 'Lady Danger.' Toni watched as she asked the barman for a glass of water. Her friend offered up a glass which Toni took, draining its contents.

She was taller than Toni. Skinnier, though a tough skinny. It was hard to tell, as she had a thick faux fur vest on. But Toni knew bodies, made it her business to know them. Despite having a fuzzy head, she could tell the girl was in good shape, and physically strong.

Vodka tonics appeared soon after. Her friend led her through the dance floor. There was no sign of Miche. She followed anyway, feeling better for being taken somewhere. The sound of the club's music was muffled as the door behind them closed. They were in the washrooms, tucked into a cubicle with a small glass shelf above a porcelain basin. Toni looked on as her friend cut and chopped lines on its surface.

A rolled note was offered to her. Toni pressed the end of it gently to a nostril and inhaled the white powdered line stretched out on glass. She felt it tickle, then quickly thicken in the back of her throat, and smiled. Her friend inhaled the second line, tapped the residue on the glass shelf with a moist finger and rubbed the contents against her teeth.

Toni was still as her friend's lips found, then parted her own. She felt herself relax, as the girl's tongue searched her mouth and a knee worked its way between her now wet legs.

'Toni … are you there? Toni? You've answered the call; all you need to do now is speak … Toni?'

Toni sat up in a tangle of sheets, blinked, then held her head. Daylight was seeping in through the blinds to the left of her bed, and it hurt to look at it.

'Toni … it's Arvin.'

Her head was pounding. She found her phone buried in the sheets alongside her. She untangled it then held it to her ear.

'Arvin? What … the fuck?'

'We've had a break-in at the office. Files have been stolen. There's no sign of forced entry to the doors, though Hadley's cabinets are a little buckled. The lock could have been picked, but we're calling around, in case anyone's had their keys taken.'

Toni opened her eyes. The other side of the bed was empty, just a pressed space that was now cold.

'Fuck! No. Hold on.'

She jumped out of bed, found her crumpled jeans on the floor. She picked them up and shook them. Plastic cards and a few loonies fell out, but no keys.

'No … no, she wouldn't have. I mean … why would she? Who–'

'Toni?'

'Fuck off, Arvin! I'm looking, for Christ's sake. I'm … they must be here somewhere. Let me call you back.'

'Right. We're meeting at the office in fifteen. I'll tell them I called. We'll see you in a bit.'

'Yeah … okay.'

Toni hung up and fell back on the bed, staring at the empty space beside her.

'Bitch,' she said aloud to no one. This wasn't good.

2 7 .

It had gone well, though I'd wanted to be one of the guests at the gallery; to see it all unfold around me, be part of something I'd helped orchestrate.

She hadn't known. Had no idea that the gems of thought I was throwing at this pretty, needy, floral-printed stick of a girl at a late night bar, would surface as her own. Ideas she would take running to a boss, who showed more arrogance than the man who'd played a part in all of this.

And why would she? She had a habit. Several, in fact. Coke was the least of them, though it was the thing that made her talk. Incessantly. It was easy to walk her from point A to point B in a conversation, in a corner booth of a club where everything and nothing made sense.

She was Trixie, the assistant, after all. One of those annoying people who take delight in keeping a digital record of anything they come across. Digital pics of good bottles of wine, of food, themselves; digital notes on the most mundane things, tapped into an oversized phone.

There were four of them. Dressed in black. I watched from across the street as they filtered in from each corner of the gallery. A chandelier exploded. Muffled screams reached me through the thick glass paneling at the front of the gallery. The street out front was quiet.

I saw him roll onto his back as one of the assailants kicked him hard in the face, blood spraying the corner window and a woman who lay beside him. I smiled at that. Then his partner was searched. I couldn't see her clearly, though from where I was standing she looked pretty, lithe, caramel-skinned, fearless. It was her I had to target. To move it all along, with maximum impact.

— ✹ —

It was always the pain that brought it back to me. He'd returned to our small apartment smelling of whisky and someone I didn't recognize. It had been late at night, and things hadn't been good between us. In fact they were as bad as they could be.

The benders had become a regular fixture, the promises he'd made long forgotten. I was pregnant and he had to know. Decisions needed to be made. He suspected something, though couldn't see it, almost seemed afraid to acknowledge anything.

I heard the door open and close downstairs. I lay on my back in bed; my head hurt from overthinking. He was still down there, like he'd hit pause, undecided as to whether he should come upstairs or head in the other direction. I lay in darkness, listening – waiting.

It was almost an hour before he appeared in his white singlet. He rolled himself onto our bed and then on top of me. I pushed him away, slowly at first, trying to free myself before I was yelling, then screaming at him.

I lashed out, heard him scream back before I was able to flick the nightstand light on. His face was covered in blood. I'd cut him above his eye and down the left side of his face. He put a hand to it, blotted what he could with his palm before pulling it away and staring at it. His eyes had rolled back into his head, and his mind followed.

I tried to defend myself, fighting then pleading with him to stop. Things escalated; I told him I was pregnant, begged him to remember what we meant to each other, though the person who dragged me to the top of the stairs was nobody I knew. Every mistake I had seen in my mother's face I knew was now etched on mine.

— ✶ —

I can see her watching me, propped up against the long bar on the other side of the room. She's drunk, though not drunk enough that I escape notice. And that's okay, I want to be noticed. She tries to order a drink and fails. Her tattooed friend is in la-la land, circling her way through a crowd of faces that move on seeing her arrive.

I give her water, then order her a drink. She's prettier than I'd thought. We're in a cubicle, inhaling coke. The ketamine will come later. For now she's alive, her hands and body all over mine, her tongue gentle, though hungry, working its way inside my mouth. I forget who I am, what I'm here to do, and fall into it.

My eyes open in darkness. I can hear her breathing deeply beside me. She'll wake with a sore head, though nothing else. I wish her no harm. I like her. I'll be a vague memory, though hopefully a sweet one.

I find her keys, retrace her steps to the office. I've followed her home before. I take what I need and head for the storage facility Chris used to place them in. I hate myself for it, but she's part of what I need to do.

The press eat it up. Chris Finch and his freshly sold works are missing. I call his bluff before he can claim any true sense of theft, while nudging him toward something someone like him would hate more than anything. I turn them into a gift. I donate them to charities. A paper trail as a means to an end. After all, they need to know that someone else is control.

'Jo?'

'Yes?'

'There's someone here at reception for you.'

'Okay … can I ask who it is?'

'I don't know. He's no one I've seen before. Lyden … Mr. Arnold Lyden.'

'Fine, I'll be right out.'

And it's him. The only one who, up until a few nights ago, I knew nothing about. *Well I do now, Arvin.*

'Arnold?' I ask.

He smiles back. 'Hi, Jo. Thanks for seeing me at such short notice, I really appreciate it. You're a fan of Son Goku?'

Of course, he's an escape artist.

2 8 .

Toni submerged her head in freezing cold water, momentarily blanking out all other sound and feeling as she pushed her face toward the bottom of the basin. After almost a minute she pulled herself free, sucking in air as the water ran from her face. Her head was numb, giving her temporary relief from the incessant pounding inside it.

She threw on something casual, grabbed her things, found her spare keys and headed for the door. They'd be waiting for her.

Toni lived north of High Park in the West End of Toronto. She took her time following Dupont St down until she hit Spadina. The streets were backed up, as the tracks for the street cars were being torn up and replaced.

She parked a block north, deciding to walk, wanting fresh air and time to think. Chinatown was its usual busy self with salted fish, plucked ducks, and fruit she couldn't name being loaded onto trays, or onto hooks at the front of the stores.

The roller door was up and the lights were on when she walked through the entrance to the gym. The rest of them were grouped in a corner, holding coffee. The conversation stopped as she entered. Hadley studied her face, handed her a drink and pointed to a corner.

'Right then, we're all here. Guys, I know we're going through a rough patch right now,' he said, turning to face Paul.

Paul's swollen nose was covered in a white-plastered x. 'A fucking rough patch? Jesus,' he said, staring at the ceiling, shaking his head.

Hadley ignored him and kept going. 'What with Jordan suspending his tour, Arvin and Leroy having issues – sorry Arvin, he did call me,' he added facing him now, 'and with last night's robbery at the gallery, not everything is going our way.'

Paul snorted, before draining the rest of his coffee, being careful to hold it away from his nose as he did so.

'But we've been here before and we always punch through it,' Hadley said, looking at the rest of the team. 'What does concern me,' he said, circling the floor with a finger in the air, 'is that we had a break-in here last night. There was no sign of forced entry and we all have our keys,' he said, indicating the other two. 'Toni, have you got yours?'

Toni felt heat course through her face as they turned to look at her. She shook her head.

'Where were you last night?' Hadley asked.

'Probably some fucking dyke parlor,' said Paul.

Toni gave him a solitary finger.

'A bit of focus here guys, please,' said Hadley.

Arvin was his usual quiet self, standing, his body braced against a wall to one side.

'Toni?' Hadley probed.

'Look. I was pissed about the robbery. Chris losing his works and all that. So I went out for a drink with a girlfriend,' she replied, watching as Paul began to smile and nod. 'Then on to a club.'

'Okay,' Hadley said. 'Then?'

'Then I went home.'

'Alone?' Hadley raised his hands. 'Sorry, I to have to ask.'

Toni sighed. 'No.'

'What time was this?'

'Late,' she said, shaking her head. 'I couldn't say.'

'Try.'

'Fuck, I don't know! Maybe two? Three?'

Hadley took a step closer. 'Toni, did you know them?'

Another sigh. 'Not really.'

'Ho' bag,' said Paul.

Toni shot him a dark look.

'Paul, not now – please,' said Hadley. 'Can you describe them?'

Toni searched the room, then lowered her eyes to the floor. 'All right, okay. She was tall, a little taller than me. Dark hair, wore heavy mascara. She was a little pale, kind of skinny, though muscular.'

'Did she have a name?'

She let out another sigh. 'I'm sure she did.'

'Anything at all?'

Toni shrugged her shoulders. 'It was all pretty hazy, I–'

'Okay. Would you know her if you saw her again?'

'I think so. Though she was pretty heavily made up.'

'How's your head?'

'Been better.'

Hadley pushed on. 'Were there drugs?'

'Getting a bit personal here, aren't we?'

'Where our lives depend on it, yes.'

Toni nodded. 'I might have dabbled, though nothing heavy.'

'Toni, what you do in your own time is yours to do, so long as it doesn't jeopardize what we do here. Do you think you were drugged?'

Toni rubbed her head, thought about the drinks she'd had. There had only been one line, though a lot of drinks. She'd had sex and had passed out. Comatose, which wasn't normal for her. 'Yes.'

'Right. Grab a piece of paper, write down as much detail as you can remember. I'll need to file a complaint with the police.'

'What? What are you going to say?'

'Don't worry, I'll only say what I need to. Our files were taken, Toni. Someone came in here last night and took a lot of sensitive info on our clients. Think alarm codes, phone numbers, pseudonyms they use, places they go. Take the day off, Toni. Don't beat yourself up too badly here. It sounds like you were targeted. That said, I expect better behavior from you, regardless of the situation.'

'Hadley, I'm–'

He gave her a hug. 'Get some rest, honey, it'll be okay. Call me if anything else comes to mind.'

She searched the faces in the room before quietly leaving.

'Chris … it's me.'

'Toni.'

She was sitting looking out of the large windows of the Belljar, a cafe on Dundas St West with retro lights and decor. She was onto her second espresso of the day, staring out at the trees.

'Look, about yesterday,' she said. 'I'm really sorry how it all went down.'

'Yeah. It wasn't good.'

'I'm … I'm sorry. I – we – I mean Paul and I did all we could. It was the last thing I expected to be faced with.'

'Hmmm.'

'Hmmm? What the fuck is that? What we were supposed to have done? They had guns, for fuck's sake!'

Toni checked herself. A few patrons were peering at her from behind papers or their coffees. She got up and walked out through the glass doors onto the street. 'There were at least a hundred people sprawled on the floor. They could've–'

'Toni. Stop. Paul broke the guy's fucking arm, for Christ's sake!'

'What? What do you mean, the guy's arm? The fucking gunmen? Is that what you–'

The phone was quiet as Toni processed what she'd heard.

'Wait a second. You … you hired those idiots?'

Chris wasn't saying anything.

'Are you fucking kidding me? You put lives at risk for some crazy … lunatic … fucking shakedown? For … for what? You sold everything!'

Toni could hear herself breathing heavily down the phone.

'Notoriety, Toni. Followed by profit. Any fucking artist can sell something. Not everyone has their work stolen in front of a hundred witnesses.'

'Jesus fucking Christ!' Toni raked a hand through her head. 'This is fucked up. You are … just–'

'Unbelievable, right?'

'Sick is probably closer.'

'Think of the press, Toni. Good coverage, elevation in status for me, which is good for you. Terrific PR.'

Toni felt her heart hammering in her chest. Her head was beginning to pound again. This was rapidly turning into a morning for the books.

'What I'm not happy about is the storage facility that was planned to hold all of my works, post their removal. What do you think they sold for last night, Toni?'

'I dunno, Chris. A million? Two? Who fucking cares?'

'Well you should, Toni. Two-and-a-half million. I've just had a call from Hadley. I understand your place was robbed last night. He told me files were taken which might have been … sensitive?'

'What? You had them pull a double shift?'

Chris spat. 'If only I had. Hadley mentioned it may have been your keys that were taken. They included keys to the storage facility I'm talking about. Do you know where I'm going with this?'

'No … you can't mean–'

'I fucking do! The works are gone, Toni. Some fucking opportunist has taken the lot.'

'Then you got what you wanted.'

The line went quiet.

'No. Not quite, though I'd better. Otherwise the work your team does will be done by somebody else. You're paid to protect. Get off your ass and find my shit or you'll be fucked. That much I can assure you.'

Click.

'Hadley?'

'Yeah, Toni.'

'We need to talk.'

2 9 .

Trixie wore a bright green floral print dress, with a black leather jacket draped loosely over her shoulders. She looked immaculate as ever as she approached the glass entrance doors to Chris's gallery. She eyeballed Hadley and Arvin carefully, then unlocked and opened the doors, allowing them in.

The place felt cold. Its walls were empty. Large blank canvases with no story to tell. Hadley and Arvin scanned the room and the doors leading into and out of each space. Trixie walked them to a small rectangular wall, where a hidden door opened to reveal a staircase beyond.

They followed her up a single flight of stairs. Music drifted down from above. The staircase entered a large attic space that had been converted into an office. Chris was seated in front of an oversized Mac, coffee in his left hand, tapping keys with one finger from his right.

He ignored Hadley and Arvin as Trixie seated them on a vintage couch in front of the windows. They declined coffee and waited for Chris to be done. He wasn't. It was a full ten minutes before Hadley coughed himself into being.

'Feeling sick, Hadley?' Chris asked, looking up at him.

'Chris, listen … I know this situation isn't a good one. Toni's pretty cut up about it. The thing is–'

'What's the thing, Hadley?' he said, cutting him off, his shock of red hair framing a face that looked anything but impressed. 'Is it that I've lost two-and-half-million dollars? Is that the thing?'

'Well, I get that, though I don't–'

'Do you, Hadley? Because while I know I pay you well, I'm not sure you understand what that kind of money looks like,' he said, screwing up his face. 'Well … do you?'

'I'm not saying–'

'Then don't say. Say nothing at all.'

Chris leapt out of his chair. 'What the fuck am I supposed to do?' he said, pacing the room. 'Do you realize that I have twenty – no, make that fucking forty – high-end buyers who've paid a small fortune for works that no longer hang … on my fucking walls!'

'I realize–'

'What do you realize, Hadley? What do you and your Asian friend here realize? Because I'm coming up with a few realizations of my own, eh?'

Hadley got to his feet. 'Why did you have them stolen?'

'Sorry?'

'You heard me, Chris. Why did you have them stolen? Why did you put two of my staff in a situation they couldn't hope to control?'

Chris stopped pacing. 'Are you telling me you had nothing to do with this?'

It was Hadley's turn to get up and stride around the room.

'Why would we? We're in the business of protecting, not stealing. You wanted security for the night, and we provided that.'

'Did you? Because if that's the best you've got, you've been found wanting.'

'This is bullshit, Chris. Do you trust Toni?'

'I did … though now, I'm not so sure.'

'Well, you'd be a fool not too.'

'Am I a fool, Hadley?'

'Between you, me, and my Asian friend Arvin here, yes, I think you are. And I don't say that lightly. Who did you hire?'

'Who? What?'

'Who did you hire to steal your own works with a view to publicizing your own exhibition?'

Chris took a long sip of his coffee. 'I'm not liking where you're steering this conversation, Hadley.'

'The direction it's taking has nothing to do with me, Chris. This is your own ego talking. Toni and Paul were here. They're well and truly capable of securing your safety, as well as the safety of your patrons at an art exhibition. Now tell me who you hired, so that we can help find your stolen works – free of charge, I might add.'

'Well that's fucking generous of you,' Chris spat.

'Given the circumstances, I'd say that it is,' Hadley replied.

Chris stared out the window at the street below. 'I like her you know – Toni.'

'So you should, she's a good girl.'

He said nothing for a few minutes. 'Jonas. Jonas Strong and his team. Gaunter … Giant, or something like that.'

Hadley sighed, turned to face Arvin and shook his head. 'Gauntlet. Yeah, we know them. Well, that's a start.' He sat down again. 'What were their instructions?'

'Secure the works and place them in a storage facility that only they, Trixie, Toni and myself had access too.'

'Do you trust Trixie?'

'She'd remove her teeth and blow me if required.'

'So that's a yes?'

'Fuck off. Talk to your girl. I understand she's had her keys taken. By who, I don't give a damn. Find my shit or, as much as I love her, she can kiss this fucking assignment goodbye – comprendez?'

Hadley nodded.

'Next time, leave your silent Asian assassin at home, eh?'

Arvin stood. 'Just quietly, Hadley, I'm not a fan.'

Chris ignored him, sat himself down and resumed his single-digit typing, coffee restored to his hand.

Trixie led them down the stairs and showed them out onto the street.

'Thanks, Trixie, appreciate you finding the time.'

The glass doors closed. They watched as she locked them, then headed back toward the stairs hidden behind her.

'Well, I've got a new appreciation for Toni and what she does,' said Arvin, turning away.

Hadley nodded. 'Let's track down Jonas and sort this shit out once and for all. My guess is he's clueless, though he might have met someone or done something that warrants our attention.'

'Do you think Chris is hiding anything?' Arvin asked.

'Probably. Though I think the PR coverage was all he'd aspired to here.'

'Trixie?'

'Can't say that I know the girl, but from what I've seen and what Toni has said, I doubt it. Either way, we figure it out, or half our clientele are no longer paying us.'

'Right, onwards then,' replied Arvin.

3 0 .

Toni spotted Jonas sitting in a corner on the other side of the room. He looked sick. A little peaky and pale, like he hadn't doused himself in spray tan, or applied oil, or whatever it was he liked to do. He was sweating lightly, alternating between drinking and inhaling the steam rising from the large porcelain cup of green tea he held.

Jonas smiled as Toni appeared, but his smile faltered when he saw her face.

'Hi, love,' he said, pushing himself up from his chair.

Toni ignored him. She seated herself at the bar, then ordered a beer.

'What? No hug for an admirer?'

Her beer arrived. She drank deeply before placing it quietly on a coaster.

'Toni, sweetheart … what did I do?'

The bartender looked up from where he stood.

'That remains to be seen.'

'And here I was thinking the call had finally come.'

She turned to face him, focused on the shape and movement of his eyes. 'Where were you on Wednesday night?'

'The night before last? Was that after the paintball? Just before? I don't know. I'm not sure, I mean–'

She slapped him hard on the side of his face. Jonas fell backwards, knocking the tea into his lap.

'Fuck! Ouch … Jesus!' He brushed himself down. 'What the fuck was that?'

What had she expected from him? He was anything but a straight shooter. She studied his face, saw his cheek reddening, noted the shape of her palm, her fingers stretched out across his face. She couldn't take him seriously. He was self obsessed. It was like nothing mattered.

'Is everything okay here?' asked the bartender, his hands now planted across the bar top.

Jonas looked at her, then raised his palms. 'Sorry … just a misunderstanding is all, nothing we can't-'

'Ma'am? Are you alright?' the bartender asked. 'Is this guy bothering you?'

Jonas couldn't help grinning as the bartender sized him up. Toni saw his back straighten. It was like he'd already forgotten why she was here.

Toni raised her hands. 'No. No problem here.'

The bartender backed away to serve another customer.

'Don't fucking lie to me, Jonas. It took me a while to figure it out – that was you groping me the other night, wasn't it? You took my fucking knife.'

'Toni … honey, I don't know where this is going.'

'Stop being a dickhead, Jonas. I could smell that shitty cologne of yours. Why did you do it? You knew he was my client. You and your cronies know us. Why would you put everyone's lives at risk, including your own?'

'Don't flatter yourself.'

'Then why?'

He shook his head. 'We needed the money.'

Toni slapped the top of the bar. She stared at his face, searched for reason in it and failed. He was dumb. She had to accept it and move on.

'As bad a run as you guys have been having, ours has been worse,' he said.

'So what, you sabotage us?'

'No. We did a job for a client that was contained and managed without injury, at least to everybody outside of our team.'

'And publicly ruined our reputation in the process.'

'How? Does anybody know who you are, other than Chris? The patrons wouldn't. You're not branded.'

'It was a fucking publicity stunt! What do you think publicity is meant to do?'

'The focus is on his works, not the security team behind it!'

'And you're in charge?' she said, screwing up her face. She couldn't believe what she was hearing. 'Christ. I could lose my job. Once the word is out, and it will be, the backstory on us – on me – will be brutal.'

'It'll blow over. Once they're found–'

'Did you take them?' asked Toni.

'No … I didn't.'

'Do you know where they are?'

'I know where they *were*.'

'So … what? Chris pays you to rob his gallery, to hide his works in a storage facility,' Toni said surveying the bar, 'and you promptly lose them.'

Jonas cleared his throat. 'Point the finger at your own face, honey. As I understand it, the keys to that facility were held by myself, Chris, Trixie, and you. Our keys can be accounted for. Yours are missing, am I right?'

'Surely they've got CCTV cameras all over the facility. Has anyone checked them?'

'Not much more than a shadow, covered head to toe in black.'

'Any suspects?' Toni asked.

'Only one,' he said, looking the other way.

Toni got to her feet. 'Are you fucking serious? Why would I rob my own client? I was there, for Christ's sake, on the threshold of blowing your fucking brains out!'

Jonas just smiled at her.

'I'd get rid of that, before I punch it,' Toni said, finishing off her beer.

'Who were you with, after the robbery?' he asked.

'Oh, you mean after you fucked us over? A friend.'

'Anybody I know?'

'Lucky for her – no.'

'Her? Really?'

'A friend, shithead. Listen, there was a girl. She's tall, about five-eleven, dark eyes, good-looking, pale skin, thick lips. Bubbly girl. I'd say quite fit. No one I've seen before. Ring any bells?'

'No one I know. I'd like to meet her, though.'

'Can you keep your dick out of your head for a second?'

'I'm teasing, Jesus! No, I don't know your girl. Though she sounds like the type that Chris's assistant would likely run around with.'

'Who, Trixie?'

'She's a dyke, isn't she?'

'How the fuck would I know?'

'Well, I'm still waiting, so I have to–'

'What? Assume that because I'm not falling all over that well-oiled body of yours, that I'm gay?'

Jonas grinned back at her.

'You are such an asshole,' said Toni, getting to her feet.

'Toni, honey? Don't go, I–'

'Thanks for the beer, Jonas. Do anything as stupid as you and that fucking collection of idiots you call a team have done again, and next time, it'll be your face that gets broken.'

'Give Paul my love, by the way. I'm sure his face looks all the better for it,' he replied, smiling.

She ignored him and left.

31.

Contagious – Jo Reid

What's your take on art today? I love it. Have done since I was a wee thing and my father told me how good my first family portrait was. Five people with stick arms, stick legs and moonheads. I put a smile on each face and a giant yellow sun in the background, which bagged me hugs from every quarter.

So for me, art was emotional. It generated feelings, made people experience different emotions, evoked or provoked something inside them. And that hasn't changed. Though, like everything else, there's so much of it now. In so many formats.

Why? Because each and every piece has a price tag attached to it. How big or small do you want it? What's your favorite colour? Hard, soft, digital or an audio copy? What language do you speak? Would you like to see something similar? Do you want the back catalogue or the box set? CD, DVD, or just rent it from IMBD?

This I hate.

Hate being represented by the digital camera; the scanner; the plagiarist that takes things, reproduces, replicates, steals pieces of things that don't need to be stolen. Don't need to be replicated or repurposed. Can't they just – be?

There are those that have embraced this change. Artists like Chris

Finch, Damian Hirst – let's work backwards – Andy Warhol, even Salvador Dali. A slew of well-known faces (the latter being a personal favorite) who I believe have done as much for art as they have against it.

They have seen dollar signs. Turned their unique perspective into something ugly, something akin to an advert. And have merchandized the ass-end out of it.

It's not them, I hear you say?

Isn't it? It's their license. They or their agent have been given free reign to flog said pieces of art as they see fit. Chris Finch doesn't, you say? I beg to differ.

We all read the unfortunate news of the robbery at Chris's gallery in Scollared St a few days ago. Now I wouldn't wish that on anybody. There can't be anything worse than selling every piece of art on your freshly painted white walls, then seeing it being taken at gun point.

Or is there?

Can I pose a theory? There's no question that Mr. Finch is a talented artist. Though I also think he's a canny businessman. Mr. Finch is a PR dream. He's quirky, loves the camera, and let's be honest, he's an arrogant son of a bitch. He can afford to be. Which makes great fodder for anybody like me with column inches to fill and an audience to entertain.

This writer's theory (disclaimer … disclaimer) postulates that our Mr. Finch has been a naughty boy. Rumor has it PR and robbery were dating last week. To what end? It begins with N and ends with Y. If you think that's New York, stop reading now. Notoriety, my friends. Sadly, I'm contributing to it right here, right now, with your eyeballs. What better way to self-promote than to have your own already sold works stolen?

But wait, there's good news.

The works have been found, and donated. You read right. Donated to various charities, both domestic and international, who now plan to auction off the works for a range of causes. These range from child abuse, to foster care, to animal cruelty or just helping the impoverished.

I take it all back Chris. If this was a PR stunt, its been well played. You might have just single handedly restored my faith, and I'm sure the faith of my readers, in what it means to be an artist. Maybe the entire act is a piece of art in itself? One that, it has to be said, is being sold off in pieces that make a better whole, flying in the face of what I've written here.

If so, I applaud you.

Comments:

(This is a forum for feedback, please be courteous, not abusive with your responses.)

Sal: Thanks for the read Jo, I liked it. Though I can't say there are too many artists I like today. Chris Finch IS an arrogant son of a bitch. He gives the impression of being someone who cares for no one else but himself. I'll take a step back and watch the developments. I'm prepared to eat my words, though I'd be confident he's got nothing to do with these donations, which in my mind, makes it that much sweeter.

Jo: Thanks for the note Sal.

KJ: I f*$@ing love Chris Finch! Your article's a sad one Jo. It smacks of jealously, which seems to be a common thread in all of the crap you write. Maybe your parents did you a disservice by giving you a hug in your formative years?

JO: Lovely KJ.

Ed: @KJ – What a dumb thing to say. Did nobody hug you?

PS: @Jo – I represent a charity and I can say that's it's a hard slog for all of us out there. Children of Africa is a Toronto based group that/

Jo: @PS – Sorry to put the brakes on there PS. This isn't a forum for advertising or promoting charities. That said, I'm sure if you make enquires with those parties that have already received donations, maybe they can point you in the right direction. All the best. Jo

 KJ: @Ed – I bet you suckEd dick.

Jo: @KJ – Clever KJ.

This thread has been frozen and will be screened. No further comment can or will be posted.

3 2 .

'Christ! You've got to be shitting me,' said Paul. He ran a hand over his head as he entered the room.

A tall red-haired guy with a heavy moustache and a gray suit smiled a little too broadly. 'Looking good, Samuels. Having a bit of work done on your nose?'

'Thompson.'

Paul turned toward a woman in a black suit and a tailored white shirt. 'I can't imagine your day is easy with this guy around. We're happy to wait if you want to bring someone else in,' he said, smiling.

She didn't smile back. 'Take a seat, please.'

Toni joined him on the other side of a white square table. It was midday and they were at the 51st Division of the Toronto Police Service, located off Parliament St. They'd been summoned for questioning the previous day. Toni thought hard about what she knew, what she hadn't already shared with Paul. Too many revelations and she would look bad. They all would. She'd said as much to Paul before walking in. Fingers crossed he'd keep his composure, and his gob shut.

'This is Detective Thompson and I'm Senior Detective Simons. We understand you're both part of a company called The Security, a local security firm that was on detail last Wednesday night. Ms. Rodriguez, we further understand that you're a contracted worker for Mr. Chris Finch, the artist,' she added, checking her notes.

Toni cleared her throat and nodded her agreement.

'On the said night, Mr. Finch was holding an exhibition. His guest list included approximately one hundred patrons. What time did this function get underway?'

'We were there from six thirty pm to help with the set up, and guests began arriving a little after seven.'

'Do you know the space well?' Simons asked.

'I do. I spend a lot of time with Chris at his exhibitions, and occasionally when he's showing in other provinces or out of the country.'

'Why were you there, Mr. Samuels?'

'As back up to Ms. Rodriguez. Most functions of this size typically have two of us on detail,' Paul said, straightening himself in his chair.

'Aren't you working with Jordan Franks any more?' asked Thompson.

'He's on a sabbatical.'

'I heard.'

'Then why ask?' replied Paul.

'Ms. Rodriguez, can you take us through the night in question please?' said Simons.

Toni relayed the events of the evening, though was vague in her description of their assailants. She described the way the group had entered the building, how they managed the raid, and the time they took to get it done.

'Were they professionals?'

'I'd say they were. They knew what they were doing. They dissected the room and disabled us.'

'That can't have been easy,' said Thompson. 'How did you break your nose, Samuels?'

'I was kicked in the face.'

'I can understand that. Do you know why?'

'Because I'd snapped one of their wrists,' Paul replied, staring straight back at him.

'And then what?' asked Simons.

'They drove off in a vehicle parked behind the gallery and left us with a bag of phones beside the back gate,' said Paul.

'Do you know who they are?' she asked Toni.

'How would I?'

'You work in the industry, you see this kind of thing all the time. Did you recognize anyone? Sense anything at all?'

'They wore balaclavas and were dressed head-to-toe in black. How could I?'

'What do you think they did with the artworks?'

'Haven't a clue. Would I be sitting here if I had the slightest idea?'

'You might if it was you who'd taken them,' said Thompson.

'Really? Is that what you've come up with?' Toni asked.

'You knew the layout of the place. You had Chris's confidence and you know the industry,' he pressed.

'Well, it wasn't me. I had nothing to do with it.'

'Maybe your buddy here?' said Thompson. 'Bit short of funds, aren't you, Hammer? Wasn't that why you were working alongside Ms. Rodriguez on Wednesday night? Probably blown a few too many wads down at that parlor of yours, am I right?'

'Why is this man a detective? Honestly, I can't think of what my tax dollars are paying for. No, Thompson. I didn't orchestrate the robbery, and yes, I have seen your girlfriend wrapped around a pole down there on occasion.'

'Fuck you, Samuels! If you think–'

'Detective,' said Simons, placing a hand on Thompson's shoulder. 'Why don't you get our guests some water.'

Thompson eyeballed Paul, and chewed his bottom lip as he rose quietly from his chair.

'Sparkling, if you've got it, thanks buddy,' said Paul, winking at him.

The door opened to the sound of phones ringing, keyboards being tapped, and voices blaring from an office filled with workers, before it closed again, returning them to silence.

'Apologies, Mr. Samuels. My partner has a tendency to–'

'It's quite alright, Senior Detective.'

'What did you do after the robbery, Ms. Rodriguez?' she asked.

'I … we called the police. We helped clean up the scene after they'd been by. Managed the people out and spent time with Chris and Trixie.'

'Trixie Feldon? Chris's assistant?'

'That's her.'

'And after you left the gallery?'

'I had a few drinks with a friend and went home.'

'Your friend's name?'

'Look,' said Toni, leaning forward on the table. 'Why are we here? We spoke with police on the night, and we're both as devastated about the events as anybody who was in the room is entitled to be.'

'I'm not denying that.'

'Then why? Am I … are we, really suspects here?'

'There are all sorts of rumors flying around at the moment. I'm sure you both appreciate the value of the works in question. Is this something your employer would have done?'

'Chris? Why would he steal his own work?'

'Publicity.'

'He'd sold everything. I know Chris, and if there's anything he loves more than himself, it's money. So no, I don't think it's something he would have done.'

'We received a theft complaint from your offices via your boss, Mr. Hadley Peters. We understand that your place was broken into and files were stolen on the same night in question. Seems like a remarkable coincidence, don't you think?'

'What? That we were robbed twice in one night? Or that we reported both crimes to the police once they had occurred? What does seem odd to me is that in both cases, we were the victims, with, I might add, absolutely no benefits.'

'Do you know which files were taken?'

'That's a question for Hadley.'

'Then that's who I'll ask.'

The door opened and Thompson arrived with the water.

'Is that all?' asked Paul.

'For now,' said Simons. 'Thank you both for coming in.'

Paul picked up his glass and held it to the light. 'Did you spit in it?'

Thompson rolled his eyes.

Paul got to his feet, placed his own full glass on the table, picked up Toni's and drained it. 'Be seeing you buddy,' he said, patting Thompson on the shoulder.

Thompson stared at the wall instead of Paul's face as they walked out.

3 3 .

Arvin made his way through the front doors of the Globe & Mail and approached reception. Two girls sat behind a large desk that resembled a fort. He veered left, choosing the girl who appeared most bored. She looked all of twenty years old and had her head down, scrolling though an iPad.

'Good afternoon. I was hoping to see Jo Reid of Contagious, if she's free?'

'Sorry, who?' she said, looking up.

'Jo Reid. She writes a column for you called Contagious.'

'Right. Let me just see if she's in … She is. Is she expecting you?'

'No, I'm taking a chance. I'm a big fan.'

'And your name is?'

'Arnold Lyden.'

'Okay, then. Let me call her,' she said, picking up the phone. 'She's on a call. She'll check in with me once she's off. Take a seat, Arnold.'

Arvin sat down, picked up the latest copy of the *G&M* and scanned the headlines. A few minutes passed before he heard the phone at reception ring. He pretended to ignore the conversation.

'… I don't know. I haven't seen him before. Lyden … Mr. Arnold Lyden. Okay. Alright, thanks Jo.'

'Mr. Lyden?' she called.

'Yes,' said Arvin, looking up.

'Jo will be right out.'

'Great. Thank you.'

She looked as Arvin had expected – confident. She approached him with a broad smile, her hand held out. She was tall, with thick lips, striking blues eyes, and blonde hair. Her skin was lightly tanned, which was odd, given the time of year. He assumed it was fake.

She wore blue jeans with Converse sneakers, and a gray business jacket over a T-shirt featuring the familiar figure of Son Goku.

A smile crept across his face.

'Arnold?'

'Hi, Jo. Thanks for seeing me at such short notice, I really appreciate it. You're a fan of Son Goku?'

Jo looked him up and down, then grinned back at him. 'Love the guy. Can't beat the energy and chaos of a great Manga movie.'

'Agreed. I was in the area and I love your column and I wanted to say hello. Is there somewhere we can speak?'

'Ooh. I'm intrigued, I thought this was a friendly handshake. Follow me.'

They walked behind reception into a larger space that had been divided into itself several times.

Jo took him into a small windowed meeting room. It was ordered, though cluttered with mini stacks of magazines piled around the floor. Articles were stuck to the glass, obscuring what might have been a nice view.

'Grab a seat. What's on your mind?'

'As I said to one of the girls on reception–'

'Amy.'

'Yes, ahh … Amy. I'm a fan.'

'Thank you.'

'I love your style of writing, and I like the fact that you engage with the feedback in the thread that follows. All too often it's the funniest part of the article. No offence.'

'None taken. It'd be rude not to engage, so I do what I can.'

Arvin leaned forward. 'Your last article talked a bit about the dilemma facing Chris Finch.'

'Okay,' she said. 'I'm not sure it's much of a dilemma, but keep going.'

'I've read the headlines around the theft. You mentioned rumors that it might have been something a little more sinister, like a PR push?'

'Well, a girl writes what she hears. It's an opinion, after all. I'm not sure if you know Chris Finch, but if you did, you wouldn't put it past him.'

'The other thing that caught my eye were the donations. You mentioned his works were popping up across the country with various charity groups. I hadn't read anything anywhere about that, can you tell me more?'

'Arnold,' she said leaning back. 'I'm not sure you're being entirely honest with me here. This isn't really a fan visit, is it?'

'Oh I'm a fan, though I'm also curious.'

'Well, so am I. Who do you work for?'

Arvin leaned back, giving himself more space. 'Habitat for Humanity. We build homes for low income families across the GTA.'

'Really? Good for you. So this is about trying to source one of Chris's works?'

Arvin nodded.

'As I mentioned in my article, the best way to source them, if any are left, is via those who've already received gifts.'

'That's the thing. I've met a few, though their donations all came from anonymous sources.'

'Donor's prerogative I guess. A lot like my sources. If people don't want to be known, then they aren't – simple as that. Sorry I can't help you here, Arnold. If there's nothing else, I do have another appointment that I need to get to.'

'No, that's it. I appreciate the time, Jo. Thanks for seeing me.'

'I'll see you out then.'

Arvin waited in a cafe across the street. It was a full twenty minutes before Jo Reid appeared. There was a lot more to this girl than she was letting on. He'd follow her to see if he could learn anything else. She was on foot, which was a bonus.

He waited until she took a right on Draper St before he fell in behind. He had to hustle, she was moving quickly. She zig-zagged across Wellington onto Portland St before Arvin found himself jogging. Her blonde hair was an easy trace, which he was thankful for.

A crowd of kids were coming toward him, and he stepped off the footpath to get past them as she turned a corner. He followed suit, having gotten round the flow of kids, but found the street empty. There were lanes to his left and right. Nothing. She was gone.

The roar of an engine caught his attention. A bike appeared, yellow with black powder-coated exhausts. Its rider was slight, dressed in a heavy leather jacket, leaning into a wide tank. The helmet was tinted black, blonde hair hanging loosely from the base. Arvin dove into a stack of boxes to avoid being run down.

A white gloved-finger rose in his direction before the biker turned the corner. He recognized the jeans and Converse before she was gone.

34.

Paul knew it was late. His friends had bailed, though he felt there was more to be had from this night. He was still thirsty, but given the hour – it was well after one – he'd take what he could get.

The thick chrome writing on the side of the brick building said *Flesh*. He smiled at that, nodding to himself, as if he'd answered the question his own head had been unable to come up with.

He had no idea where in the city he was, though he knew the lake was at least twenty bucks in a cab south, so he wasn't that far removed from the CBD. He lifted his head, straightened his back, then did his best to conjure up a smile, mentally ticking off all of the signs he'd been paid to look for as a bouncer, all those years ago.

A tall, slim guy stopped him. He was dressed in black and wore a white Blue Jays cap turned backwards. On his feet were the obligatory shit kickers most bouncers wore – soft soles with steel-capped toes. Paul was confident he could snap his neck in less than three seconds.

Paul's smile extended across his face, and he nodded politely before being ushered in.

Dickhead. Get a real job. I was doing that when I was five years younger than you.

The lights inside the club were brighter than he'd hoped for; a rainbow kaleidoscope of strobed color he had to shield his eyes from before making his way directly to the bar, doing his best to navigate the plethora of sweating bodies working themselves up on the dance floor. He slid onto a seat and ordered a beer. A cold Molson was all he needed right now.

They didn't have any.

What kind of fuckin' club doesn't have Canada's most popular beer, for fuck's sake?

He somehow managed to keep his mouth shut, and chose something else. He missed its name; what looked like a pig and spade stared back at him from the label on the side of the tall brown bottle. At least it was cold.

It disappeared too quickly. He ordered another, pushing aside the bucket of champagne that some fat bastard beside him had ordered.

He surveyed the dance floor. The talent looked pretty scant for a late-night bar. For a second he thought he saw a familiar face, though dismissed it just as quickly.

There were way too many guys in here. He had to look hard to spot the odd girl. This town was going to the dogs. And the music – what was that they were playing? It sounded like an eighties band. Duran Duran, or someone just as bad.

His head was spinning and he needed to piss. He slid himself off the seat and searched for the washrooms. A weak *Restroom* light on the far side of the dance floor told him he'd have to wade through it to get there.

It was during this walk that he became concerned. There were almost no girls on the floor. They were all guys, hanging off each other. Several wore hats and half of them wore sunglasses, despite the darkness.

It wasn't, was it?

More fleeting glances to his left and right as he pushed his way through sweating bodies. More than a few were in suspenders. Fuck. It couldn't be.

Just get to the washrooms buddy, do your business and get the fuck out of here.

Paul turned the corner and walked down a small passage. Two guys had tongues locked down each others throats, their arms entwined. The closest to him had the other guy's hand on his ass.

His head wouldn't stop spinning. Paul pushed past them, forced his way through the doors and found an empty cubicle toward the back of the room. He threw himself inside it, kicked the door shut and vomited into an open bowl.

His head and face broke into a sweat as he fumbled for the door's lock and twisted it shut, before another wave of nausea washed over him. He wiped his face with toilet paper, gave himself a courtesy flush before unbuckling and turning to sit on the toilet. He needed to calm down. His bladder purged itself of its contents as he held his head, doing his best to stop the spinning.

Just get it done and get the fuck out of here, Paulie. This is the last place you want to be seen in.

He jumped as something hit the side of his cubicle. He could hear the unbuckling of belts. It was definitely more than one. No. Please. God no.

God refused to listen. Paul's shared wall moved with the weight of a body being pressed against it. The sound of bodies slapping each other was loud enough for Paul to hear before another wave of nausea coursed through him. He had to switch positions as everything he'd eaten reappeared. His neighbors weren't stopping, in fact they'd gotten louder. Groaning as they worked their way toward a result.

Paul's head was clearer. He flushed the toilet, ripped the door open and headed for the basin. He buried his face in the cold water pooling between his cupped hands. He filled them again and covered his head.

In the mirror he saw the door behind him open, and Hadley walk out of the cubicle, followed by a younger man with blond hair who headed straight for the door.

'What the fuck?' said Paul.

Hadley's head snapped around.

'Paul? Wha … what are you doing here?'

'I might ask you the same thing, though I think I already know you … you sick fuck!' he said, launching himself at Hadley.

Hadley blocked his punch and threw him against the wall, cracking the mirror beside them.

'You're drunk. Go home and sleep it off.'

'Fuck you … faggot!' Paul replied, swinging and connecting with the side of Hadley's face.

He cut it open. Blood trickled down Hadley's left temple. Hadley wiped it away before throwing himself at him. Paul fell to the floor and then Hadley was on top of him, driving his huge hands into the side of his head, cutting Paul's lip open. Then his fists were hammering deep under his chest, driving the air from his lungs.

Paul rolled from his back to his knees, gasping, before he threw up once more on the tiled floor.

'You done now?' Hadley asked.

Paul wiped the residue from his face; blood had mingled with it. 'If anyone's done, Peters, it's you,' he said, spitting through bleeding lips. He laughed. 'No wonder this operation's falling on its face. My boss is fucking queer.'

3 5 .

'C'mon, Toni, get your hands up,' said Hadley, moving quickly around the ring.

Toni replied with a quick jab to his face, followed by another to the left side of his rib cage. She smiled on connecting. 'Keep your mouth shut and box, Hadley.'

'There you go, she means business now.' He lowered his head gear, faked left and boxed right, catching her hard on the side of her own helmet.

'You like that?' Hadley said.

Toni shook it off, using her lips and tongue to work her mouthguard back into place. She loosened her arms with a shake and raised her hands again. Arvin watched from the couch alongside the ring. There was no sign of Paul. Hadley had come in this morning with a shiner that he refused to talk about. Arvin couldn't help but think Paul's absence was somehow linked to it.

Hadley looked off today. Not because of the way he was boxing, just how he'd gone about things. Quietly, saying very little, like something odd had somehow crept into his day without him being aware of it.

The front door was thrown open and Paul appeared. The midmorning sun caught the side of his face; it was bruised. He wore black tracksuit pants with a red and white Lonsdale singlet. A pool of sweat circled his neck. He had his white runners on and was breathing heavily.

He walked straight to his bag and took out his headgear and gloves. He pulled his helmet and gloves on, then held them out to Arvin to lace up.

Hadley waved Toni away and hung his arms over the side of the ropes.

'Paul, what are you doing?'

Paul ignored him and swapped hands, letting Arvin lace up the second one. He walked to the side of the ring, climbed up and pulled the ropes aside.

'Get out,' he said to Toni.

'Come in and drag me out, bitch,' she replied.

'It's alright, Toni,' said Hadley. 'Let him in.'

Toni passed through the ropes. 'Looks like you made some more friends last night.'

'Paul … listen,' said Hadley, raising both gloves.

But Paul was on top of him, swinging wildly at his head. Left and rights slammed into the side of Hadley's head as he tried to bat them away. He pulled back, but Paul kept coming. Seeing no other way to slow him down, Hadley brought his knee up and drove it hard into Paul's thigh.

'Fuuuucck! You cunt!' said Paul, doubling over.

'I'm sorry, Paul, but what are we doing here?' he replied.

'You want to fight me drunk? Now you're bringing fucking knees into the equation? You fucking coward!'

'Whoa! Calm down boys,' said Toni, standing outside the ring. 'What's going on here?'

'What's going on? What's going on … is this right here, you motherfucker!' replied Paul, charging at Hadley again.

Hadley ducked and came around with a huge right hand. Paul's face crumpled under the connection, dropping him to the floor.

Paul rolled onto his feet. 'You think that's going to stop me … you bitch?'

Paul put some more distance between them now, one arm raised high, the other held slightly below it, his legs evenly spread. Now they were trading blow for blow. Paul forced his way in with brute strength, landing some hits to Hadley's chest before pulling back and delivering a brutal upper cut.

Hadley fell back against the ropes.

'You like that, cocksucker? Paul said to him under his breath. 'Think I should tell them what you are? What you do?'

Hadley shook it off. Paul switched to southpaw and threw a left jab that Hadley easily ducked. Hadley rose and drove a straight punch into Paul's left cheek. Blood dripped onto the floor.

'What do you want, Paul?' he said, pulling back.

Paul came back at him. 'What do I want?' Paul moved further forward. 'What I want … is you gone!' he said, throwing a fierce combination of lefts and rights.

Hadley was forced back against the ropes. Paul wouldn't stop, he was spitting with each punch now. Sweat covered his face and ran with the blood as he worked his way in. Hadley slid to his left and spun himself free.

'You want to tell them … or am I going to?' said Paul, breathing hard.

'Tell us what?' yelled Toni.

'Guys, stop fighting. Please. Let's just talk it out,' said Arvin, joining Toni beside the ring.

'Fuck that!' Paul ran at him, throwing haymakers and roundhouses at his target. He meant to put an end to it. 'Come here, bitch!'

Hadley rolled to his right, dropped his arms low and let Paul come at him. Paul launched himself off his feet, putting everything into a right-hand punch which Hadley managed to avoid by the narrowest of margins. He was quick enough to know where Paul would end up. Hadley dropped his right shoulder and brought his left arm up quickly, just as Paul rebounded off the ropes. The uppercut slammed hard between Paul's jaw and his helmet. Paul fell to the ground. He was still, but breathing. Hadley stepped over him, walked to the side of the ring and climbed out of it. He held his hands up to Arvin, who unlaced him.

'What the fuck was that?' said Toni.

Hadley was breathing hard. 'I bumped into Paul at a club last night. He was drunk and stupid.'

'And?' she pressed.

'He saw me with another guy.'

'What? You're gay?' Toni said, screwing her face up.

'And?' he asked.

'It's … it's nothing. I'm … I'm … just surprised, is all. I always thought you–'

'Were … what? A straight hard man?'

'I guess. Does it matter?' she asked.

'Depends on who you're talking too. He's right about one thing, though. It's probably not the smartest thing to admit to in this industry. I'm leaving.'

'Hadley … wait,' said Arvin. 'Can we regroup and talk this through?'

Hadley turned to look at Paul, who was now holding his head in his gloved hands. 'Not today. Maybe just keep an eye him. See you guys.'

'Hadley!' yelled Toni, following him toward the door. 'Hadley?' This is crazy, don't just … I mean you can't …'

He pulled the door closed and was gone.

'Damn,' said Toni, looking round the now quiet room.

3 6 .

Arvin picked up the phone and rolled onto his back, the soft blue light illuminating his face as music blared through the speaker. Leroy's name was on screen, along with pale white digits reading 3:15 am.

'Keanuuu? Keanuuu? Thaat youu?'

'Leroy?' Arvin replied, sitting up.

'Who elssee is gonna call youuu this time o' mornin'? Ya thought it was a booty call – didn't ya? Haaahaaa.'

'What's wrong?'

Leroy was drunk. Arvin could hear loud music in the background, as well as cheering and screaming. It sounded like Leroy was at some sort of club.

'Oooh, that's gooood sugar, I like that. Yeah … yeah, keep doin' that. Give the girl some money … no, nah man … that one, with the … yeah.'

A strip club.

'Leroy, what do you want?'

'Easy, Keaanuu. Why isss … that fucker Paul callin' on me?'

'What do you mean?'

'I don't like him, at all. Know what I'm sayin'?'

'Yeah … okay.'

'Anythin' I need ta know? I mean, where's Hadley at? I ain't heard from that boy for an age.'

Arvin turned on the lamp next to his bed.

'Don't worry about it, Leroy. Hadley's okay. He's just … taking a little time out, that's all. I'll have a chat to Paul, I'll tell him to leave you alone.'

'You do that. I never liked that motherfucker. That face o' hiss … it pisssses me off. It's an angry face … ya know?'

Arvin smiled, despite himself. Another cheer went up in the background.

'You're at a strip parlor, aren't you?'

'I'm where you shhould be. Not at home tucked up in bed.'

'Just tell me you're with friends and have it under control.'

'I'm with frieeendss and I have it *hic* … under control.'

'Sounds like it.'

'Whaaat?'

'Nothing.'

'Hey, loookss like I might be getting sssome PR.'

'Good. With who?' asked Arvin.

'Forget her name. Had a drink and a chat, earlier. Magazzine, Outraegousss, Consciousss or ssomethin'.'

'Contagious,' Arvin replied, his hand squeezing the bottom of his chin.

'Yeah … yeah, thatss the one.'

'So a girl interviewed you?' Arvin asked, bracing himself against the headboard.

'Yeaaah … cute one, too.'

'Where did you hold it?'

'Where d'ya think?'

'Don't say there.'

'Right here, baby. She loved it!'

Damn.

'When? Did it go well? I mean … what did you say?'

'Of courssse it went well. Who do ya think you're talkin' too?'

'Are you sure?'

'Sssure about what?'

'About what you said. That girl – Jo, wasn't it?'

'Yeah … I think ssooo.'

'She's a sharp customer. Pulls no punches, if you know what I mean. It might not come out favorable. Was there anything–'

'Sheee loved me. Though she did asssk me about ssomeone … ssome dude named … Arnold … Arnold Lyden?'

'Oh shit.'

'What? Who iss hee?'

'No one. Nothing you need to worry about. Ask her for a transcript of the interview before she prints anything.'

'Ask what? I can't hear you man, the mussic … ouch! Terry, who is that? Get her name. Yeah the one with the … yeah, that one.'

'I said–'

Click.

Jesus. So she knows who I am and what I do.

Arvin gently slid the drawer out of the night stand. He found an old rectangular tin tucked deep in the back, carefully opened the lid, then unfolded a piece of red velvet cloth secreted inside it. He hated and loved its contents. A glass pipe and a small vial of heroin. His habit was a small one. He smoked it, would never inject it, regardless of the high. You needed a modicum of control with these things.

He stared at both items for longer than he needed too, torn by the fact that these things had already stolen so much of what his life should have been; diverted his hopes and dreams from a steady clear path to something that was becoming increasingly distorted.

And yet, here he was. He tapped the powder gently into the bowl. A scratch of flame and he was drawing the thinnest of vapors toward him, a glass elevator that would lift him beyond the life he wasn't sure he wanted, would propel him forward into a lighter dream state, thoughts of a previous life, a previous hope that had somehow left him.

That done, he switched off his light and lay back, having restored his habit to its hiding place. He closed his eyes and before he knew it, she was there in front of him. Once more in her blue dress with its red and white flowers fluttering in the warm city air. Her pale arms extending to his own, hands clasped between his fingers as she pulled him along beneath the bright lights of Shibuya in all its neon glory. Tugging him slowly at first, then dragging him between streets, headlights and street vendors as they laughed, dodging it all, fluid like pieces of paper being buffeted on urban winds, untouchable to anything that might attempt to slow them.

The lights began to blur, faces began to blend into one another, his hands began to hurt as she pulled him through a curtained entrance off a side street, the lights growing dimmer as faces faded from view. He tried to resist, asked to her to stop, to slow down. She wouldn't.

His hands were slick now, from the sweat of running and the heat of their palms being pressed together. Was it sweat? A halogen light blinked on overhead, illuminating himself and everything else around them. They were following pipes under concrete streets; his arms were covered in blood. Now he was yelling, then screaming at Myoki to let him go, to give him the forgiveness he sought. She stopped running. Her hair hid her face with its long strands.

Arvin reached forward to brush it gently away; she turned quickly to look at him. It was Jo staring back, laughing gently at first, before reaching up and clawing the skin from his face. He was screaming now, tears mingling with disbelief. He could only watch as her smile broadened before her free hand stopped him cold with a knife she pushed hard into his chest.

Arvin woke in a pool of sweat, ran his hands lightly across his chest, searching for the knife's handle, blood, proof of anything residing in his head.

Relief arrived with reality. He tapped his phone's face to life: 5:30am. It was pitch black outside, though there was no sleep left to him. Nothing good would come of this.

37.

Pocket sixes and the King of Spades arrived in the flop in front of Toni. Chips hit the table as the betting made its way around the circle of five. She placed her own bet and smiled as the croupier reached for the fourth card, to make the turn. For just a second his eyes locked on her own. She wondered what he saw. What he had seen on the faces of so many others. Was it excitement, or tension?

She checked her phone for the time. It was well after midnight. Her head was spinning. She shouldn't be here, though Paul's altercation with Hadley and his departure ensured she couldn't be anywhere else. She wanted space. A place to escape the bullshit that was somehow mounting in her life and was now at risk of collapsing.

Toni searched the faces around the table as the next card fell. The King of Hearts. There was a quick intake of air on either side of her. This was a dangerous hand.

Toni checked her own draw, the Ace of Spades and a club six. She had a full house, but did her best to suppress a smile. She needed this hand. Toni signaled the waitress for another drink, a vodka, which she knew meant her night was almost over. Her stack of chips was light, bought on credit in her position as a long-running client. They sorely needed refreshing before she was shown the door.

She did her best to keep her hands resting on the table, conscious of the faces studying one another, looking for any sign of confidence, advice to walk away. There were plenty of faces in behind the table as well, a gallery of people that had swelled as the pot had grown. One, she thought she recognized.

Her attention snapped back to the final card – the river was placed on the table once the last round of betting stopped. Toni's heart skipped a little as the Ace of Diamonds was placed neatly at the end of the row. Her full house had just gotten a little bigger.

She drank deeply from her vodka, excitement beginning to rise in her as two of the five other players folded. A young guy with a Yankees baseball cap and sunglasses pushed all of his chips into the center of the table. The fifth player folded, collected what was left of his stack, and left.

She had this.

'Ma'am?' asked the croupier.

'I'm all in,' she replied, pushing the remainder of her chips forward.

The pot was huge. This is where she liked to be. In that precarious place. A place that took her away from all she had known, staring at a pool of money that was more than she'd ever seen as a child; money that could be all hers, or which could just slip through her fingers. It was the chance, the opportunity of it all, that she relished.

Her stack was smaller, she'd been called. Toni turned over the six, then smiled as she turned the ace over alongside it. A few of the players tapped the side of the table in appreciation. She leaned in, eager to see her opponent's cards.

The guy adjusted his own cap and turned over the five of diamonds. Toni eased back in her chair, confidence growing, though focused on his last card, her heart beating steadily in her chest.

The King of Clubs dropped lightly from his fingertips to the green felt. She closed her eyes as the faces around the table turned to look at her own. She drank the rest of her vodka as her chips were added to the oversized stack in front of the prick with the Yankees cap.

She smiled graciously at him, stood up and walked away on unsteady feet.

'Ma'am? Ma'am?' repeated the croupier, following her from the table.

Toni looked confused.

'Mr. Faris would like a word.'

She glanced to the side, and saw one of the larger staff members standing quietly against the wall. Nodding, she followed him toward the stairs at the back of the main floor. She was pissed with herself. After quickly scanning the punters on the floor, she focused on her feet. Most patrons stared at their screens, the hand of cards they held, or at the ceiling, as more money left their pockets.

The face appeared beside a bank of slot machines to her left. Toni was sure it was her – the girl she'd spent the night with. She wore a leather jacket over a gray hoodie, and black skinny jeans. Toni darted to the left, hearing the security man grunt behind her as she started to run.

The girl was heading toward the exit, having seen Toni chasing her. She was quick, but Toni knew the room better than she did. She scooted right, in behind a side bar, the fog in her head quickly clearing as she gave chase. Then she was on top of her. She reached out and caught the girl's waist before she could slip through the door.

'Hi,' said the girl, smiling at her as Toni spun her around.

'Are you following me?' Toni asked.

She searched Toni's face. 'Is there any crime in that?'

'Depends on why, I guess?'

'Curious, is all.'

'Yeah? Well I'm curious too. Did you take my keys?'

'Keys? Keys to what, I'm not sure I follow ...'

'Stop being a bitch.'

'Ms. Rodriguez. We need you to come with us,' said the security guard, having caught up.

'One minute, please. Who are you?'

'Just a girl, who likes another girl.'

'And the girl's name is?' asked Toni.

'You don't remember? That's a bit disappointing, Toni.'

Toni stared at the security staff gathering behind her.

'I'd like to know.'

'Well that's nice to hear.'

'So tell me.'

'Another time, looks like you're a bit preoccupied.'

She turned to walk through the door. Toni reached for her before the staff took hold of an arm and spun her in another direction.

'How do I reach you?' Toni called.

The door closed as the girl passed through it.

'This way, Ms. Rodriguez. Keeping the big guy waiting won't do you any favors.'

She sighed, resigned herself to it and followed them upstairs. People stared at her as she was led to a side door.

'Toni,' said Faris, from behind a large desk.

His office was dark, a green lawyer lamp lighting up the paperwork he'd been hunched over. He pushed it aside and stretched himself out as she approached.

'Andrew,' she replied.

'Another loss, as I understand it?'

He stood up, towering over her. Faris was tall and skinny, and dressed in a gray suit that sat uncomfortably off his shoulders. He spoke with a high nasal pitch that seemed incongruous, given his size.

Toni held his gaze as he reached for a steaming cup of tea. His lips stretched around large crooked teeth as he took a sip, then placed it gently on his desk.

'What should I do?'

Toni lowered her eyes, opting to stand in silence.

'Nothing. Is that it?' he said, arms held wide apart. 'Am I to sit back idly and watch you play my tables with money you don't have? I like you, Toni. That, I think, is part of the problem. I've let things slide where I normally wouldn't. You're done with this casino, and I'll be letting those across this province, as well as Quebec, know that you're not good for it. You're gone. You have two weeks to front up with the cash, or you'll be getting visitors.' He looked sideways at one of his team. 'Are we clear?'

'I'm not sure I can–'

'Are we clear!' he barked at her, slamming a fist into the table.

Toni nodded.

'Good,' he said, sitting himself down. He repositioned his paperwork, making it clear they were done.

Toni headed for the door.

3 8 .

I've been following her for a while. I've learned her routines, where she likes to hide, the things she does, where she likes to go. And this place, at this hour, seems to be where she loses herself. I know it's a little dangerous, but there's something about her I like. Her strength.

Which is why, it's fair to say, I'm a bit disappointed. Why would a girl like this end up here? In a casino, of all places? She seems smart, clever.

What if she sees you? Do you want her to? That could get complicated pretty quickly. You've been here before.

I hide myself behind a crowd of people gathered around her table. Toni looks like she's been there a while. It's after midnight and she's signaling for a drink. There are only two players now, a mountain of chips separating them.

I watch the cards fall. I'm not much of a card player, but the faces of the people around her, their silence and body language, tell me it could go either way. I see the tension leave her face, a sort of calm wash over her. In this moment she's beautiful, serene, with her dark eyes fixed on nothing but the green felt of the table. Then me.

I feel the weight of her stare, sense recognition in her eyes before I slip behind a couple to the left of me. The final card falls and her eyes follow it. A cheer goes up as her opponent pulls the pyramid of chips toward his chest. She drains the fresh drink she was given only moments before. One of the staff whispers in her ear. She looks lost, a feeling I know only too well.

— ✶ —

I could see the red door from across the street, through tears and heavy rain. The road was flooded, the gutters ran freely. The water bounced back up at me as I weighed up my options. Blood trickled down the inside of my left leg. I had been nine weeks along. I'd told him I was pregnant. The fall and beating had hurt me as badly as he'd intended.

I wasn't sure if I was ready, and didn't know if I wanted to keep it. Clearly, he didn't. He didn't want me. Just fucked me and left. All charm and love – then nothing. Is that what they do? What my dad had done to my mother?

Well I couldn't and wouldn't do what she did. I wouldn't bring a child into this world and this shitty life. It was done, anyway. He'd ruined it. That much I was sure of.

My ankle was broken, and I supported my arm and fingers that were too sore to move. I was bleeding heavily as I dragged myself toward the building, cradling my stomach, hunched over, protecting and hiding myself as I moved.

Cars passed by, pushing water onto the footpath as I waited for the road to clear. My shoes were soaked through as I did my best to avoid the flooded potholes as I crossed. I was sure there were better clinics than the one I'd found on Gerard St East, though I was delirious and dehydrated.

I walked slowly up the green-carpeted stairs. I could hear the sound of a xylophone being struck, along with a string instrument, through a fuzzy speaker at the top of them. My heart was racing.

You don't have to do this.

You do and you will.

The room was darker than it should have been. No bright lights and posters of smiling families in here. Fine by me, I didn't need either. My financial situation didn't lend itself to anything better.

I was given a gown by an elderly doctor of Asian descent. He was slightly stooped with a wrinkled face and smiling eyes. I studied his gloved hands before a mask was dropped over my face and an overhead light was switched on.

Darkness.

— ✖ —

The croupier points to a larger staff member, and it's clear she's being escorted away from the tables. Does she owe money? I follow her from a distance, being careful to avoid being seen, ducking between banks of slot machines as she passes.

I step into a gap between rows, and her eyes catch mine. Her face changes; she's alert.

I bolt. I hear someone grunting as I leap a side table and sprint past a couple arguing over lost money. I can see the exit and make for it. *Get out, Kat, you shouldn't be here.* My heart is racing. I look sideways, and she's gone.

I reach the exit, but feel a hand catch my jacket and pull me backwards. She's caught me. I let her study me. She asks who I am, what I'm doing. She's angry, made the more beautiful for it.

I give her nothing; listen as she struggles to remember my name. I repeat hers. She mentions the keys I stole, convinced I took them. That makes her dangerous. She tries to stop me leaving, but they hold her.

I step out into cold air.

She will be your issue, as will Arvin. You have to take bold strides, otherwise this all goes nowhere.

I make my way to the back of the building, pulling on my helmet, and leap on the bike. The moon is out and cold air washes over me as I tear up the road, leaving behind thoughts of what lies ahead.

3 9.

It was late in the day. The light outside had all but faded from view through the skylights above the boxing ring. It was cold out and the roller door had been pulled shut. Paul checked his watch for the third time in less than ten minutes. Neither of them was here. He cracked the lid of a second can of Coke Zero.

Were they coming? Or would he just be ignored? They'd have to listen or risk losing everything. Hadley wasn't coming back anytime soon, that much was clear. And even if he did, would it matter? It didn't to Paul. They shouldn't care either. This was about preservation; ensuring they all had an income. There had been no sign of Hadley. It was like he'd just picked up and vacated. Maybe he was embarrassed about being outed. And so he should be.

The door to the gym opened and Arvin walked in.

'Arvin! Glad you could make it,' said Paul, jumping to his feet. 'Is Toni with you?'

'Hi Paul. No she isn't.' He dropped a bag near the door. 'She's five minutes away.'

'Okay. Great … that's good. That'll give you and me a chance to talk. Have you heard from Hadley?'

Arvin shook his head.

'Me neither.'

'What are we here to talk about, Paul?'

Arvin looked a little paler than usual, slightly drawn, like he'd been out on a bender or something. 'You okay?'

'Yeah, just a few things going on is all.'

'Anything I can help with?'

'No, just a few things I'm sorting out.'

'Good,' said Paul. 'Well, that's why we're here. We need to figure out what our next move is.'

'What move?'

'What we're doing with the business. Making sure our clients are happy, building new ones, ensuring the business is safe.'

'Isn't that something Hadley–'

'And that's the kicker … he's not sure Hadley's coming back.'

They turned to see Toni standing at the door.

'Right, Paul? That's what this is, isn't it? A fucking coup?'

Paul walked toward her. 'Glad you could make it.'

She stood her ground, arms folded.

'No Toni, it's not a coup. It's a discussion.'

'Does your discussion involve the leadership of this business?'

'It probably needs to, don't you think?'

'I think all parties need to be here to talk it through. Has anyone called him?'

'I've tried,' said Paul. 'Have you?'

'I have, but I didn't get an answer.'

Paul started walking the room. 'Listen, we've got a business with some well-known and sought-after clients. If those clients sense anything's being dropped, or we're slipping in any way, we're done. Am I right?'

'I agree,' said Arvin. 'Though you calling my client is a bit presumptive, Paul, and needless to say, not very helpful. Leroy told me to tell you not to call again.'

'Okay. Maybe I was bit hasty there, though–'

'Hasty?' said Toni. 'No one has fucking elected you boss, Paul. Don't go wading into something that hasn't been talked through at length.

Tell me you haven't called Christie?'

'I might have left her a message.'

'What the fuck are you thinking?' said Toni, raising both hands skyward. She walked to one side of the boxing ring and sat on a padded corner.

'At least I'm trying to think,' said Paul 'To do something about the situation we find ourselves in.'

'Are you?' asked Toni. 'Or is this some sort of opportunistic grab for power that we've all come to expect from you?'

'That's hardly fair. I'm–'

'You're the fucking reason our boss isn't here! It's because you're a homophobic shithead with an ego that outweighs your fucking talent.'

'Sorry? As opposed to what you're doing, Toni. Which is what, by the way? Wallowing in depression while your client gives you the cold shoulder? Racking up debt at the local casino with that fuckhead Faris?'

Toni blushed.

'What? You think you're the only person who knows a few faces in this town? It's time to pull your head in and do what we need to do … together. To ensure that what we have isn't lost.'

'And what have you got, Paul? Where is your fucking client? Why do you think–'

'Guys. Stop beating each other up. He's right, Toni.'

They both turned to look at Arvin.

'All of us have tried to call Hadley. I've left messages and haven't heard anything back. We're in limbo – though Paul, calling clients without consulting any of us isn't helping our situation.'

'Okay. I apologize,' said Paul, raising his hands.

'We do need a game plan, though. We can't just jump into something without taking a step back. I'm convinced there's a lot more going on here than we think,' said Arvin.

'What do you mean?' asked Toni, taking a seat on the small couch.

'Doesn't this run of unfortunate luck we're having strike you as being a little coincidental? I mean the attack on both of you. The theft of Chris's art?'

'Fucking Jonas,' Toni muttered under her breath.

'Hadley being forced to pull Christie out of a drug bust at her own show. I mean, how many shows do you think Christie has taken drugs at?'

'All of them,' they replied in sync.'

'Yet, right now she finds herself in trouble with the narrowest of escapes? How long have we all been doing this? And what? All of a sudden Paul's client decides to try and kill himself?'

'To be fair, that had been boiling away for a while,' said Paul.

I think we would all be well served to take it slowly and think about what might be happening here.'

'What did you say about Jonas?' said Paul, staring at Toni.

'Nothing,' said Toni.

Paul straightened himself, sure he'd missed something. He tried to focus. 'What about Leroy?'

'I'm watching Leroy,' replied Arvin.

'You think we're being targeted?'

'No. I don't think, I know. What I don't know is why or by whom. Though what I'd suggest is that each of us keeps close to our clients. It could be a vendetta against any one of us. There's one thing we need to understand.'

'What's that?' asked Toni.

'That Hadley's okay.'

Paul and Toni nodded in agreement, both struck silent by Arvin's revelation.

4 0 .

'I need coffee. Right fucking now!'

Marleena Riley was reclined on a lounger beside the rooftop pool of the Thompson Hotel. Behind her, the CN Tower bisected the skyline, the white lid of the Roger's Center to its right.

It was the middle of the day and the sky was bright, though it was way too cold to swim.

Marleena's yellow bikini glittered under the photographer's lights and reflective umbrellas. A turquoise-and-white-striped robe hung open, revealing the tanned body that meant she was in hot demand from designers across the northern hemisphere.

'Christ! Can someone hook this bitch up with something to shut her up?' said Christie under her breath. She was seated in a spectator's chair behind the photographer's screens. 'We've got less than half of what we need, and I'm not paying her ransom for another fucking day!'

'Christie? Christie?' Marleena called from the other side of the pool.

'Yes, honey?' she replied in her softest voice.

'Do you mind if I take a look at the prelims? I'm not convinced Harlow's shooting me from the right angle. I'm sure the last thing any of us wants is a reshoot. And it's fucking cold up here. Can I get some slippers or something? I get that you need nipples, but do you have to have goosebumps as well?' There was a smile on her too-perfect face.

Christie bit her lip, then smiled back, nodding at her model in the most congenial way she could manage. The scissors on the chain around her neck felt all the more solid as she held them tightly in her right hand.

'Harlow, take Marleena through a few of the prelims,' she said. 'Reassure her that I'm happy with what I'm looking at and that I'm paying for this shoot – would you?'

She paused as a new face appeared on the rooftop of the closed shoot. Her staff held him up at the entrance before Christie waved them away. Arvin made his way over to her side of the pool.

'Mr. Reeves, you're almost right on time. There's a model over there that I might need you to evict if she doesn't change her tune.'

He leaned forward and gave Christie a polite peck on both cheeks. 'Thanks for seeing me at such short notice, Christie. I really appreciate it.'

'That's okay. I'd ask why, though I'm guessing Hadley's still in hiding.'

'Something along those lines. Has he been in touch?'

'A while ago. Just to say he was taking a little time out for a few weeks.'

'Did he mention where he was going?' Arvin asked.

'No. He wasn't that forthcoming, and when I see someone I like appear to be a little unsettled, I'm not inclined to push.'

'Fair enough.'

'Is anything wrong?'

'We're okay. I wanted to make sure all's well with you?'

'I did get a call from Paul. Don't really know him, but he wanted to get together.'

'Ignore that. Just someone getting a little power hungry at our end.'

'Right.' She laughed. 'Are you okay? You look a little a pale.'

Arvin used a fist to cover his mouth and coughed. 'No, I'm good. Just the change in season is all.'

'Don't I fucking know it. Wouldn't it be nice to shoot summer in summer for once,' she said through tight lips.

'Listen, I'm sure Hadley's fine. If there's anything you need, feel free to call me and I'll be there where I can.'

'Great, thanks Arvin.'

He was about to walk away, then stopped. 'One small question.'

'Fire away.'

'Do you know a columnist called Jo Reid? She writes a piece called Contagious for the *Globe and Mail*. She seems to know a few of us, and I wondered if Hadley had ever mentioned her, or met her, perhaps.'

Christie stared directly at him.

Arvin pulled out his phone. 'I've got her picture here.'

Christie took the phone off him and looked at the photo. Arvin could tell she recognized her. It was the smallest of expressions, though he'd caught it.

She smiled through it before shaking her head. 'No … I'm not sure I do. Should I? I mean … has she done something?'

'No, not at all. I'm just curious is all.'

Christie gave him back his phone and took his free hand. It was damp, though warm to the touch.

'Go home Arvin. You don't look well,' she said, studying his face.

'I'm fine, it's nothing.'

'Looks like withdrawal to me.'

He pulled his hand free.

'You can't fool a user, Arvin. You know that. Stay in touch and be good to yourself.'

Arvin turned to go.

'Christie. Christie!' yelled Marleena from the far side of the pool.

Christie sighed, then muttered, 'Skinny ho-bag. Thanks for coming by.'

Arvin walked toward the doors. Christie knew Jo, of that he was certain. How? Coincidence? There had been way too many of those. The girl was at the center of it all. He needed to know why. What her motives were. Before all of that, he needed to straighten himself out; things were getting out of hand. He had to get across Jo's blog about Leroy before it went out. Nothing good would come of it, that much he was sure of. He took the lift down and crossed the street.

41.

Contagious – Jo Reid

I love a good film and everything that goes with it. The night out –
ideally with rain, a cheap eat followed by the obligatory rush to a
movie. The smell of butter on salted popcorn and seeing something
new – hopefully original, en masse with friends.

The issue I have is what happens when the film is done. With those
on screen, who are then forced to leave it behind. The actors almost
seem to believe they're still in there. Do you know what I mean?

Our exposure to them is somewhat limited. I mean they're
squirreled away behind giant fortresses, tucked up in tinted limousines,
managed by agents and PR consultants to ensure their exposure in
market is tempered. Sure they appear on talk shows, laugh inanely
at the simplest of jokes from hosts who do what they can to make it
interesting. You get salacious tidbits in magazines, usually driven by
the media, revealing stories with the most tenuous of links to scenarios
we willingly devour.

Though are we really seeing them? Understanding who they are? I
don't think so. Which is why it was quite refreshing to get the chance
to chat to up and coming actor Leroy James. Do you know him? You
should. He's never short of headlines.

He's the guy who outed director Will Rogers' on-set affair with

Veronica Paul at this year's film festival showing of *Behind A Dark Cloud*. While on stage during the Q+A session for the film's premier, no less.

I caught up with him at his local strip parlor. You heard right. Charlie Sheen in the making. Though let's be honest, at least like Charlie, he's not hiding. This is less of an interview and more my take on what I heard.

Yes, there was the usual rhetoric around new projects, people he likes, outnumbered by those he hates – not surprisingly, Will Rogers is one of them. Rumor has it the feeling's mutual. What was concerning was his take on women. Probably not that surprising, given our location, chatting with drinks in hand with Lady Gaga singing about her Pokerface, lots of tassels, legs covered in oil, writhing around brass poles behind us.

He eats it up and the girls react to it. He's borderline lecherous. He's arrogant, but I think that comes with the territory. His view on the world is a little disconcerting. Is it his background? His upper-class upbringing? He's the youngest child of six, his successful parents able to afford a large family. His father's in insurance and his mother's in real estate, both earning good coin that meant a slew of nannies doing the hard yards.

Leroy believes he's earned success through hard work. What he's got now has almost become an entitlement. He has self-confidence that builds as the whisky disappears. And they fall quickly. Maker's Mark – Hollow Kentucky, if anyone's asking. He's a believer – in himself.

He tells me you have to be. Imagine it? Everyone telling you you won't make it; that you're wasting your time. Both of your parents from studied, learned business backgrounds, the rest of the family all workers; classes upon classes; the endless parade of lucky stories – right place at the right time, the other 99.5 percent having missed it.

So what was his lucky moment? He tells me it was the right audition for a small part with a director who knew him. He gives persistence as his reason for getting lucky. I remind him he's up and coming, yet he's pissed off two directors in less than six months, not to mention being fired/walked out of (depending on who you talk to) his latest film.

Is he at risk of blowing it all? He waves his finger for another drink and grins at me with large white teeth that easily push everything else aside. You can't help but like the guy, despite the fact he's laying down what looks to be a clear path to inevitable self-destruction. I tell him this, and he laughs it off.

My sense is he's got it all. And keeps getting it. Now we can't belie the hard work that it takes to become successful in this field. Unless your last name is Spielberg, Coppola, or these days Nolan, you probably won't get much of a look in untested. The talent has to exist.

And Leroy has it. Though I think attention becomes the enemy. They get too much of it. Bad behavior fuels it with headlines, notoriety and inevitably paints a profile picture they themselves devalue.

And it's happened again. *It's You, Or Me,* is the next film you won't be seeing him in. Leroy bowed out after an on-set stouche with the film's director, Pierre Fields. This time over a stereotype in the script Leroy didn't like.

Didn't you read it, Leroy? Anyone with half a (sober) brain would have seen it for what it was. That said, we need to give him props for walking away from it. He has an idea of where he wants to go and, fingers crossed, we'll see him get there. His face is still intact, which his security needs to be applauded for, though there was a fairly decent king hit from Mr. Fields to the side of his face, which was still slightly bruised when I caught up with him. Age is on his side, though this guy is tough to handle.

My question to you reader is this: do we as a society want him there?

Comments:

(This is a forum for feedback, please be courteous, not abusive with your responses.)

Pod: Jo, I've been an avid reader for a while, though all too often you seem to walk a fine line between wanting to write about celebrities and hating them. Is that what we've got here? I would liked to have heard what Leroy had to say versus being force-fed your opinion, which, in all honesty, didn't add up to much. I will however answer your question. Yes, I'd like to see him there. The guy seems real to me, not laminated like the rest of them.

JO: @Pod. Thanks for being a regular reader. Sorry if you didn't get what you wanted here Pod. It's a column and an opinion piece after all. I don't hate Leroy, I thought I said as much in there. The arrogance and the girls bother me, but it is what it is.

Si: Good piece Jo. The guy sounds genuine. He needs to be there!

JO: @Si. Thanks Si.

KJ: @JO. This piece is as bad as the last two. Your writing is shit!

JO: @KJ. Welcome back KJ. Giving the doll a little time out to put your thought down can't be easy. I'll let you know when the next one's ready.

AL: @Jo. I've read the last couple as well. You mention the security teams in every piece. Have you had a bad experience with one, or is it just a fascination of yours?

KJ: @JO. Don't bother, this will be my last. Bitch!

JO: @AL. Is that you Arnold? Probably just a fascination.

AL: @JO. Can we talk?

JO: @AL. I'm thinking – no.

JO: @KJ. Miss you already honey.

42.

Hadley pressed himself into a corner. He could feel the concrete of the jail cell against his cold skin, the left arm of his shirt having been torn when he was forced to the ground and arrested. He could hear and smell the others in the cell he shared, though he refused to look at them. He chose instead to hang his head between his arms and legs, staring at a damp, filthy floor.

Not for the first time, he told himself he was an idiot. A mess. Even that thought hadn't been easy to shape. His head was aching, dehydrated, and recovering from the drugs he'd taken at a club he couldn't quite remember the name of, on Bloor and Yonge. His regular club had been forever tainted by the fight he'd had with Paul. He doubted his friends on the door would let him through it again, hence the episode in the park.

They'd caught him running, stumbling, out of his head, his jeans halfway down his legs as he tried to escape the toilet block he'd just vacated. The other person involved in his early morning liaison had managed to break right, having followed him out and sprinted as soon as he heard the shouting. Hadley had been tackled within less than a hundred yards, pinned to the ground by two burly cops while his counterpart had vanished.

Hadley stared at the floor, not because he wanted to hide from the reality of where he was, but because he wanted to disappear. While being brought in, he'd spotted a former soldier who used to report to him. The soldier was now a police officer. The last thing Hadley needed. There was no time to reminisce on what had gone wrong, he told himself. Focus on now. Sort this mess out.

'Peters,' called an officer with a clipboard. Those in the cell looked at each other to see who'd been called out.

'Hadley Peters?' said another officer, stepping forward.

Hadley looked up. It was the face he'd being hiding from, the solider.

'Come on out. We need to go over your case file.' His face showed no hint of recognition, though Hadley knew he'd clocked him.

Hadley hung his head and stepped out of the cell, falling in behind the officer holding the clipboard. The soldier – Myles – followed quietly as they walked to the end of the corridor.

Hadley was led to a matte black door. The first officer opened it and motioned them in, handing the clipboard to Myles before leaving.

'Take a seat, Hadley,' Myles said, closing the door behind him. 'How long has it been?' he asked, with a sad smile on his face.

'I don't know, five or six years?'

'I heard you were running your own security team here. That still happening?'

'Yeah, still doing that.'

'You want to tell me what's going on?'

'What's to say? I'm gay and I met someone.'

'At a toilet block near Asquith Park? Is this a … new relationship? Or one of several?'

Hadley rubbed his head. 'To be determined, I guess.'

'What the fuck happened to you, man? You were revered. A stand-up guy that all of us looked up too. And now you're … I mean … what are you doing, man?'

'I'm bent. What can I say? I don't like it, but despite my best efforts, there's not much I can do about it.'

'That's bullshit, Hadley. You were high. There will be repercussions. You understand that, don't you?'

'Do there have to be, Myles?'

Myles' eyes were focused on him. 'They want to take a blood sample. Any idea of what they'll find?'

Hadley shook his head.

'Give me one reason to tell them no.'

Hadley stared silently at the concrete wall behind the officer.

Myles leaned in. 'Is this about James? I ask, because that can't have been easy, man. You became a topic of conversation when you left, though it wasn't your fault, buddy.'

Hadley had the good sense to nod and keep his mouth shut.

'I think you'd benefit from some sort of counseling. I'm no doctor, but there's got to be something in it, doesn't there? Some kind of release that's better than this, right?'

Hadley was rigid, but remained silent.

'Here's what I'm going to do. You get to go home. Though I need an assurance that you'll get help. That you'll sort out whatever the fuck is going on inside your head. What I am going to insist on is that you get a friend or a colleague, with no priors, to come in here and collect you. I'll be asking them to help you sort your shit out. Understand?'

Hadley nodded.

'You'll get a phone call, and we'll hold you until I'm satisfied you'll do something about this. Sound fair?'

'It is. Thanks, Myles. I appreciate it and I'll do as you say.'

'Great. The phone's in an office across the hall. Let's go.'

'Hello?' said a sleepy voice on the other end.

'Toni? It's me.'

'Hadley? What the fuck? Where have you been? Do you ... are you okay?'

He looked around at the gray concrete block walls to the left and right of him.

'I'm okay, just ahh ... well, I'm being held at 53rd Division in Eglinton.'

'For what?'

'Can we talk about that later? I need you to come and get me.'

'Will you talk to me if I do?'

Hadley sighed. 'Can we do that in the morning?'

'It *is* the fucking morning.

Hadley checked his watch, it was almost three a.m.

'Do you want to stay here?' asked Toni.

'If that's easy.'

'It is. See you in fifteen.'

'Thanks, Toni.'

Hadley hung up the phone and nodded to the guard, who escorted him back to his cell.

4 3 .

'Do I just sign here?' asked Toni at the front desk.

'Your signature and a smile ought to do it,' said the cop on duty, from beneath a thick brown moustache.

'Forget it, Ron Jeremy.'

'Ouch! Ron? Really? I mean, his moustache was black and I look nothing like him. The guy was large and I have a full head of hair.'

'Do I wait here or go somewhere else?'

'Okay. Just trying to be polite is all. This is the nightshift.'

Toni straightened herself. 'Do I need to go in, or does he come out?'

'Alright already. I'll call him out,' he said, picking up the manifest. 'Ms. Rodriguez … no surprises there,' he added, giving her another once over. 'Take a seat. He'll be out in a few minutes.'

Toni sat in a corner chair at the back of the waiting room watching the headlines on CNN. She was knee deep in yet another Syrian assault when Ron called her back to the front desk.

Hadley stood behind a glass door looking broken and disheveled, dressed in what would have been a decent outfit had it not been stained with grass, mud, and sweat. She tried to avoid his eyes, which wasn't easy. She took yet another clipboard off an officer who led Hadley out in cuffs.

The officer's eyes were focused on her own. They took their time, studying her from top to bottom, in a careful manner rather than in a lecherous way.

'You okay?' she asked Hadley, handing back the clipboard and taking his hand.

Hadley folded his gently around her own. 'I'm good.'

'Great. Then let's get out of here.'

Toni turned right and headed west toward her house. They drove for ten minutes before she said anything. She had questions that would lead to decisions needing to be made. She couldn't put them off any longer. His silence was frustrating.

'So what are we doing here?' she asked.

'I don't know,' he mumbled.

'What do you mean, you don't know?'

He turned his head and stared out into the darkness.

'What is this? Some sort of spiritual guide into your fucked up part of the universe? We need you to come back, Hadley. Park this fucking soul-searching, loss-of-identity shit. I know you don't want to talk about it, but you need to get over yourself. Who cares if you're gay? You're leaving us in limbo here. With a fucking moron who wants nothing more than to sit in your seat!'

'Can we do this in the morning? Please, Toni? I just can't right now,' he replied pressing his face sideways into glass.

Traffic lights flew past as they crossed a few blocks. The homeless were prolific out here. Silhouettes crept from one streetlight to the next.

'Sure. I'm sorry, I just … I mean we're all just struggling with this shit, Hadley. You know? Paul has lost Jordan; Chris is fucking furious at me with the loss of his art; Leroy and Arvin, well, who the fuck knows? As for Christie, I haven't–'

'Pull over.'

'What?'

'You heard me, pull over!'

'Hadley, I didn't–'

'You did, Toni. I left for some space, and you're not giving me any. Now pull over.'

She did as she was told, pulling into a cab rank under a tree on Eglinton Ave West. Hadley wrenched the door open; cool night air rushed in.

Toni reached over and grabbed his arm before he could stand up. 'Please, Hadley. I get it … I get it. At least, I think I do.'

His face turned toward hers. It was folded and creased in all the wrong places.

'Don't go. We need you. I, more than anyone need you … to stay. Can you just, please come and stay with me. Just tonight. I'll make you coffee, or just give you a shower and a bed. I promise not to say anything else.'

She saw him hesitate.

'Please,' she added, gripping his hand tightly.

He closed the car door and slumped back into his seat.

'Thank you,' said Toni, pulling away from the kerb.

They said nothing as they drove the rest of the way, Toni with the easy distraction of the road, Hadley staring out at the black shadows of the trees, and the streetlights appearing then disappearing like flashbulbs as they passed by. He was hurt, that much was obvious. Lost was probably closer to the mark.

Toni's apartment building was a tall dark block against a black sky. Garden lights lit the narrow path to the entrance. They took the lift to the tenth floor and quietly made their way to her door.

'You sure you want me here?' said Hadley. 'I could easily head home.'

'And do what, exactly? My shower's a good one. Clean yourself up. I've got a robe for the occasional gentlemen caller. It might even fit you. You can take the spare bed and you'll wake up to eggs and fresh coffee that I bought yesterday.'

'Thanks, Toni. I appreciate it. Really, I do.'

'Good. Get some rest.'

The sun was well and truly up by the time Toni got herself out of bed and dressed. It was the sound of a door being pulled shut that woke her. She washed her face, pulled open her door and said half a *Good morning* to an empty room. A fresh cup of coffee steamed gently alongside a plate of scrambled eggs.

She opened a folded piece of paper that said, *Thanks. Promise I'll call you.*

'Dammit,' she muttered to herself. She sat down to drink the coffee. Fortunately it was good.

44.

'How long have we been doing this for, Toni?' asked Chris, seated behind his desk.

He was dressed in a bright green suit and thick gray sunglasses, both of which hinted at a meeting she knew nothing about. He always dialed up his colour pallet when he had something big on.

They were in his Scollard St gallery, both looking out of the window as the sun worked its way down behind a thick stand of trees.

'Five years, I think. Maybe a little longer.'

'And in that time, how much shit have we gone through?'

This wasn't a conversation she wanted to be having. 'Plenty, Chris.' She smiled as wide as she could, trying to keep it together.

'Have I always trusted you?'

She nodded.

'Do I have any cause not to now?'

'Not at all.'

'Then why do I feel like you're holding out on me?'

'I'm not holding anything back. What makes you think I would?'

'Search me,' he said, leaning forward. 'All I know is, I've got this fucking shit storm floating around me because some shit bag has stolen something that belongs to me. Something, I might add, you were supposed to look after.'

There was colour in his cheeks she hadn't seen in a while. He kept going. 'Artworks, that are now being devalued through every fucking dime-store charity I've done my best to avoid!'

Toni got out of her chair and started pacing, a puzzled expression on her face. 'Haven't I always worked hard for you, Chris?' she asked. 'Haven't I always put my body on the line when it was needed?'

'Yes, I pay you too. And?'

'So where's the trust you and I have built up over the years? This whole fucking thing was to be supposed to be some sort of … PR exercise. And for what? More money? Exposure for shit you'd already sold?'

'I'm the fucking client here! Don't lecture me on what I choose to do!'

'I will lecture you … you prick! That was my life out there and a hundred more that were placed in jeopardy because you wanted a few extra column inches. Fuck, Chris! Why couldn't you have just told me what you were doing? I could have run this and made it all that much simpler. Tighter, for fuck's sake!'

Chris raised his head and just watched for a while. Watched her pace from one end of the room to the other. 'Would you have done it?'

'Maybe, maybe not. Though I might have, if I understood what was going on.'

'You're right. Okay, I'm sorry. I should have told you. Though I'm not sure you could have sold it. Call it intuition.'

'And where exactly has that gotten you now?'

'Take a look around,' he said, smiling.

'Point taken.'

'What did you do afterwards?' he asked.

'Got drunk. I was gutted. What else did you expect me to do?'

'I'm not sure,' he said, straightening his arms. 'Find my fucking stolen works?'

'Well you didn't exactly look cut up on the night. Now I know why. You thought they were in storage with that circus you hired, right?'

'You know them?'

'I do.'

He slumped back into his chair. 'You lost your keys. The keys, I understand, that were used to take all of my works. Who was he?'

Toni sighed more deeply than she'd intended.

'I didn't lose my keys, they were taken. And … it was a girl.'

'Really?'

'Don't give me that face.'

'A girl? What girl?'

'I don't know, but I'm doing what I can to find out.'

'So what? You meet some girl during some post-I've-let-some-fuckwit-steal-all-of-my-boss's-shit-self-pitying session, and she knows to steal your keys and my fucking paintings? I hope she was cute, honey, because she sounds a little more conniving than any bitch I've ever met.'

'You're right. None of it adds up unless it was premeditated, including my own–'

'Well, at least one of us got something out of it,' he said, staring at her. 'I won't be pleased if it all goes, though there's one picture you need to get back. I don't know how you do it, and I don't care. It's a black and white photograph called *This is me.*'

'The prostitute with her knickers around her ankles.'

'Of course that stayed in your head. A precursor to your evening, by the sounds of it.'

'And yours, if we're being truthful,' she replied, gently laughing.

'Not that funny, Toni. Just get it done, and you might still be lucky enough to be gainfully employed.'

'Right then, I'd better get to it.'

'And Toni, love you, but don't come back without it. We clear?'

She nodded.

'One other thing.'

She looked up. He was facing the window, his back to her as he spoke. 'Give up that crap you've got going on at the casino. Nothing good will come of it, and you can't afford it.'

Trixie was there to show her the door and lock it behind her. She looked immaculate as ever, though Toni could see traces of last night's truths covered lightly by makeup.

They turned away from each other as Toni left. She wrapped herself tightly in her jacket as she walked the street. The wind off the lake was getting up, forcing a chill down her front.

Why the prostitute photo? Surely he had a negative he could reproduce? Was there something else about it?

She had a sell sheet at home. There were thumbnails of each piece shown beside the listings. She'd take another look. This whole saga was one giant fiasco. She'd start by listening. Staying the fuck away from the casino and doing what she had to do to get a few more faces on side. She'd focus. She'd track that bitch down.

Arvin knew something; she'd speak to him first. Hadley was of no use to anyone yet. She'd work with Paul, much as she loathed the pig, but she'd start with Arvin. He knew more than he was letting on.

4 5.

'Who's there?'

'It's me, Arvin.'

'Well don't stand out there, get your ass in here!'

Leroy was seated in front of an oversized mirror surrounded by enough bulbs to make him sweat. A large girl with bright blue hair completely shaved on one side and pinned at the other, worked frantically around him, applying foundation. Leroy's own hair was covered in latex in preparation for an oversized blond wig that sat on a white plastic head to his right.

Arvin watched the girl work. She wore thick red glasses and a tight white T with the words *If you don't, I will* stretched across oversized breasts. She was a living mural, with tattoos covering her forearms, the back of her neck, and what he could see of her legs between her black and white striped pants and her short pink socks.

'Can you believe this shit, Keanu? A fucking trannie! That's what they've got me playing. Delores, for Christ's sake!'

Arvin grinned, despite himself.

'What? You think this shit's funny?'

'Leroy, can you sit still please?' said the girl in the gentlest of voices. 'I need you to breathe, you'll cool down if you do.'

'I hear what you're saying, Fran. It is Fran, isn't it?'

'No, it's Phoebe.'

'Sorry. What I really need, Phoebe, is a drink. Can you–'

'I can't, Leroy. Director's orders, I'm afraid. We're dry on this set.'

'What? I mean, what the fuck is that? Can you believe this shit, Keanu? It's late in the day, we've been at it all morning. Least a man can get during lunch is a small–'

Someone knocked at the door.

'What?' Leroy asked.

'First call reminder, we shoot in fifteen.'

'Great.'

Arvin checked his watch, it was eleven a.m.

'Fran, you got much more to do?'

'It's Phoebe, and we're almost there.'

'Sorry. Thanks for coming, Keanu. Fran, can we speak in confidence?'

'It's Phoebe, and I'm here to do your face. My eyes are open, ears are closed.'

'I like this girl,' he mouthed to Arvin in his mirror. 'Did you read it?'

Arvin took a seat in an opposite corner. 'I did.'

'And?'

'I thought it was okay.'

'What?' said Leroy, attempting to turn around.

'Please. Leroy, if you could keep still.'

'Sorry, Fran.'

'Phoebe.'

Arvin watched as she applied thick mascara beneath light blue eyeliner. Leroy's eyes seemed to grow with every stroke of her pen.

Leroy reached for a glass of water. Ice cubes and mint leaves jostled for a position near the rim.

'Take a big drink, we're putting on lipstick next,' said Phoebe.

'Yes, ma'am.'

'So the bit about me being lecherous, arrogant, and full of myself slid past you?'

'It didn't. What do you want me to say?'

'That it's bullshit! That it's unfair.'

'Is it?'

'Are you–'

'Leroy, can you please sit still.'

He repositioned himself, held his head up. 'Are you saying I am?'

'No, *you* did. You agreed with her.' Arvin pulled out the article, folded it back and read, '*He's a believer – in himself. He tells me you have to be.*'

'Well, you do.'

'Then roll with it.'

'What about all that other shit, about me drinking and blowing up with directors and crap?'

'Do you think you're alone?'

'No.'

'Have others been affected by similar stuff?'

'I guess. It depends on who and what.'

'The short answer.'

'No.'

'Then take that stance. Stand by what you've said. You're sitting in a chair about to do another film, aren't you?'

'I am.' He nodded, getting to his feet. 'You're right. If I can't–'

Knock knock. 'Second call, on in ten.'

'Will you sit the fuck down, before I knock you down!' screamed Phoebe.

'Whoa. Christ. Alright … sorry–'

'Phoebe,' said Arvin.

'Phoebe,' said Leroy.

They sat in silence as she finished up, packed her things, then left the dressing room.

'Damn! What got into her knickers?'

'The trannie sitting in front of me, I think.'

Leroy smiled with those enormous white choppers of his. It was disconcerting under all that makeup.

'You need to step back, pause before you start mouthing off. Think about what they're doing and what the outcome might be before you say it. And don't do another interview out of your head in a strip club.'

'Listen to you, telling me the way of the world.'

'You're asking. I'm answering truthfully.'

'I'm glad you raised that.'

'Raised what?' asked Arvin.

'Truth. And that's something I need from you, Keanu. I'm with you on the whole notoriety, watch-my-mouth thing. I can't keep running it and expect no fall out. Though what you didn't read in the report was her question about you. You're Arnold Lyden, aren't you?'

Arvin looked around the room, at the large white lilies blooming in the corner, and answered. 'Yes.'

'Why?'

'I've been watching her. I'm not confident she's who she pretends to be.'

'What? Not a journalist?'

'I'm sure she's that. I just don't think we're getting the whole story.'

'Well she's suggesting I'm not getting all of yours.'

Now Arvin's back was up. He could feel his shoulders tensing, bracing themselves, ready to resist what came out of Leroy's mouth.

'In what way?'

'Are you a drug addict?' said Leroy, turning to face him.

Be careful, Arvin.

'What? No ... no I'm not.'

'Do you take drugs? Because I, in my notorietal, unsober state, need someone to look after me. And while I'd like that person to be you, despite whatever shit is going down at your place, I can't afford to be wrapped up in a drug scandal. I'm not saying the drinks aren't an addiction, but have you ever seen me take drugs?'

Arvin shook his head.

'That's right. And you ain't gonna. It's easier to piss into a cup and talk about a hard night on the drink, than be called out over a failed drug test. I may be a loud-mouthed, lecherous, arrogant son of a bitch who chases headlines, but what I'm not and will never be, is a junkie. If you're dabbling, walk away, or you're done. You got that?'

'Got it.'

Knock knock. 'Five-minute call to action, you're required on set.'

'Good, then let's do this.'

Leroy wore a turquoise sequined dress with shiny black heels. He placed the wig on his head, adjusted the sides and smacked his lips into the mirror, before turning to face Arvin. 'Fucked up, isn't it?'

Arvin got up and opened the door.

4 6 .

'Damn! Here he is!' said Paul, getting to his feet, all but galloping toward Jordan as he entered the restaurant. Jordan had his arms out. Paul went under them, picked him up and pulled him in.

'Whoa. Don't think I've had a hug like that since the Showbox in Seattle, when you and I were just starting out,' he said. 'Remember that gig?'

'I do,' said Paul, laughing. 'That neo-Nazi group tried to pull you off stage. You were fucked up that night. I'm surprised you remember anything.'

'I do. I'm sure the fucker that started it all, and his broken nose, remember it well too. Speaking of which, what happened to you?'

Paul smiled back. 'Ah, nothing. Just disgruntled competition is all.'

They took their seats at the far end of the room. Paul seated himself door-side of Jordan to make sure he could manage any approach. Jordan was wearing a gray sweatshirt with a hood bunched around his neck. A black denim vest was open over the top of it.

'You're looking great, man. Your eyes are clear, skin looks good. You look revitalized, dude!'

'I feel good, Hammer. Its taken a while, but I'm feeling almost new.'

'Well fuckin' hip-hip hooray is all I can say. So it was okay in there?'

'Yeah, wasn't easy. Few curly moments, though you sweat those out.'

'You hungry?'

'I ate already, but I'll grab a drink.'

'Bourbon?'

He shook his head. 'Herbal tea.'

'What the fuck?'

'Don't I know it.'

Paul signaled a waiter. A small, thin, young guy with his hair pulled back into a man bun approached.

'Can I get a beer? Molson will do, and a herbal tea.'

'Sure. Any particular tea?'

'Pomegranate, if you've got it,' replied Jordan.

'Bagged or loose leaved?'

'Loose leaved would be great.'

'Okay then,' he said, turning on his heels and heading for the bar.

'Loose leaf?' said Paul.

'Some hard yards in rehab, buddy. Not something I'm gagging to repeat, if you know what I'm saying.'

'Ten-four, Jords, whatever you need, man. Just tell me what we've got lined up, because I'm dying to get back to it.'

'That's the thing. We were dropped by Capitol.'

'Really? Cunts,' said Paul, his jaw tightening. 'Their loss, buddy.'

The drinks arrived. Paul chopped his in half as he watched Jordan pour steaming tea from a blue and white porcelain pot. Jordan blew on the surface of an equally delicate cup, then took the smallest of sips.

'Fuck, dude. It's strange to see you … drinking tea, man. Don't get me wrong. I get it's a good thing, just … odd, you know?'

'Yeah, well, not all by choice, I've got to be honest. We've signed with Universal.'

'Well alright! Now you're talking. They're fucking huge, like one of the biggest. Aren't they?'

Jordan nodded, looking past Paul's shoulder at the rest of the restaurant. They had gotten there ahead of the lunch rush, though it was starting fill up.

'It is good news, but it comes with some caveats.'

'Caveats? Like what?' asked Paul, finishing his beer.

'Changes I need to make.'

'Well that's okay. Change is good, right? I'm sure they'll be for the better.'

Jordan looked to his left out a nearby window.

Paul pushed his empty glass away from him and spoke. 'I'm part of these changes, aren't I?'

Jordan slid his tea clear of the space between them.

'You are, Hammer.'

'Fuck!' said Paul, slapping the table. 'Why? I mean, haven't I been here for the whole thing? Beside you whenever you've needed me? This is fucking … bullshit, Jords. What am I suppose to … I mean, how can they just–'

'Hammer, please stop. Think, okay? One of their caveats is a new team, and that includes my security detail. They need reassurance that I won't slip. So part of the deal is that they appoint their own team, to help manage me and the rest of the guys.'

Paul slumped in his chair, stared into space then ran both hands over the skin of his head.

'You've had it good, haven't you? For the longest time. But the parties, the drugs, the girls … they need to be pushed aside if I'm to keep going.'

'So I get pushed with them?'

'I can't sugar coat it in any way … so yeah, I'm afraid you do.'

'That's fucked!' Paul said, hitting the table a little harder.

A few patrons close to them turned to stare. Paul stared back. He signaled the man-bun waiter, pointed at Jordan, who shook his head, then ordered himself another beer.

The restaurant was louder now. Paul could see people standing, pointing and sneaking in the occasional picture of himself and Jordan. Paul couldn't give a shit. *Take a photo of the tea-drinking motherfucker for all I care.*

They sat there saying nothing until his beer arrived. Paul drank from a fresh glass, then spoke. 'So what am I supposed to do?'

'That's for you to figure out, my friend.'

'Friendship is all about loyalty. I'm not seeing much of that here, Jords.'

He shook his head. 'That's not fair, Hammer. It's out of my control.'

'The fuck it is! You could change it. Change yourself. Why sink everyone else around you? It's not our fault, is it? And where's that fucker Riley at? Eh? He's the real fuckin' reason this goddam train came off the rails. Right? Don't tell me that motherfucker is going to be anywhere near the team?'

'He's gone, trust me. I get your frustrations, Hammer. And you're right, it should be me that changes. It is my fault, I invited it in. Though now I'm seeing it out.'

'Now I'm seeing it out,' he mimicked. 'Well hooray for Jordan Franks and the Vaulted fucking Ceiling. Long may it stand, because the fucking walls have just been pushed down!'

Jordan could see several waiters starting to whisper to one another over Paul's shoulders.

'Calm down, Hammer, please. The last thing I need is a scene.'

'The last thing you need? What about what *I* need?'

'This is my fucking life, Hammer, not yours. I'm pleased you've been a big part of it. I've paid and treated you well, haven't I?'

Paul finished his beer, stared at the table without raising his head and spoke. 'Sorry, Jords. You're right. It's just there's … a lot going on. This is the last thing I needed to hear. I'm just disappointed is all.'

'Listen, mate. I'll give you a decent chunk of change to thank you for all your hard work. That'll tide you over for a while. If I hear of anything going, I'll be sure to give you a shout, eh?'

'Yeah.'

'One other thing. Do you remember the groupies from that last ill-fated gig?'

'A few, though not really. Why?'

'My last night at the Four Seasons.'

'What, when you–'

'Slit my own wrists? Yeah,' he said. 'The girl I ended up with, she was tall and I think she had long red hair. I keep getting flashbacks.'

'Of what?'

'It's hard to say. I was well and truly out of it. The cops told me I had a fucking lethal combination of acid, ketamine, and coke in my system. Acid and coke, sure. Ketamine? I'm not even sure I've tried it. Though what I'm almost sure of, because its been replaying itself in my head through out the whole of fucking rehab, is that I'm confident I wasn't holding the knife.'

'What?'

'I'd like some closure, Hammer. Find the girl. Help me unravel what happened on that night. Show me it wasn't a suicide attempt, and I'll double this,' he said, dropping a check onto the table.

Paul picked it up.

He studied each figure slowly, then whistled under his breath. Along the bottom was typed: $125,000.

47.

It was a sports bar Toni didn't recognize, somewhere well north of Dupont and Bathurst. She should have come across it, given its proximity to her neighborhood – but she hadn't, which made her perception of it even worse.

It was one of those places with dark bricks and small table lamps that made everyone inside it melt away. A small well-stocked bar was backlit alongside old Budweiser and Coco-Cola neon signs that were a throwback to yesteryear. The fact that it was raining cats and dogs on an already dark night made it easier to want to be inside. A jukebox tucked in a corner near a few pool tables was playing 'Gold on the Ceiling.'

Toni spotted Paul and Arvin in the corner, saw they had drinks and ordered herself a beer. She'd need it to get through this.

'Thanks for coming,' said Paul. 'How is everyone?'

'Fuck off, Paul. What are we doing here?' said Toni, necking her bottle.

'Lovely as always,' he replied. 'Okay. I've been fired.'

'What?' replied Toni, almost choking on her drink.

Arvin said nothing.

'I had lunch with Jordan yesterday. He's out of rehab, was dropped by Capitol and resigned with Universal, along with a whole new entourage of good guys to keep him clean. As it turns out, I'm not one of them.'

'And what? You're surprised?' said Toni. 'You've been boozing with him and fucking his groupies since you first met. The line of professional conduct has been well and truly crossed. So no, I'm not.'

'Thanks for the kind words of support.'

'So what happens now?' asked Arvin.

'The bigger question here is, what's happening to us all?' Paul replied.

'We're employed, you're not,' said Toni.

Paul ignored her and took a large pull of his beer. 'I've been thinking about what you said when we last got together, Arvin. There's been a slew of unfortunate events, for Jordan, Chris, Christie, and to some extent, Leroy. I'm convinced there's a common thread to all of these, and I know both of you are too,' he said, tapping the table.

Toni stared at Arvin; watched as he nodded his head slowly.

'Who is she, Arvin?' Toni asked.

'Jo Reid. At least, that's her alias. She's a journalist for the *Globe & Mail*, writes a column called Contagious. She's written recent articles on three of our employees, and they seem to be vaguely linked to us. Paul, you read the one about Jordan that Hadley gave you a while ago. She's covered Chris's stolen artworks and has interviewed Leroy.'

'Okay,' said Paul. 'Anything on Christie?'

'Not that I know of.'

'Have you approached her?'

'I did. Went in posing as a charity worker asking about the donations for Chris's stolen artworks.'

Toni straightened herself. 'And, what did she say?'

'Not much, really. Just denied any knowledge of the whole scenario and told me her sources were unknown.'

'Bitch! She's lying, has to be. What does she look like?'

'Tallish, about five-eleven, blonde hair, blue eyes, an overdone spray tan. Kind of what you'd expect in a news office.'

'Right.'

'Did you follow her?' asked Paul.

'Tried to. She disappeared on me before reappearing on a motorbike. She gave me the fingers as she rode around the corner.'

'I like her already. Have you spoken to her since?' asked Toni.

'Tried to, via a thread on her last article. I asked if we could talk. She fobbed me off. She mentioned me to Leroy, though. She knows who I am.'

'How? I thought you went in posing as a charity worker?' asked Toni.

'I did.'

'Hmm … I guess she is a journalist. Thanks for sharing, Arvin. It's probably best I do too,' replied Toni.

'Before you do, I'll get another round in. Same again?' asked Paul.

They both nodded.

Paul returned with drinks. Toni and Arvin pulled back from close conversation.

'Okay. You're not going to like this, Paul.'

'So tell me anyway.'

'Chris hired Gauntlet to steal his works the other night.'

'What the fuck!' Paul said, a little too loudly. He leaned back in the booth and hissed through his teeth. 'Jonas? That fucking little grease ball. I knew that outfit was trained, albeit badly. Cunts.'

Toni noticed Arvin was very quiet. 'You knew?' she asked.

'I did,' he said, his eyebrows raised. 'Hadley and I went to see Chris a few days after it happened. We wanted to know where his head was at.'

Toni bit her bottom lip. 'And no one thought to tell me?'

'I'm sorry, Toni. Hadley organized it. I went along as an extra set of ears.'

'And?' she asked.

'It went as badly as he thought it would. Chris threatened to drop us unless we found his artwork. He gave us two weeks. Hadley confronted him on the whole thing being an organized robbery, which didn't go down well.'

She snorted. 'I got the same treatment when he called me in.'

'Hats off, seriously. He's a tough customer,' added Arvin.

'There's more. I've spoken to Jonas,' said Toni.

'What did that little fuckwit have to say for himself?' said Paul.

'Not much. They locked everything up in a storage facility owned by Chris. He, Trixie and I had keys to the place before mine were taken. Jonas had already returned his.'

'The place must have had cameras. Was there any footage?' asked Arvin.

'Not much more than a shadow,' she replied.

'So the girl you went home with. Does she look anything like the girl Arvin described?'

'Same height, though she had dark hair, dark eyes and pale skin.'

Arvin showed them a picture of her on his phone.

'It's her,' said Paul.

'What makes you so sure?' asked Arvin.

'The conversation I had with Jordan. He said that while he was in rehab, he kept having flashes of the groupie he slept with on the night of his alleged suicide attempt.'

'More like hallucinations,' said Toni. 'Why alleged? He called it in. He slit both wrists while he was in the bath, out of his head on coke, acid, and ketamine.'

'The last one is a substance he claims never to have tried,' replied Paul.

'How would he know? And even then, so what … he's drugged, rolled into a bath, someone slits his wrists, then he phones the police?' asked Toni.

'Don't get me wrong, it all sounds pretty odd. Though Jordan's adamant that he wasn't holding the knife. He described the girl as being tall with long dark hair.'

'Damn,' said Arvin.

'I don't get it. What's her motivation?' asked Toni.

'Who the fuck knows?' said Paul. 'Why does anybody do anything to anyone?'

'Well one thing's clear, it's not them she's after,' said Arvin. 'It's us.'

4 8 .

Paul could see him through the misted glass windows on one side of the hall. By the look of things, his session was almost over. There were only a few cars left in the lot out front. It was a cold night. Paul wore gloves with their fingertips cut off. These weren't your standard kind, they were reinforced through the knuckles. They were made to cut faces.

It was a karate class. No doubt one of those feel-good things Jonas did for himself. Parading around at the front of the room with his two yellow stripes on his black belt, like he needed to remind himself how good he actually was.

He was a fucking tool.

Maybe he is, buddy, but one of his guys broke your nose last time you bumped into him.

Yeah? Well, there were three others with him, and all you had was a lesbian for support. Some fuckin' contest, right? Let's see how good he is tonight.

'Damn right,' he said to himself, steam rising from his face as he talked to darkness.

Paul walked toward the hall's entrance. It was lit by halogen lights. A few people stared in his direction as they headed for their cars. He ignored them. He walked through the double doors and into a corridor that opened up into the hall.

He could hear Jonas talking to someone near the front of the hall. Paul didn't stop to listen, he just kept walking in. They were two young girls. Jonas had his arm wrapped around one, while the other looked on.

Jonas stopped talking as he saw Paul come in. It wasn't so much the look on his face that gave Jonas pause, more the speed at which Paul was walking, in a straight line toward him.

'Excuse me, girls. I think this guy wants to talk to me,' he said, pushing them gently to one side. 'Paul? What are you doing here?'

He didn't respond.

Jonas raised his hands, palms forward. 'Paul, if this is–'

He ducked as Paul lashed out with a vicious right hand.

The girls screamed, and ran for the entrance. Paul swung again, this time bringing his knee up at the same time. The knee found its mark in the side of Jonas's right leg. He grunted, though gave nothing else away. He bounced backwards and braced himself in a defensive position, fist clenched, stance wide.

'What the fuck is this?' he asked.

Paul pushed forward. 'Been to Chris's gallery, lately, you fucker?' he yelled, swinging a fist at his head.

Jonas ducked. 'I didn't know you'd be there!'

'You knew she would be,' he said, circling him.

'Who? Toni?'

'You fucking coward!' Paul connected with the side of his head. A spray of blood covered the blue mats beneath them. Jonas wiped the blood away from his face with a black-clothed forearm.

'Fuck,' he said to himself, shaking it off. 'You're going pay for that.'

'What, you got people coming?' Paul replied.

Jonas moved forward, threw himself into a somersault before bringing the heel of his foot hard into the side of Paul's face, narrowly missing his healing nose. 'That what you came for?' he said, spitting blood on the floor mats in front of Paul.

Paul could sense the faces pressed against the windows. Let them watch. Jonas deserved to be embarrassed in front of his fan club. The guy was quick, he had to give him that. He was small, agile. Paul needed to corner him, catch and hold him.

Paul began circling first to his left, then right, watching the leg he had gotten to earlier. He'd hurt him, despite his acrobatics, he could tell by the way he moved.

He feinted left and struck right, though Jonas saw it coming. He dropped and swept his leg, knocking Paul off balance and onto the floor. He drove an elbow into his face. Paul heard his nose break once again, ignored it and threw himself on top of him, pinning him with his body. Their faces were almost touching each other.

'I'm going to kill you! Never liked you … you're just a little shithead,' Paul spat through clenched teeth.

'No fan of yours. No one is!'

Paul lifted a hand and drove it into the side of Jonas's face, then used it as leverage to push himself away. He wrapped his free hand around Jonas's arm and wrenched it the wrong way with a sickening crunch.

Now Jonas was yelling, and there was screaming from the far side of the hall as Paul got to his feet, wiping blood from his face.

'You see Jonas, you're just not that good.'

'Ugggh … fuck you.'

'Don't think so, buddy. It's you that's fucked.' Paul kicked him hard in the side of his head, knocking him out.

More screams from the front of the hall.

Paul left as quickly as he'd arrived. He didn't want to be there when the cops turned up. His nose hurt, but he couldn't help smiling through it as he headed for his car, parked a few blocks away.

He jumped in, searched the street, but saw no one near him. He pulled off his gloves and plucked a cigarette out of his glove box. He didn't smoke often, though when he faced a challenge and prevailed, it had become a tradition.

The light from the glovebox lit up the seat in front of it. A white envelope with his name on it had been left in the middle of the passenger seat. Puzzled, he picked it up, and studied the street a little more carefully as well as the trees and bushes down one side of it. Nothing.

He focused on the envelope and teased open the flap with bloodied hands. A folded picture was buried inside. It was a scanned picture of Toni. The words *She'll ruin you all* were written in red marker across her face.

He knew the photo – it was clipped to the top of a page in her file. He could see the outline of one of those oversized paperclips Hadley loved to use. It was a mugshot of an earlier arrest in some place he couldn't pronounce.

He threw it in the passenger well and spat through his driver's window. He'd always suspected something was wrong with that bitch. Hadley must have known. One homo looking out for another, he thought, smiling to himself, before wincing at the fresh pain it caused.

He got out and checked the lock on the passenger side. Intact. Nothing wrong with the windows. Whoever had left it knew how to break into a car.

He rechecked his face in the rearview, gunned the engine and pulled into the street, hearing the distant wailing of sirens a few blocks over. His thoughts moved from Jonas to the note. Someone was watching him.

4 9.

Toni's sleep had been broken. She'd been in bed for what felt like hours, and had managed to roll from one side of it to the other, drifting in and out of dreams that threatened to become nightmares. The latest had her fighting over one of Chris's pictures, with hundreds of homeless people chasing her through the city's streets.

She rolled herself awake, breathing heavily and sweating in the darkness.

She'd turned the AC off before going to bed, as it was cool enough without it. She preferred clean air to the shit everyone else in her building was inhaling. She pushed herself out of bed and reached for the bathroom door, feeling her way in darkness. She turned on the soft lights hidden beneath the basin and stepped into the shower. Jets of water warmed her skin, stripped away the worries her mind kept throwing at her. She turned her back to the shower and put her head under the jets, letting the water fill her ears, pushing reality away.

Toni dried herself and pulled on a robe. She was thirsty, so she walked from the bathroom through a second door connected to the lounge and kitchen, before stopping in her tracks. The low light from the bathroom lit up a large dark silhouette standing against the wall. Her stomach flipped, throat turned dry as she pulled the robe's belt tighter around her waist.

'Hi, Toni. Good shower?' asked a deep voice from beside the front door. She looked toward the voice, and another shape materialized from the darkness. He was much larger, thick through the waist, almost fat, his arms folded.

'Bad time?' the first guy asked, pushing himself off the wall. He switched on a floor lamp and sat down in a chair by the dining room table. He had closely cropped hair, blue eyes, tattoos, and a small cross on the right side of his neck.

'For what?' she asked.

'A house call, I guess. Why do you think we're here?' he said, reclining in the chair, a gun resting on a knee.

She stayed silent, breathing gently. Her own gun was in the bedroom, strapped to the back of the left-hand door of her wardrobe. Her knife was in a sock drawer, her phone – charging on a small table next to the sofa.

'You tell me.'

'Faris isn't happy. You owe him a lot of money. As I understand it, he gave you some time, which you've pretty much used up. Thing is, he hasn't heard from you. Have you got it?'

Toni exhaled as slowly as she could, willing herself to be calm. 'No, I don't.'

'Well that's too bad. I guess we're on to plan B,' he replied, signaling to his friend.

'Listen … guys. I'm not disagreeing with you. I want to work with you to get it. To pay back in full what I owe Faris.'

'And what's he supposed to do, honey? Sit patiently by while you get your shit together? Do you think you're the only bad debt in town? What does your lack of payment – no,' he held up a finger, 'make that total disregard for his business, say to others?'

Toni shrugged. 'I don't know, but I'm sure you'd like to tell me.'

'Disappointing, Toni,' he said, snapping his fingers.

The large guy stepped forward. Toni grabbed the floor lamp and ripped the cord out of the wall, plunging them all back into darkness as he lunged at her. The lamp struck him hard on the side of his head, shattering the bulb inside it. He batted it away with a thick forearm, though the cord wound its way around his shoulders.

Toni dived at him, fumbling in the darkness for the cord. She pulled hard. It tightened, and the steel bar of the lamp forced its way up under his neck. She moved to him and launched a knee into his balls, heard the air rush from his lungs, then pulled as hard she could on the cord.

She could hear him choking, struggling.

A light blinked on in the doorway. She tried to look over her shoulder at the other assailant, before his gloved hand smashed into the side of her head. She dropped the cord and fell to the floor by the sofa, taking the small table with her.

Toni could hear the big guy choking, gasping for air, not far from where she lay. She saw her phone on the floor beneath the broken table. Her outstretched finger found the home button, and she held it there until the phone unlocked. She saw it activate to diction. The silent icon blinked on screen. Thankfully she always turned it down at night.

'Hadley,' she said, through a mouth filling with blood.

She could see the call being made, connecting. Then her feet were being pulled and she was being dragged across the floor, her robe bunching, then gathering around her breasts. She was naked, screaming as they pulled her in.

'No good saying his name. Queer and silent, isn't he?'

'What did you say?' She was dazed, uncertain of what she'd heard.

'Your buddy, Hadley. He's queer, isn't he?'

'Says who?'

'Does it matter? Neither of us are,' the talker said to his mate.

Fuck. Paul had done this. Faris didn't know where she lived.

She tried to reach out and claw her way free, but she was held by her feet. She tried to writhe, to turn. She was exposed.

'Let go of me! Take your fucking hands off me!'

The big guy she had almost choked struck her hard in the face with a boot. She rolled onto her back, clutching her face. The tattooed talker with the cross on his neck spoke again. 'Shut up, Toni. Stop struggling, keep your mouth closed and this could all go a lot smoother for you.'

Her jaw felt numb. Her left eye was rapidly swelling.

'We're going to search your apartment for anything we think might be worth taking. Let's call it a deposit.'

His large friend cut the cord from the floor lamp while the first guy forced her onto one of the four wooden chairs. They made her kneel on the seat, then tied her hands below the chair and her feet to the front legs. Mercifully, her robe still covered her body.

'After that, well, I guess it depends on what we find.'

They trashed her apartment. They kept the noise down, though with thick brick walls, no one next door was waking up anytime soon.

Time seemed to crawl. Toni felt the blood running to her hands and feet; the cord was cutting off her circulation, forcing her to stop struggling. Her clothes and belongings were spread across the floor. A vibrator she kept hidden was placed on a table in front of her.

'Looks like we're wasting our time here, Toni,' said the tattooed guy. 'Is there anything you want to share with us? Chris's artworks might be a start. What? Nothing to say?'

Toni stared at the floor.

'Too bad,' he said, undoing the belt around his pants.

She was tense now, her back rigid as he circled her. Toni watched him pick her stockings up from the floor. Watched him stretch them around his knuckles before he forced them over her mouth. She turned her head from left to right, before he finally managed to gag her.

She felt her robe being lifted, exposing her backside. He struck her hard on her ass with his belt. She bit down on the stockings, but didn't make a sound.

'The thing I hate about girls like you is, you think you're better than everyone else. Like you're entitled. Well I'm going to show you exactly what you're entitled too. Right, buddy?'

His fat mate nodded, and grinned at her.

Toni heard the unbuckled belt fall to the floor, felt his knees then his erection on the back of her thighs, before the door exploded inward.

'Get the fuck away from her! Right now, before I put a bullet through the back of your head,' said Hadley, a gun in his hand.

'Whoa … listen, man,' he said, trying to pull up his pants. 'This bitch–'

He turned to face Hadley, his cock pointing at him like he was its next target.

'Keep your hands in the air,' said Hadley. 'You …' He waved his gun at the large guy standing beside the wall. 'Get rid of the gag and the cord.'

He didn't move.

'Now!'

The guy did as he was told, then wrapped his arm around her neck and threw himself on top of her. The chair collapsed under their weight, and as it did his accomplice escaped from the room.

Toni cried out as she hit the floor. His hands were wrapped firmly around her throat, squeezing the life out of her.

Hadley sprang forward, grabbing him on either side of his head. When that failed he shot him in the leg. That didn't stop him either.

Hadley pistol-whipped him across the back of the head, knocking him out.

Toni gasped, choking down pockets of air, trying to fill her lungs. She began untying the cords that hung from her wrists, before the other guy burst back into the room, gun in hand.

Hadley dove at his feet and rolled into him, knocking him to the floor. A shot rang out and plaster fell from the ceiling. Hadley fought him for control of the gun, and another shot embedded itself in the brick wall not far from Toni's head.

Then she was on him, twisting his wrist then wrenching it backwards until it broke. He cried out. Toni drove a fist into his face. Blood burst from his nose, the gun flew from his hand. Hadley had him pinned.

Toni was on her feet now, her hair hanging in strings, wet with sweat. He was looking up at her now, the tattooed cross on the side of his neck pulsing. Her robe was open, her body exposed.

'You're not entitled to anything, you fuck!' she said, kicking him hard in the face with the heel of her foot. And he was done.

Toni was sobbing now. Tears streamed down her face as her body started to shake.

Hadley wrapped his arms around her and whispered in ear. 'Sorry I've been gone, Toni. I'm back, promise.'

She buried her head in his shoulder, as they heard sirens outside.

5 0 .

Jo had left the *Globe & Mail*. At least, that's what the receptionist told them. She'd recognized Arvin, telling him Jo had switched to freelance status, which meant she couldn't be reached. She point-blank refused to give Arvin any of Jo's previous numbers, though she surprised him by handing him a sealed white envelope with his fake name typed on it: *Mr. A. Lyden / Reeves.*

Arvin thanked her and left, with Toni in tow.

'What does it say?' she asked.

Arvin pulled a yellow Post-it note out of the envelope. Toni saw something scrawled on it in blue pen. Arvin couldn't quite make it out, and handed it to her as he opened his car door.

'A Post-It note?' she said. '*Evergreen*. What the hell is that?'

'It's a charity. The Evergreen Brickworks. They're based just out of town in the Don Valley.'

'That community thing? With the lakes, organic produce and stuff?'

'That's my guess.'

'So what? She's sending us toward one of her donations?'

'Seems to be.'

'Well, they're his artworks and I need to find one of them. Best we get going then.'

The Evergreen Brickworks were the lungs that Toronto had seemed hell-bent on depleting. Acres of lush green grass with pathways encircling ponds, cycling tracks and food stalls set up to preach organic to weekend visitors. It was quiet now, though several people milled about, just wandering, enjoying time out in a nature wonderland of yesteryear.

Toni and Arvin made their way up to the equivalent of an oversized pack house. Huge iron beams stretched from one side of the building to the other like some sort of giant animal carcass, its ribs now devoid of skin, facing the sky.

The surrounding structures were roofed. One side looked to be set up for a wedding. Large antlered chandeliers hung from the ceiling. A long table covered in a white cloth sat on a raised dais overlooking a collection of smaller tables.

'Can I help you?' asked a girl in a white jacket and black pants.

'Sure. My name is Toni Rodriguez and this is Arvin Reeves. We work with The Security, representing Chris Finch.'

The girl adjusted her shoulders, holding her chin a little higher.

'We're not here to get in the way of the donation of Chris's works, though we would like to see what was sent. If that's possible?'

She nodded, but looked unconvinced. 'I can't tell you who donated it, or if it came from Chris himself, but a place like this is very pleased to receive it.'

'Can we see what you've got?' asked Arvin.

She walked them to the main entrance and to the wall at the end of the foyer. There under a single bright light was the large photograph Toni remembered seeing on the night it was taken. The ninety-story concrete block next to the quaint little cottage, complete with the white picket fence beside it.

'Amazing, isn't it? And apt, you'd have to say, for us I mean,' she said.

They both nodded.

'You realize this was stolen, don't you?' said Toni.

'I have read the press. It's since been donated, and until Chris presses charges or publicly asks for it back, our understanding is that we can legally keep it.'

'What are your plans for it?' asked Arvin.

She pinched her chin with her left hand. 'We should sell it. The money we could make would allow us to complete several projects here, though there's no rush. For now, we'll just appreciate it.'

'Did anything come with it? An envelope, or anything stuck to it at all?'

'I don't think so.'

'Do you mind if we take a look?'

'Help yourself, though break it and consider it sold.'

They each took a side and lifted it gently off the wall. There was nothing on the frame they could see, so they spun it around and searched the back. It was Arvin that saw the small corner of folded paper sticking out from the top right of the frame. It looked to have been pushed into the frame with tweezers or a knife. Toni pulled her own knife out from her left boot and prised it loose.

'What is that?' asked the girl.

Toni ignored her and gently unfolded the small square of paper. On it was a picture of Hadley, with his service record below, and there was a short note written across it in red ink. In the photo, Hadley was in full uniform, his face raised to the light. The writing said: *You are as bad as the people you work for. Look at each other.*

'What's that supposed to mean?' said Toni.

'She doesn't like us.'

'Really? I get that, genius. So what the fuck is she doing?'

'I think she wants us to know that there's one of us she really doesn't like. Who or why is a mystery to me.'

'Is it linked to the picture in any way?' Toni asked, getting Arvin to flip it over.

'Excuse me,' said the girl. 'If you're finished, can you please put your knife away and put the picture back on the wall?'

They rehung it and stood back, studying the image again.

'What does it say to you?' asked Toni.

'That there's no regard for the quality of life, its future, past. Nothing but progress matters.'

'Wow. I just see Chris stumbling across two opposing buildings that he finds interesting. He pushes the button on one of his flash cameras and moves on.'

Arvin laughed. 'Now what?'

'We call the team and let them know to start searching for other donations. It's the messages we want. She's playing with us. Best we follow her lead and get whatever she wants us to do, done.'

'Right then.'

51.

Arvin hated himself. Hated his need. It was in his head, under his skin, and out of his reach. His head hurt, his body ached. Things had taken a turn, that much was clear. His habit had its claws in him. The self control he'd held so close for so long, through so much, was slipping.

He didn't know the name of the club he was in, though he'd been here before. It was on the fringe of Chinatown. The lights were low and the place was packed. He wasn't here to dance. He needed to find someone. He scanned the crowds for any sign of him. He'd been told he wasn't a hard guy to spot – tall, with white hair.

Arvin checked his watch. He was early. He headed for the bar, grabbed himself a beer and surveyed the scene. He always felt so old in these places. He was only twenty-eight, but felt years ahead of this crowd. They wore nothing. The girls were writhing, grinding, inviting in whatever they wanted.

I shouldn't be here. I have to put an end to this.

How is what you're doing any different to what happened to Ren? Or Myoki?

He'd been getting through it faster, that much he knew. When had he last bought? Three … four weeks ago? Maybe it was longer, had to be.

Her face appeared in front of him for a brief second. It was fleeting, though he was sure he'd seen it. Arvin pushed his way through the crowd. It couldn't be her, not here, not now. He followed anyway, needing to prove to himself it had been a mistake. She had no reason to be here. He was hungry, desperate for the drugs that would straighten him out.

He must have been hallucinating. Sweat trickled down the side of his head; he was overheating. The beer tasted wrong, nothing seemed right. He had to get out of here, some fresh air would help. Arvin worked his way through the crowd, past the stage and toward a door at the back of the room. He left his glass bottle on a bench, opened the door and found himself in an alleyway.

He had no idea where he was going. There were couples and a few stragglers moving between a few doors further down the alleyway. He stumbled through to a heavy black door. A large security guy dressed head to toe in black blocked his way.

'Help you?' he asked.

'I'm looking for someone.'

'Aren't we all,' he said, through a grill of golden teeth.

'A tall Asian guy with white hair.'

'Yeah, I know him.'

Arvin could hear music behind him. 'Is he inside?'

'Depends on whether or not he wants to be.'

Arvin reached inside his jacket pocket and pulled out a business card. It was blank, pure white, crisp. The guard flipped it over, studied Arvin again before running his thumb and forefinger over the indented corner of the card. Arvin's regular dealer had given it to him on another dealer's recommendation. He'd warned him about it, but had said if he was desperate, he'd be looked after. He just had to present a clean face, cash, and he'd be seen to.

The hidden words were Japanese. They said nothing more than 'This way.' The guard recognized them and stood back. 'Look after yourself,' he said to Arvin as he passed by.

The room was a large, with lots of small spaces off it. There was music, though it was more sedate, considered; live versus being played through a mixer. A three piece playing the sax and a cello, led by a raven-haired girl in a turquoise dress. She glided gently from side to side on a small stage, delivering vocal acrobatics with ease.

Arvin took his time, did his best to compose himself while he surveyed the room. No sign of him. The guy must be seated, as Arvin had been told he was tall with stark-white hair. Unmissable.

A tap on the shoulder from a passing barman took him to a small compact bar with low lights, hidden around a corner. The staff here obviously knew him well. He pushed through curtains and found himself in a smaller space with thirty to forty people. There at the head of the room, in a circular booth to the right-hand side, was a man in a blue suit.

Arvin could only see half of him, as he was leaning back in the booth. A long leg with a brown leather boot attached to the end of it was folded over his other leg. Every so often Arvin would see a head of silver-white hair as he reached for his drink.

Arvin slowed himself down. Forced himself to rethink a mad dash in, followed by an equally quick request for the drugs he sorely needed.

Why do you need to do this right now? There's too much going on. You've lost control, Arvin. Get it together.

His need wouldn't let him leave. He ordered a drink – vodka – clean and sharp to wake him up. He took the top off it, then forced himself to take his time as he walked into the curtained room. The dealer was standing now, head and shoulders above the rest. A thin silver metal bracelet encircled his drinking hand. He looked to be all angles as he turned to face Arvin.

Drawing closer, he could see the clean smooth surface of his face had been punctured on one side, his cheekbone slightly sunken and twisted around an old injury. His eyes were dark, focused, drawn to Arvin's own face, which he studied carefully. Arvin showed his white card, the tall Japanese man noted it and extended his hand.

'I'm Arvin. I understand you might be able to help me.'

'Moshki,' he replied in a deep voice.

'I need something you have.'

'I can see that you do. Come with me.'

Arvin tucked the bag inside his jacket and left as quickly as he could through the curtained wall. It had cost him a small fortune, though he'd make it last. He would get through this current mess and he'd work hard to put this shit behind him.

Moshki watched him go.

A slender girl appeared alongside him. 'So what happens next?' she asked.

'That will depend on how much he takes. He either wakes up in hospital or not at all.'

She looked alarmed. 'I just want him exposed, not dead,' said Kat.

'Don't worry, he realizes it's bad, though he's not over the edge yet. He would have to take it all to die. I can see that he won't.'

'Good.'

Kat paid him twice as much as Arvin had, bowed and departed. Moshki made sure she'd left before he returned to his seat and his drink, disappearing through the curtains that hid him from the rest of the room.

52.

'Christie?'

'Yeah,' said a husky voice on the other end of the phone.

'It's me.'

'Hadley. Finally! Welcome back. Where the fuck have you been? I feel like I've been dancing around in circles covering all sorts of shit without ... sorry ... are you okay?'

'I'm good, thanks. Though, I wanted to apologize. Things got a little out of control.'

'So I hear. But you're okay now?'

'I think so.'

'Great.'

'And you?'

'You know, doing my thing. Putting clothes on drama queens.'

'Dare I ask, how's your security detail?'

'Robotic and fucking useless. In a holding pattern until you come back.'

Relief washed over him. Hadley pushed himself back in his chair. 'Thanks, Christie. Did Paul organize that?'

'Paul? Fuck no! He did call me, though as I said to Arvin when he called by, I don't want to hear from him. Why do you employ that dickhead?'

'Good question. Though in this line of work, you've sometimes got to push through the attitude so many of us carry.'

'You see. Those are the wise words of the sage I've been missing. Let's grab a drink when you're free and we'll catch up.'

'Sounds great. Thanks for understanding, Christie.'

'Bye, doll.'

Hadley ended the call. He placed his phone on the desk beside the files he had been studying. He was at the office. It was getting late. The boxing ring was in shadow, as was the rest of the space. A solitary desk lamp cast a halo of light around him.

Somewhere in these papers was a clue as to why and who was being targeted within their group. He pulled the files apart and studied them one at a time. Whatever had happened, it must have been bad. Why drag everyone else down? Or was it something they'd all done? He couldn't think of anything. Could it be what they represented?

Hadley got up and grabbed a bottle of water from a fridge behind the couch. He stood over the desk and studied their faces one by one. Toni? Things were pretty cut and dried there. Fascination with money, driven by a background of poverty. Yet she had a willingness to lose it all. It was the risk and potential consequence she was attracted to.

Dangerous, though who was she harming, other than herself? They would have Faris to deal with, sooner rather than later. Gambling aside, she was a good girl. Was there somebody else she owed money to? Hadley pushed the thought from his head and Toni's file aside, then dropped the next one on top.

Arvin. A bit of an enigma. Level headed, reliable, his go-to guy. No priors whatsoever. The death of a former girlfriend in Japan drove him away from his home country. The press he'd found as part of his background checks linked her death with drugs.

Did Arvin share her addiction? Not that he could see.

Then rule him out.

That's why you shouldn't.

What do you actually know about him?

I know that he's a good guy who has nothing more than the best of intentions. He's never slipped, not once.

Hadley leafed through the rest of his file. There was nothing in it he judged to be a concern.

Then leave it at that.

Paul was the obvious choice.

Why, because he's loud, arrogant? He's never been like that to a client.

Christie doesn't seem to think so. You don't like him either.

Who does? The guy's a pain in the ass at the best of times.

Hadley ran his finger over Paul's history. Insubordination. Assault. Drunk and disorderly. He'd been on the end of that one.

Only because you were on the end of something else.

Hadley chuckled to himself.

Can you blame him? The guys' homophobic.

Is that where it ends, though?

He'd have a raft of people who hated him. He'd worked as security in a juvie center here in Toronto in his youth. Seemed that's how he got his start. Who knew what he was like as a kid.

You're missing something. Yourself.

Hadley studied his own folder. He'd asked a consultant to dig up any dirt he could find when he set up the business. You should never ignore your own stake and exposure. He had his own drunk and disorderly charge.

He remembered the girl. Her father had stumbled across them together in a back room. He'd been stupid then, arrogant, thoughtless about any impact he might have had on the girl or her family, which, by all accounts, had already been under strain. They'd fought. Hadley had broken her father's nose and had been arrested. His last act before his parents had finally given up on college and sent him to military school.

Decorated war hero. Sergeant on the rise. Then MIA with the loss of his brother.

Hadley got to his feet, stretched his back and walked quietly through the dark silence of the office. He was lucky not to have added public exposure to his sheet. Outed to the world as a gay man. Wouldn't that be great?

So what. There are others. Face it head on.

'I plan to,' he said aloud to no one.

You're forgetting something else. Your clients.

Hadley walked back to his filing cabinet. He stared at the top drawer, where the original files had been stored. It was twisted and bent. The stolen keys had gotten the thief through the front door, but not into the cabinets he alone held the keys for.

His phone buzzed to life, jerking him away from his thoughts. He checked the screen. Leroy.

'Hi Leroy, what's happening?'

'Thank god! Fuck. Hadley, I need you to come … I need you to come right away.'

'Come where? What's happened?'

'It's Arvin … he's overdosed.'

'What?'

'He collapsed on set. We're at Toronto General on Elizabeth. Be quick, he's fucking dying, man!'

'Okay okay … alright, I'm on my way.'

Hadley grabbed his jacket and keys, ran to the desk and switched off the lamp, though not before taking a quick look at Arvin's folder. He shook his head, collected the files and ran for the door.

5 3 .

'We're at an impasse here, Hadley,' said Leroy, presenting the pipe he'd found in Arvin's bag.

'Please put that away, Leroy,' said Hadley, searching the room.

Through the double doors he could see police talking to hospital staff in the corridor.

'I know this isn't good,' he whispered under his breath.

'Isn't good?' Leroy said, standing hard up against him. 'It's fucking heroine, Hadley. He's been smoking it. I get that it's a step down from injecting the shit, but it's heroine all the same. I warned him just a few weeks ago. I told that motherfucker, if he–'

'Please, Leroy. I understand this isn't a good situation. By the sounds of it, I'm even more surprised by it than you are. Though we need to be cautious here.' Hadley looked over at Arvin.

He was lying asleep, pale-faced, connected to a drip, a panel of screens above him displaying his vitals. He looked pained, drawn. His dark hair was matted to his head in thin strings. His breathing was light; his body, normally so poised and alert, lay helpless under light blue hospital covers.

'Tell me what you saw.'

'I didn't see anything. One minute I'm on set, there's a five-minute call for a washroom break ahead of the next take, then there's no sign of him. I hear a scream behind the stage from one of the makeup artists. I walk around and find him lying face down, sprawled across the floor. The set is shut down, someone calls 911 and we're done for the evening.'

'Was there anyone else with him?'

'No.'

'Did anybody else see the pipe?'

'No. I found it in the bag he leaves in my dressing room.'

'Good. And the gear?'

'I made sure that was there as well.'

'So he wasn't using when he collapsed?'

'If you're asking if he was caught inhaling this shit, the answer is no.'

'I appreciate that, Leroy. Can I have it?'

Leroy discreetly handed both to Hadley, who slid them carefully into a coat pocket.

'Do you need to be here?' asked Hadley.

Leroy studied him. 'You want me gone? Because right now I want him gone. I warned him,' he said eye-balling Arvin. 'Point blank. I told that motherfucker that if he was dabbling, he was done. I'm–'

'Calm down, Leroy.'

'Calm down? Is that what you want me to do, Hadley? Because if this shit impacts me in any way, you'll hear about it. I'm not fucking–'

'Leroy,' said Hadley, grabbing his shoulder. 'I would like you not to be associated with this, if we can help it. Have they asked you for a statement?'

Leroy dropped his hands on his hips and stared at the floor. 'There were plenty of people there, so no.'

'Good. Keep it that way.'

'He'll test–'

'Leave that with me. And Leroy?'

The actor turned to face him.

'I'm sorry for all of this. It's news to me. I promise to get to the bottom it, to straighten him out.'

Leroy shook his head. 'Straighten yourself out, Hadley, then work on your staff. They won't be working for me.' He looked sideways at Arvin, unconscious in his bed, then walked through the double doors and took a sharp left, before disappearing from view.

'Dammit, Arvin. Why now?' said Hadley to no one.

He checked the screen. Arvin's vitals were steady. The nurse had come and gone.

'Excuse me, sir, may I have a word?' said a tall policeman entering the room.

'Yeah, sure officer.'

Be caring but nonchalant, Hadley. Don't fuck this up now.

He flipped a notebook open. 'Your name please, sir?'

'Hadley Peters.'

The policeman glanced at the time on his wrist and jotted both down. 'And your relationship with the injured person?'

'He's an employee of mine.'

'And that line of work is?'

'He works in a security team for me.'

'Was that Leroy James I saw earlier?'

'Yes, sir.'

'And his connection here?'

'Arvin, the patient, works for him. I understand he collapsed on set.'

'Any reason why that might have been?'

'He's been working some long hours. I don't think he's been in the best of health, though I'm surprised he's ended up here.'

'I see. According to the staff, his symptoms seem to coincide with drug use. Can you shed any light on that?'

'None I'm afraid, officer. He takes care of himself. He's one of my best employees. He may have been taking medication, though my staff are routinely tested against anything that might influence their performance. It's not something we can afford.'

'And the last test?'

'Would have been conducted two weeks ago. There was nothing reported. I can share those results if–'

The policeman waved the offer away. 'I understand he's stabilized, though it was hit and miss there for a while. Any next of kin to be notified?'

'None I'm afraid, officer. He's originally from Japan; relocated some years ago.'

'Thanks for that. I'll leave him in your care.'

'I appreciate that.'

Hadley took a plastic cup from a water cooler nearby, filled it and drank deeply as he watched the cop go.

You've got to call them, Hadley. Get them both in here. He's been targeted. You're all falling apart. They need to see what's being done to us first hand.

Paul made it through the door first. He wore tracksuit pants and a heavy jacket. He stopped on seeing Hadley, and nodded his head before speaking.

'Is he okay?'

'Not really, but he will be.'

'And you?'

'I'm good. You?' He looked at Paul's bruised face and his taped-up nose. 'Been making more friends?'

'Getting rid of a few, actually. Not all of us can sit by and do nothing while the rest of the world fucks us.'

'Jonas?'

'Maybe. And what now? You back to preside over this?' said Paul, his hands pressed against the back of a chair.

'Yeah, I am. Problem with that?'

'Does it matter if I do?'

'Makes no difference to me. You found another client yet?'

'I'm working on something.'

'Good. How's Faris?'

'What?'

'You heard me.'

'Are you fucking kidding me?' said Toni, appearing through the doors. They swung gently closed behind her. 'What the fuck is this piece of shit doing here?'

'Hi, gorgeous,' said Paul, smacking his lips together.

'I'm going to knock your fucking–'

Hadley caught her before she got any closer. He pushed her back and held another hand out toward Paul's chest. He could see the nurses on the other side of the doors staring at them.

'I called you both here because this,' he said, pointing toward Arvin, 'is the result of somebody else's thinking. As I understand it, we've got a sense of who, though no idea of why. But I can tell you this. She wants all of us to go down as one. We need to put our heads together, push everything else aside, in order to understand. Attacking each other is what this person wants us to do.'

Paul shuffled his feet, while Toni stood in silence.

'We need to be open, honest with each other about what we've done, or I can assure you we'll end up alongside him, and we might not be as lucky.'

5 4 .

It's getting colder as the sun disappears behind the buildings. Shafts of light refract off large glass windows near the upper stories and bounce off other skyscrapers. What's left of the light touches the cold stone bench where I'm seated. By the time it reaches me, its warmth has left it.

I watch people go in and out of the doors of the precinct. It's almost four thirty in the afternoon, so I have less than thirty minutes before they close. There's been no sign of her. Her name is Senior Detective Simons. She drives a black BMW, license plate CBTU256. It's her I need to speak to. I figured leaving it late in the day might mean a quick turn around, with everyone trying to leave. I want my case to be heard, but I don't want to be scrutinized.

All I have is a certificate and a small plastic container, though I'm confident it will be enough to prosecute him. After all, I want his punishment to be enduring. To give him a chance to think about what he's done. With any luck, he'll get the same treatment inside as I was given.

I went to see Madame Rai's brother. For a fleeting second he seemed pleased to see me, whole once more. That expression left him as I got closer, as he realized I was there for more than a thank you. He hugged me all the same.

He took photos of me the day after the concert. The day after I'd slept with Paul. The canister held samples of Paul's exertions. The graphic photos I asked him to take, it's fair to say, were of my own doing. None of them were pretty. They were time stamped and medically sanctioned.

Toni was battered and bruised last time I saw her. I feel guilty about that, knowing Paul probably acted on the note I'd left him. Arvin collapsed not long after, the drugs having taken their toll. He came calling at the *Globe & Mail*, which I had to leave behind me. I feel bad about my early exit, they had been nice to me there, but it had been time to move on. It had served its purpose.

Hadley's nowhere to be seen, and besides, he's done plenty of damage by himself.

It's now or never. I check my phone once more, only to look up and see her car pulling into the driveway and disappearing behind the building. I give it five minutes, blink tears into my eyes so as to smudge the eyeliner beneath them, tousle my hair, then stride in through the front doors and demand to see her.

— ✠ —

An older woman was hovering over me when I woke. Her hair was pulled back tightly in a bun, framing a face with gray eyes and thin lips. She held a cool palm to my forehead, then felt the pulse in my neck, checked me over, studied various bits of me before speaking.

'My name is Madame Rai. You're in my brother's clinic. He took what little money you had and relieved you of your burden. I see there is much more that you have lost. Things that won't be recovered, but which can be understood and dealt with.'

I tried to speak. My mouth and the tongue inside it were dry.

'Your body had almost shut down, but you are far from being broken. You've been with us for several days, yet no one has come looking for you and your phone has been silent. That tells me you are on your own.'

She took me by my arms as I tried to turn away. 'That's a good thing. You are free from distraction. Solitude will allow you to focus, to rebuild and connect yourself with things that matter, to heal.'

I remember movement, lying in the back of a car as we drove for what felt like a day to somewhere I didn't know. The sun shone through the back window, lighting up the red skin of my closed eyelids. I lay sideways across the seats, propped up against one side, occasionally opening my eyes to watch trees pass by as we drove. I counted them before my head throbbed and darkness took me again.

— ✖ —

In here is all that's wrong in the world. The place I left all those years ago. Different groups of women sit in separate corners, most crying while a few are stone faced, ashen, or just expressionless. Several are bruised, battered, or wear sunglasses to hide their misfortunes.

Men position themselves as far away as they can, lest they be implicated through association. Young kids who should be at home with parents sit here by themselves, nervously checking their surrounds while officers hover nearby. I see myself as a young girl in their faces. How many are orphans or in foster care? Are they at the beginning of the journey I took? I hope not.

I check the contents of my bag with a solitary finger, feeling the edge of the certificate I was given, the soft plastic lid of the canister secreted in the bottom.

One final lie, Kat. Sell them your story. It should't be hard, you've lived it. Its telling has just been delayed. And doesn't he deserve it? How many people has he hurt over the course of his life?

The doors behind the office desk open and she walks through it, a tall ginger-haired guy beside her.

'Patricia Stevens?' she asks the room.

I take my time, survey their faces as they search for the person being called. I raise a hand to my face, wipe it across my eyes for maximum effect before standing. She takes my hand and leads me through the double doors.

55.

Paul made his way through the entrance of the 51st Police Division on Parliament St. It was cold out in the early morning. The sun hadn't yet risen above the surrounding skyscrapers. He rubbed his hands together, inspected the cuts on his knuckles and reminded himself to keep them out of sight. He shook a heavy head, having had a few too many beers the night before. He'd had cause to. The state of Arvin. Hadley reappearing like fucking nothing had happened. Well it had.

The beer had helped push the raging thoughts from his head. Though he was regretting it now. This was the last place he needed to be. Jordan had offered him a golden opportunity. He just had to find the bitch who'd done this and he'd be off. Out of this fucking, sordid mess.

But he'd do more than that. He'd drag her kicking and screaming to Jordan's feet. He'd appreciate that. They both would. Didn't Jordan deserve that? Hadn't they both worked hard to get to where they were? And for what? Some fucking groupie psychopath to get in the way of it all?

An early morning call from the precinct had summoned him in. Questioning, he'd been told, would be focused around the night of Jordan's home-coming concert.

Haven't I done all of this shit already? The fucking kid in his blue jumper, leather jacket and stupid knife. You'd think I'd turned up with an uzi or something. Christ! What was there to know?

No doubt it was that fuckwit Thompson and his detective buddy, the bitch he worked for – Simon or whatever her name was.

Just keep your head down and your hands in pockets. There's nothing more to talk about.

Thompson was there to greet him. He wore the same gray and white checkered suit and stupid smile.

'Hammer,' he said, scratching an ear.

'Clearly my tax dollars aren't going far enough. Have you washed that shitty suit since I last saw you?' Paul asked.

'Someone else disagree with your face?' he replied.

'Gentlemen, can we just take a seat and get on with it?' said Senior Detective Simons. 'Thank you for coming in again, Mr. Samuels. I can assure you this is related to an entirely different matter.'

'I understand it's around Jordan's home-coming concert.'

'It is. I believe that was October twenty-third?'

Paul shrugged his shoulders. 'Something like that. Is this about the kid? Because everything was all over the press, on TV. Those bastards really went to town on me, so I can't really see–'

'Can you tell me what happened afterwards?' she asked.

'Afterwards? You mean after the show? Following the attack?'

'Please, Mr. Samuels. What happened once you'd left the venue?'

'The usual, I guess. I don't know if you read any reviews – it wasn't his best performance. In fact he wasn't in good shape at all. We took him back to the penthouse suite at the Four Seasons.'

'Who else was there?'

'I don't know, a few friends. Fans, I guess. The usual entourage that follows him from one city to the next.'

'And what time did all of this wrap up?'

'What time?' His head was aching now. 'Look, that was ages ago. Like I said, there are regular after-parties, people come and go. I couldn't say. Maybe check in with the staff at the hotel. I'm sure they have logs, complaints or whatever. They'll probably be able to tell you more than I can.'

She leaned forward in her chair. 'Can you tell me what you were doing?'

'Me?' he replied, a little puzzled. 'Well … keeping an eye on things, I guess. Like I usually do. Everyone gets drunk, celebrates another show and I'm paid to make sure no one gets hurt.'

'So what happens when everyone leaves?' asked Thompson.

Paul didn't like the way he was looking at him. They were searching for something. Something relating to him. From the look on his face, behind that stupid thick moustache of his, Thompson thought he had it.

Watch yourself, buddy.

'Can I get some water please?'

'Sparkling, isn't it mate?' said Thompson, heading for the door.

Paul waited for him to leave the room. He left the door open, and Paul could see him moving between cubicles, zig-zagging his way through to what he guessed was a kitchen. Phones rang, people were shouting from one side of the room to the other.

'Listen, Senior Detective Simons. I'm not sure where you're going with this. All I–'

'I'd prefer to wait for my partner ahead of further discussion, Mr. Samuels, if you don't mind.'

'That's the thing. I do. I don't know why I'm here or what I've done.'

She stayed silent.

Paul looked up again. He could see Thompson talking to someone in the distance – a girl. She had long legs, red hair, and wore a short black dress and jacket.

'If you could just–'

She was staring straight at him. Her face looked somehow familiar, though he couldn't place it. She was too far away for him to see with any real detail.

No. It doesn't make sense.

'I didn't do anything–' he whispered.

'Sorry? Mr. Samuels? What did you say?' asked Simons.

The redhead. He'd slept with a girl that night. There was nothing … it had been consensual. There was no reason to …

'Here's your water, buddy,' said Thompson, closing the door.

'You were saying?' said Simons.

'Nothing.' He studied their faces. He knew then that he'd been brought in to be sighted.

'Well allow me, Mr. Samuels,' said Simons, now standing. 'You have been called in and are hereby accused of rape.'

'What? This is fucking–'

'Mr. Samuels, we have a witness who has come forward and is willing to testify, that on the night of October twenty-third, you drugged and raped her.'

He was on his feet. 'This is fucking bullshit! I didn't rape or do anything to anyone–'

She kept going. 'You have the right to an attorney. Anything you say …'

The rest he knew. He was roughly turned by Thompson, felt the metal cuffs circling his wrists, being fastened together. He'd knocked the cup of water over as he stood. He watched as it pooled, then trickled slowly toward the table edge.

5 6 .

Hadley opened the door to the interview room. Paul looked up from where he was sitting, his cuffed hands on a small square table. He opened his mouth to speak before Hadley held a finger to his lips to silence him. He circled the small room, looked under the table, got Paul to stand and checked under each chair.

He placed his phone on the table between them, then tapped an app that allowed him to scramble their conversation. He waited until he could see a small, white, radar-like dot emitting signals from the center of the phone, before he punched Paul hard in the side of the face.

'What the fuck!' Paul said, trying to stand, holding his cuffed hands to his lips, which were now cut and bleeding.

Hadley said in his ear. 'That's for speaking to Faris, you silly bastard. I don't know what you were thinking, giving him Toni's address. What happened could have been a lot worse.'

'I don't know what you're–'

He struck him hard in the face again, this time almost knocking him to the floor.

'Fuucckk!' Paul said, spitting blood from his mouth.

'They were about to rape her! Did you know that?' he said through gritted teeth, standing over him.

'I didn't–'

'I've read your file. You worked for him, prior to coming to me. So stop your bullshit! What were you trying to achieve?'

Paul hung his head, let the blood trickle down one side of his chin.

'We're a team for god's sake. You need to start behaving like you're in one.'

Paul spat out more of the blood pooling in his mouth. 'I thought she was the reason all of this was happening,' he mumbled.

'Why would you think that?'

'I had a run in with Jonas.'

'So I heard. He called me.'

Paul allowed himself a small smile.

'You didn't have to do that,' said Hadley, shaking his head.

'That fucker deserved it. One of his monkeys broke my nose, not to mention putting all of us in trouble. And where does it leave Toni and Chris?'

'Don't pretend you care. Why do you think Toni has anything to do with this?'

Paul stared at Hadley, leaned back in his chair and wiped the sweat away from his head. 'A note.'

'What?'

'A note was left in my car. It was a copy of Toni's file. One of the files that was probably stolen the night–'

'I know which night. What did it say?'

'It was a photo of her. Someone had written *She'll ruin you all* in a red marker across her face.'

'Jesus! And you acted on that shit? Where are your loyalties?'

'I … I just wanted to see how she'd respond. I thought maybe her and Faris were–'

'Were what?' Hadley was up and pacing the room now. 'Colluding against the rest of us? Figuring out how they could appropriate funds through our client base to repay her debt?'

'I don't know, maybe. Something like that. I wasn't sure.'

'Are you sure now?'

'I'm sorry. I was angry. And you were doing … whatever the fuck you were doing. The company was–'

'In disarray, I get it. Though what good is a team if you can't trust your own people? To have them act against your own interests?'

Paul didn't look up at him; he just stared at the surface of the table between his cuffed hands. His knuckles were cut and bruised, his nose the same.

'Why am I here, Paul?'

He took his time. 'I know … I don't deserve you being here. The truth is, I didn't know who else to turn to.'

'I was told what you're in here for. Is it true?'

'No. No it's not! I've been set up, Hadley. Some fucking groupie from one of Jordan's after-parties. It's total bullshit.'

'When did it happen?'

'Last year, late October.'

'Did you sleep with her?'

'I did, and it was consensual. Nothing I did on the night could have led her to believe anything else.'

'Were you sober?'

'Straight as a dime. I'd been working all night.'

Hadley kept staring at him.

'Alright, I had a few. I might have dabbled in a few bits and pieces, though only once I was off the clock.'

Hadley ran a hand through his hair and sighed. 'Did she have any cause for a grievance against you?'

'Not that I can think of. Though she was teasing me from start to finish.'

'So she was at the show?'

'Yeah. Out the back, part of a larger group of–'

'Okay. Did you know her, or had you met her before?'

'No, I … I don't think so.'

Hadley grabbed one of his shoulders and shook him. 'Don't think. Be sure,' he said, pacing the room.

Paul thought of the red hair, the smile on her face. 'No. I don't know her.'

'Could you place her if you saw her again?'

'I'm sure I could.'

The door opened. 'Time's up, gents,' said Thompson, coming into the room. 'Paul, we need you to come with us–' He stopped, staring at Paul's cut lip and reddened face. 'What the hell?' He looked at Hadley. 'Hadley, I understand you're his requested call. He's to be lined up for identification. Let me get a towel so he can clean himself up. It's your privilege to stay if you'd like.' He left the room.

They sat in silence, processing the situation.

'I'll stay,' replied Hadley as Thompson reentered.

'Okay. Paul, walk to your left with the guard by the door please. Hadley, come with me.'

Hadley followed Thompson down a corridor that looped in behind the door Paul had been walked through. Ten or more people were standing in a small room opposite. The lights were out. They were staring through a large two-way mirror into a brightly lit room where five men, including Paul, were lined up. Three were heavy set and unshaven; one quite tall, another short.

A girl stood near the front of the glass, waiting for her cue to speak. She was taking her time, no doubt aware everyone else in the room was a witness.

'Ma'am, if you could please identify the defendant, starting from left to right,' said a small guy with no hair and glasses, at the front of the room.

She pointed through the glass at Paul. 'Fourth from the left.'

Hadley quietly exhaled and took a step backwards.

'Are you sure, Ma'am?'

'I am.'

She was tall, about five-eleven and in good shape. Although the light was poor, he could see she was wearing a white-collared shirt under a dark jacket. Her skirt was short, revealing long legs. Not really something you'd wear to identify someone you claimed had raped you. Unless you wanted the witnesses to see what he'd had.

The group filed out of the room one by one. Hadley made sure he followed her out. She carried herself well. This wasn't some meek, fragile personality. Most of the groupies he'd seen with Jordan were needy, airheads. She definitely wasn't one of them.

'Officer Shelly?'

'Yes Ma'am,' said the small guy with the glasses, turning to face her.

'I'd like to see him.'

'Sorry.'

'To confront him … only if it's possible?'

'I'm not sure that's a good idea, Ma'am. I'd recommend–'

'Not up close. At a distance. Just far enough that he can see me. To see who I am … what he's done.'

'Ma'am, I … I mean. He'll be restrained. If you think it'll help?'

Hadley stood back as she nodded. He could only see the back of her head. The rest of them had left now. Only Thompson, Shelly and another guard stood by.

The door down the corridor opened. Time seemed to slow down as Hadley watched the first man step out, followed by Paul. His head was hanging. The rest had left the room before the girl screamed at him.

Paul's head snapped round toward her.

'You fucking rapist! I hoped you're pleased with yourself!'

Paul looked puzzled, confused, then frightened as she lunged at him. Thompson and the guard grabbed her shoulders and forced her back as the rest of the guys collided with Paul in the corridor.

Hadley couldn't take his eyes off Paul's face. He looked ashen. Eyes wide, like he was seeing her for the first time. Then Paul was yelling back at her. No – it wasn't her he was yelling at, it was him.

The nearest guard wrapped an arm around Paul before he could get any closer. Another clamped a hand over his face. A baton found the underside of his chin and dragged him backwards, choking his words. The line up of men spread to the left and right of him as he was dragged away, the cords in his neck straining, his face red as he did his best to fight for release. Then he was gone.

The girl apologized to the officers. She pressed herself against a wall and brushed herself down, sobbing as she did so. The officers flanked then embraced her, leading her quietly away, though not before Hadley's eyes met hers. It was the girl Hadley had driven home more than a year ago. The only girl he'd ever known to have shaken Christie. The girl in the white latex suit.

57.

The dress was the most beautiful thing I had ever seen. It was a pale yellow, a patchwork of fabric made from discarded pieces of cloth that had somehow been dyed and stitched carefully together. The denim had been cut from jeans, which were pretty much a uniform in the juvie center. There were shoulder straps and pockets, designed to carry the things I normally had on me. The things she saw me collect.

My life up until this point had seemed like nothing more than a bad mistake. My father had died at a young age. Actually, that's a half-truth. It was my mother that killed him. A piece of broken crockery driven hard into the side of his neck. Thankfully I didn't see it. I heard it, though. Heard the mess that might have been an attempt to breathe, or a plea for escape or something. Nothing I could understand.

I was disappointed, but in truth I didn't care. He deserved it.

They say hindsight is a wonderful thing. Had I been her, I wouldn't have done anything different, apart from the obvious choice of not having a relationship or a child with him.

I walked the long corridors of the juvie center, clutching the dress tightly, hidden in the folds of a loose jacket. The center was an endgame, they had told me, a final destination following a long list of houses, relocation programs and everything else they had used as an attempt to control me.

Unfixable. That was the only word I recalled from the parole officer who'd taken the time to share my file, which had grown substantially over the years. I don't know what happened to my mother. I was taken, removed from her care the night it happened. I was informed she'd made attempts to contact me, though they had been blocked. Then nothing. Just me.

And her.

— ✖ —

I awoke in a sun-filled room to the sound of water falling softly outside. Wooden shutters had been bunched up and tied with thin cords of string. The room was empty, but for a white robe, slippers, and a set of crutches laid out at the foot of my bed. It was more of a mat. I was barely two inches above the ground.

The floor was wooden, polished. I took the robe, placed my good foot in a slipper, then used the crutches to lift myself and make my way outside. I was in a secluded garden with bonsai trees. White pebbled walkways took me from there to what looked like the main house. All of it was surreal, like none of it should have been where it was.

Madam Rai was seated on the floor at a low, simple wooden table.

'Come. Sit beside me. Share some breakfast and tea. I've brought you here to talk about you. To understand what's in here,' she said, tapping her head.

'Why?' I asked.

'Because you need it. I can see that you are lost. I am here to help, to bring you back, healthier and stronger. With purpose.'

'But why?'

'Because I choose to. I too have been lost. Now eat, then we'll talk.'

I had no concept of time or place. Both had been left behind. I just was. My broken leg healed well after her training started. I was taught to endure, to focus, to strengthen my body. Taught to defend, to fight when called upon. We spent endless nights discussing life, trading stories with one another on where we had come from, where we hoped to go.

She talked about her heritage, about the strangeness of the future. I grew to love her. The parent, mentor and friend I'd never had. I listened, worked hard, did what I was told. She taught me to quiet my mind, to focus on the simple things in front of me. To banish the hatred of a youth and a relationship that had hurt me so badly. Though in truth, I knew that darkness would never leave me. I was scarred.

She had a fondness for an anime character named Son Goku, who came from a classic Chinese monk named Sun Wukong. We watched this character on a small dated colour TV hidden behind a simple kitchen. I watched her laugh as Son Goku made his way from one calamity to the next, defying the odds with his girlfriend Chi Chi alongside.

'Do you ever laugh?' she asked.

'I try,' I replied.

'Push the darkness away, Kat. What's done is done. You can change nothing, beyond what lies ahead of you.'

She was a little older than me. How much older, I didn't care to ask. It was nice to be noticed. To be looked after.

It had never been pleasant in there. Not for a skinny white girl like me. Trailer trash was the term used by the larger girls, my inmates, I guess. Not that I'd ever lived in one. My parents could afford more than that in Winnipeg, though I guess most people there can.

I wore it everywhere. Mostly because she watched me wear it, though I loved it all the same. We fell into one another. Became inseparable. I never asked what she was in there for, though rumor had it she had a checkered history not too dissimilar to my own. So be it.

Life became tolerable. No more suicidal tendencies. Let's just call them thoughts. I could have jumped on that wagon like way too many do, but I'm too strong for that shit. What was the alternative? I just learned to take what I could get.

She called herself Francine, Frankie for short. Which I liked, though didn't entirely believe. Who was I to judge? We shared dreams, talked of lives we might one day grow into on the outside of this shit box.

Inmates left us alone. We became lovers. I'm not sure how to describe that initial feeling. Of being loved. Of being told we were lovers. How could I? I'd never truly experienced it. All I'd seen were the tragic outcomes of broken families and those who struggled with loss. Those who tried to make me fit into holes their dead, lost or unborn kids had left behind. It never worked out.

My dress had been noticed by the staff. Frankie had found herself in the sewing room, repairing anything that needed stitching back together. I worked outside, mostly, doing community projects that the center won contracts for. Putting ourselves on display for the betterment of not just our own development, our rehabilitation, but also for the society that might one day grow to accept us.

I heard a lot of bullshit from people with not much more than a uniform, or an online certificate, usually in an office they could barely fit into. I learnt when to nod, when to smile. Most importantly, when to shake my head. Not at them, with them. I paint a rosy picture, but it wasn't. Yes, there was a crimson tinge on those roses, but make no mistake, they were black.

I'd shown some aptitude for writing. A broken arm gave me the opportunity. The accident had been my own fault, according to the filed report, but half a dozen witnesses could have told any one of them something different – though they didn't.

Lucky for me it was my left arm.

A staff member landed me a job in the library, filing, preparing books, eventually responding to enquires, which they told me I had a real knack for. Those responses turned into PR pieces for the library's ongoing community work, then articles for the center. I was enjoying it, before Frankie was hurt.

Hurt through my own absence. She'd been attacked when she came looking for me, by the same bitches who'd hurt me earlier. It got me thinking. Frankie liked to see me. Liked to know I was there, not far away, right where she wanted me to be. And for the longest time, a bit like the community work, I hadn't been.

Sex that night had been rough. She had taken scissors from the sewing room, held them to my neck as she thrust fingers into me, her eyes alive. I gasped as I felt her wet hand clamp itself across my mouth, steel points being pressed hard between my legs.

'Do you love me?' she asked.

I nodded, gasping, breathing heavy.

'Then cum for me.'

I cried out between her fingers as I did what she asked. Sated, she kissed and rolled off me, clambering up the small ladder to her mattress above mine. I could hear her breathing, slow at first, then regular. She was asleep. It would be hours before it would take me.

5 8 .

He was new. A youngish man, though large, which made it hard to guess his age. I'd seen him walking the corridors, checking doors, mostly closing and locking them behind the rest of the security detail he followed. He had black hair and dark eyes, cute. He didn't seem to know what to make of us. It was odd for us to see someone a bit younger in there.

His name was Paul. He was a local, a kid like me. Though he was living on the outside, which made him different to anyone I knew. He would stare at me from afar. I wouldn't do much more than stare back.

I'd been in there for a few years. I chose to forget time. It seemed to make it go faster. I'd only discover the date when I overheard a conversation, or saw a news article. Which was why I was surprised to hear that a day I'd scribbled in red crayon on the brickwork beside my bed was less than two weeks away.

September tenth. The date I turned eighteen and became eligible for release. Frankie had been held back on a few misdemeanors, though she was due for release around the same time. We'd planned for it. We would leave this city and head north to Ottawa then on to Montreal. Our decision would fly in the face of the protocols the center had in place for our rehabilitation, though as an adult, I would finally have a say in what I chose to do. So I would choose to leave.

I'd heard it was beautiful up there. Vibrant, bagel-laden. I'd never been, though loved the thought of ice skating in the Capital on the Rideau Canal; soaking up the atmosphere of the Jazz Festival; wandering through the Bio-Dome. Things I'd only read about, experiences I'd only been able to dream of. And there was safety in knowing that if it all turned to shit, we could jump on the train and drag ourselves back to the center, if we really had to.

It was the kiss that ruined it. I should have known better. Known to push him away, to knock back his advances when things had gotten to such a pivotal point. I knew she'd been watching me. Following me. I could sense it, but couldn't see it. I couldn't push the thought of the scissors she'd held to my neck from my mind. Couldn't forget the threat she'd impressed upon me, forcing me to bend to her will. This place, my life, had all seemed to be about control. Well, I'd challenge it like I always had. I'd test her. I needed to know before it was too late.

Paul and I would speak daily, on the most mundane of things. Small talk confined to the smallest of spaces. And then one day, he leaned forward, caressed the back of my neck so gently, and guided me in for a kiss I needed to feel, to know. I was lost, savoring the warmth and the need of his touch, caught in a moment of pure bliss. As he pulled away, I saw her through the square window of the small closet we had been hiding in. Her eyes found mine, didn't leave them. She wanted to know what I'd felt.

It was then that things turned. My mistake had been to smile. They'd come for me the following day – the day before we were due to leave. 'They' being the bitches who had broken my arm. Which got me thinking – why? I hardly saw them. Had nothing to do with any of them. The days and nights of recovery led me to one conclusion: she wanted me to know it was her I needed. No one else.

I woke to the smallest of sounds. Breath above me. I could feel it on my neck, gentle, rhythmic. I could hear it. My eyes opened before my mouth did. It was the biggest of the five, Sal, the dark girl with knotted dreads wound into balls on the top of her head. I could just make out her silhouette in the darkness. She shook her head, clamped her hand over my mouth, threatened me with an order of silence. I could feel the point of a knife being pressed hard against me, breaking the skin on the right side of my neck. She forced me out of bed, to stand beside it. I looked left. The bed above mine was empty.

My throat was dry. I clawed at the walls, a handle, grip – anything to slow me down before a second unseen pair of arms wrapped themselves around me, rendering me powerless. I lost track of things then.

Snippets return to me when I least expect them. They're usually preceded by the blackouts that have plagued me for years.

I remember a dark hallway that kept on going. My naked feet being dragged across its surface. My head colliding with the walls as I was pulled along; a shower block, the concrete floor tearing the skin from my knees and elbows as I was forced to the ground, stripped of the few bedclothes I had on. Of being beaten, punched in the face until my eyelids swelled to the point of closure, sight being replaced with pain, my good arm being snapped, of being raped, assaulted by hands, things I couldn't see, shadows I knew were witnesses.

Then nothing. Just the darkness of me. I could smell my blood as I lay there, broken, disfigured, sobbing quietly, not wanting anyone to come back. I could smell her. I tried to keep quiet, to listen, through the tears and the pain of what was left of me. I couldn't speak, my throat was dry. Then she was above me. She kissed my cracked and swollen lips and whispered, 'Goodbye Kat. Lesson learned.' I tried to grab her, to reach out … agony, then nothing as I passed out.

There's something remarkable about a gray block wall. At first glance, your brain tells you what you are seeing. A slab of concrete, devoid of anything, no blemishes, smooth, nothing to see. Just repetition captured in four walls around you. A hard surface.

But given time, stare at them enough and your eyes find imperfections, like anything in life. Strokes made by a tradesman's hand. Smooth wide arcs that move from one corner of the wall to another, vein-like cracks that tease you, taunt you with thoughts of a structure's weakness.

How you define those arcs, the cracks, the patterns within them, depends I guess on where your head is at. Mine had been connected to the wall. Which was why blood trickled down one side of it. A horizontal line of red splatter marks, growing in size as I moved from one side of the wall to the other.

You see, I'd been in there a while. Left to rot, as the bitch who had kept me there walked out. Into fresh air. Set free to do what we'd wanted, while I did what she wanted.

The years that followed were the hardest. Years that would shape my thinking, underscore what I was, drive me toward a future I now understood. Yet there was a light. His kiss I'd savored. The feeling I'd had, the warmth he had given me. He had been forced to leave, and I have to assume that was down to her. That hurt the most. More than the beatings I would take, the added years I would endure.

Well, I'd find him. Love him. Then I'd find her.

5 9 .

'Thompson! Get me the fuck out of here!' shouted Paul, banging the thick metal door of his cell.

The room was bereft of anything. A single light embedded in the ceiling and a concrete bench – that was it. No natural light ensured Paul had no idea of how long he had been held there.

'Thompson, you fucker! Thompson! I need to get out of here!'

Nothing.

'Thompson? Fuck!!!'

Paul sat down on his concrete bench, held his cut and bruised face in his hands, stared at the floor. He raised his head as he heard footsteps, quiet at first, then louder as they approached the steel door. Thompson's lips appeared through a panel on the door as it slid open.

'Will you shut up, Hammer? Christ. You've been identified, you're fucked. Shut up. You'll be processed.'

The panel slid shut.

'Thompson? Listen, Marty,' said Paul, getting to his feet and walking to the door. 'Please.'

It slid open again. 'Marty, is it now? Why should I listen to anything an asshole like you has to say?'

'Please, Marty. I need you to hear it. I've realized something.'

'That you're a douchebag?'

'I am … I mean, I have been.' Paul saw his face disappear from the door, heard him exhale then saw him lean back in.

'So what's this, a sudden revelation?' asked Thompson.

'Something critical to this case.'

'What? Enlighten me.'

'That's the thing. I can't.'

'Well then, keep your mouth shut and enjoy your stay.'

'I need to make a call, Marty. Just one. Please.'

'Doesn't work that way, Hammer. You've got to give me something before anyone's going to listen to anything you have to say.'

Paul stepped away from the door, slapped a hand into a wall. He was breathing heavily, doing his best to calm himself down.

'Okay.'

'I'm listening.'

'The girl. What name did she give you?'

'Sorry? You mean the girl you raped? What? You want her number as well?'

'Can you just cut the shit! What did she call herself?'

Thomson exhaled. 'Okay. You'll hear it in court, anyway. Patricia. Patricia Stevens.'

'Are you fucking kidding me? P.S.? My initials. And you bought that shit? She's using another alias. The girl's a liar!'

'Listen, Hammer, she was ID'd, had the credentials. And besides, it's you who's being investigated, not her.'

'Kat. Her name's Kat. Kat Mathias. Search her file. She'll pop up. She was held in a juvie facility here in Toronto, about ten years ago.'

'Why should I believe you?'

'Don't. Look it up.'

'So what's your connection here?'

'I used to date her.'

'Really? She's way out of your league.'

'Apparently not.'

'That's not remotely funny.'

'Listen, Marty. Something bad's going to happen and I'm confident that if I had the opportunity, I could stop this. I just need to make a call.'

'You're staying here, but I'll look it up. I'm not promising anything. She checks out, I'll let you have your call.'

'Okay. That's all I'm asking.'

The panel slid shut.

It felt like an age until he returned. He could hear the sound of the door being unlocked. He pushed himself back toward the wall as Thompson entered his cell.

'Did you find it? She pop up?'

'Hammer. Listen buddy. I checked the system, went through everything. There's nothing on file for anyone of her description and age in that name.'

'So it's been wiped.'

Thompson groaned.

'I mean, what's the process when a youth gets released? Wouldn't they give her a clean start? A fresh file of some sorts to help her move on?'

'It's not my field, Hammer.' He held his hands up. 'You asked me to check and I've done that.'

'There must be another name.'

He thought of the girl in her patched yellow dress. Pictured her walking the corridors of the juvie center from the guarded distance between them. Being shy at first then more forthcoming. She had worked in their small library, writing pieces for the place, which he always read. That was before she'd been attacked.

'She's the fucking journalist.'

'What?' asked Thompson, his face screwed up.

But Paul heard nothing. He was lost to response. Buried in thoughts of a misplaced past. A past that seemed to be screaming toward him with no sign of slowing down. She was stalking him. The girl in the corridor flashed in front of his eyes. Her face taut, eyes bright, red hair slightly askew, nostrils flaring as she screamed at him while being held by the police, straining against their force. She hadn't been angry, she was laughing at him. Acting for him.

And he knew.

He remembered the girl he had almost loved as a kid. The girl he had later reconnected with, but hadn't recognized. Hadn't known. How could he? She had grown. Taller. Stronger. Her whole appearance had changed. It had been her again. Why hadn't she said anything?

'Hammer?' said Thompson, opening the cell door and entering.

She had chosen not to.

She wanted to know it was you. That you were still the kid she'd probably clung to the memory of, while she'd been trapped, beaten, and who knew what else inside there? And what did you do?

He was trembling now.

I treated her badly. I ignored and forgot her. I hurt her.

And yet, she had come back again. Not for love, this time. She had fucked him.

He threw up. All over the cheap gray and white checkered suit Thompson was still wearing.

'What the fuck? Hammer are you–'

'I'm sorry, Thompson.'

'For what?'

Paul lunged forward and wrapped his cuffs around Thompson's neck. He strained his arms, forcing the air from Thompson's lungs. Thompson fought back, desperate to get a hand, a finger beneath the thick links of chain and the edges of the metal cuffs that cut into his neck. He failed. Color rose in his cheeks, forced the whites of his eyes into his head before his body went slack and fell to floor.

Paul checked his pulse. It was still there. He'd be fine, but Paul needed to move quickly. He found the keys in Thompson's left pocket, undid his cuffs, slipped out of his orange boiler suit and into his friend's cheap, gray, vomit-covered suit.

He swapped shoes, thanking his friend for having the same size feet, then left, locking the cell behind him. Shielding his head with a casual rub of his hair, he passed beneath the hall camera. He swiped his pass and disappeared into the night. There was someone he had to call.

6 0.

Arvin caught the kerb with his feet as a small van cut in front of him. He was covered head to toe in black and wore a Raptors cap low over his face. His head hurt and he felt like shit, but he'd finally left the hospital.

He'd been forced to sign himself out, and had been informed he was under probation. That he'd be watched. He checked to see if he was being followed. Confident he wasn't, he zig-zagged through a network of streets anyway. It was dark and cold out, and his body felt clammy from the fluids they'd pumped through his system over the last few days.

He didn't care. He had two faces in his head. The girl, of course. He'd seen her at the club and was confident it had been her who'd set the whole thing up. The other was the tall white-haired Asian, the guy called Moshki. He would have known what he'd done. Well, now he'd find out what it meant.

Arvin pulled his phone out of his pocket and made the call he'd been dreading.

'Yeah.'

'Hey, Leroy,' said Arvin.

'Shouldn't have picked up. Honestly, I don't know why I answered. I'm pissed with you, man.'

'You're right. I was an idiot.'

'Fuck, Keanu. You gave us a big scare back there. I'm glad you're breathing.'

'I'm sorry … things got a … out of control. I apologize. I shouldn't have put you on the spot like that … on set, I mean.'

'Yeah well, it's done. Can't do much about it now.'

'Leroy, I'm sorry.'

'I'm sorry too, Keanu. I asked you … gave you the chance to come clean. You know how I feel about drugs. You fucking lied to me, man! I asked point blank if you were doing them, if you were an addict, and what did you say?'

Arvin walked through a crowd of people outside a club as he neared Chinatown. They stared at him, parted on seeing him approach. He slipped through traffic past a streetcar, crossing one side of the road to the other.

'What did you say?' Leroy asked again.

Arvin stopped walking, turned away from the road and placed a hand on a brick wall opposite him.

'I said I wasn't.'

'This thing here, our relationship, was built on trust. You've just broken it.'

'Leroy, I-'

'We're done.'

'The girl, Leroy. The one that interviewed you. It was her that set me up.'

'Set you up? How? What do you mean?'

'I'm guilty. I take drugs, have done for a while, but I'm cautious, Leroy. I'm not silly, I control-'

'You don't control shit! If you're on drugs, you're off my team. What the fuck does she have to do with anything? Where are you?'

'That doesn't matter.'

'What do you mean it doesn't-'

'I'll be seeing you, Leroy. I'm sorry. Beyond all the bullshit, you're a good guy who I've really loved working with.'

'Keanu?'

'Take care.'

'Arvin?'

Arvin killed the call, switched the phone off and pocketed it. He made his way to the club he'd walk into several nights ago. It was late, so there was a decent crowd in. Security looked him up and down, made him lose the cap before recognizing him. The larger of the two took a step forward and spoke.

'You okay, buddy?'

'Yeah, yeah, just a cold is all,' replied Arvin.

He could see the second one reaching for his radio.

'You meeting anyone in there?'

You know how this is going to go.

'Just some friends.'

'Got any ID?'

'Yeah, sure,' said Arvin, reaching into his jacket.

He took a step closer, opened his palm and drove the heel of his hand hard underneath the big guy's chin, lifting him off the ground. His head snapped back and he fell sack-like to the pavement. His friend whipped out a butterfly knife, flicking it into position about the same time as Arvin snapped his wrist.

'Fuck!' he screamed, clutching a hand that flopped on the end of it.

Arvin walked past him, through the club, ignoring the patrons, the music, the lights, the bar, heading for the back door.

The second bar had more people in it. He squeezed through them and brushed aside the curtain. Moshki was seated there, a few men and women beside him. He was dressed in a black suit, drink in hand, a cigarette poised to light in the other. He looked up, then back at the floor like he wanted to ignore him.

One of his friends blocked Arvin's path. 'I wouldn't, friend,' he said, smiling.

Arvin drove his head into the man's nose, which crunched under the impact. Blood spread from both nostrils as he pulled back in shock, his hands now covered with it as he tried to stop the flow. Arvin drove a fist under his ribcage; he folded and dropped to the floor.

A second man was on his feet with a knife as the girls threw themselves on the ground and dragged themselves out of the way. Arvin spun to his right and smashed his heel into his opponent's knee. It caved inwards, before he too was screaming, his left boot now pointing at an acute angle toward the ceiling. Moshki was on his feet now. He was tall –must have been six foot six – his gun in hand, level with Arvin's head.

'Arvin-san, you fight well.' His voice was deep. 'Can you dodge bullets too?'

'What did you sell me?'

'What you wanted. The drugs you are addicted to.'

'And what did she ask you to lace them with?'

He smiled, a toothy grin that forced its way between wide pale-thin lips.

'You would have to ask her.'

'Oh, I plan to. Who is she?'

A groan from behind him gave Arvin the pause he needed. He lunged, but not before Moshki fired. A bullet buried itself in his shoulder before his forearm caught Moshki hard on the side of his head. He followed through with a knee to his groin, which forced him to the floor. The gun sailed over the couch they'd been seated at. Arvin withdrew a knife from the inside of his boot and placed its serrated edge against Moshki's long thin neck.

'Now … Moshki-san, here we are.'

He grunted.

'I asked you a question. The fact that you know who I am tells me you research your clients. What's her name?'

'I don't know.'

'Her name!' he repeated, cutting the skin below his neck.

Moshki groaned as blood ran down the front of his shirt.

'And if I … tell you?'

'I'd say no hard feelings and I'll leave you to it.'

He was breathing hard, his eyes wild, searching the floor, considering his options.

'Jo Reid.'

'Her real name,' Arvin said, pushing the point a little harder against Moshki's throat.

'Kat. Kat Mathias.'

'Good. There you go,' said Arvin, relieving a bit of pressure. 'Where can I find her?'

'No idea. My guess is she's leaving town. Like you should be.'

Arvin let him go. Moshki pulled himself up, straightened his blood-stained shirt and jacket.

'Was she trying to kill me?

He smiled. 'You are here, are you not?'

'Stop doing what you're doing, or next time you'll die,' said Arvin.

'And you? Let me guess, a clean start from here? That is what most addicts tell me before they die.'

Arvin turned to walk away.

'Tell me Arvin-san, do you miss Japan?'

He ignored him.

'Do you miss her?'

Arvin spun the knife in the palm of his hand, turned on his feet and soared toward him, plunging the knife under his chin and thrusting it up through his jaw and into his head. Arvin heard him collapse as he left.

61.

Toni held the picture in her hand, pulled it in closer. She still couldn't quite believe what she was seeing. It was her. There, in black and white. It was unmistakable. Her hair color looked slightly different, a lighter shade than Toni remembered, and longer, maybe red. But the face and legs were definitely hers.

She ran her fingers around its black frame, traced her fingers over the glass, looked up at the second floor to where Chris' office was hidden, and thought of what she wanted to say, what she would do.

Toni had found the donated picture through clues that had led to a group she really wasn't keen on visiting. It was a clinic off the Don Valley Parkway, twenty minutes north of the city center, that dealt with addictions, including problem gambling.

It had looked like a bad hotel. A throwback to the late sixties or seventies, with an angled concrete facade. Ancient-looking patterned carpets and furniture that had been set up in round circles, or clumped together in corners of oversized rooms that had no doubt borne witness to something close to the disintegration of every soul that walked into them.

She felt close to it herself. Her control over things seemed to be slipping away, unravelling, as the moving parts she'd held onto for so long gradually loosened, pulled away from her.

The photo had been there. They'd been embarrassed to pull it out, let alone display it on their walls. She'd offered to pay them for it, but had been forced into an admission before she could take a second look at it.

Toni's jaw was black and blue, yellowing as the days had passed. The thin layer of makeup she wore couldn't hide it. They'd pressed her on what had happened. She'd been shaken by recent events, felt vulnerable, and had finally admitted to being attacked because she had a gambling problem.

She'd been invited into a group. She'd declined, before being offered the picture in exchange for a session. Begrudgingly, she'd taken a seat in a circle of friends. She was confronted with the hallmarks of what Toni recognized in her own face – anxiety for the future.

Confessions had been ugly; tears, anguish and loss on so many fronts. Disappointment from so many recurring mistakes.

Toni knew she had a problem, but her own tears and confessions weren't forthcoming. She couldn't help but wonder who'd directed her here, and to what end. Someone who cared?

They handed her a card, offered to create space for her at the clinic. Then, making good on their promise, they handed her the photo. She'd unwrapped the brown paper that covered it, and flipped it over.

She'd recognized her straight away. The girl from the club. The girl who seemed to be at the center of everything. The girl she had no name for, beyond the fake one she used as a journalist: Jo Reid. Arvin knew something, and look what had happened to him. That was his own stupid fault. Or was it?

Her head hurt. The light in Chris's office blinked on above the trees as the afternoon clouds began to coalesce, turning the sky gray. Toni carried the picture in its brown paper up the stairs. She passed Trixie, who told her he was busy. Toni ignored her and pushed past, ripping open the door, then taking the stairs two at a time.

Chris was on the phone. 'Thanks, Jerry. Look it's good to–'

He saw Toni, spotted the package in her hand, before his eyes returned to her face.

'I'm sorry. Someone's just marched into my office, unannounced.'

She could hear a loud voice echoing through the speaker on his iPhone.

'I should … though something tells me I'd better deal with it.'

Toni could see he'd lost interest in the call. His eyes had shrunk and were now focused on her.

'Hmm … yeah, I'll call. Yeah, let's do that. Ciao.'

He ended the call and dropped the phone on his desk.

Trixie entered the room, began to apologize before he waved her away. She closed the door and left.

'What the fuck are you doing, Toni? Coming in here like that. Didn't Trixie tell you I was busy?'

'Here's your damn photo!' she said, dropping it on his desk.

He stared at her, then got to his feet.

'Well thank you,' he said, peeling tape off each corner.

'Why didn't you tell me?'

'Tell you what?'

'Can we just cut the shit, Chris? I mean, what the fuck are you doing in all of this? Why is this bitch, the girl I slept with, incidentally, staring back at me with no fucking panties and what looks to be a red wig on?'

He laughed at her. 'Crazy, isn't it? That's not bad, Toni. The photo's black and white, you've got a good eye. She was indeed wearing a red wig when I fucked her.'

Toni felt her cheeks color. She could see he was enjoying himself. She began walking the room.

'So what? You organize some fucking … dumb-ass plan to have your works stolen from you by a bunch of security monkeys – our competition, by the way – then you have some bitch … who you slept with after you took her picture–'

'Don't hate me because I beat you to it.'

'… drug and seduce me, then steal my keys so I'd be implicated? You're my fucking client, for Christ's sake! And then what? You … you drag my boss, and me, through your fucked-up plan, balling us both out, to what end?'

'I know! Nuts isn't it?' he said with a straight face. 'What's crazier is that it was my blonde-haired assistant who came up with the idea.'

'I doubt that.'

'Of course the PR piece, through my buddy Jo, she was a bit borderline with that blog of hers. Man has she got some balls. To lay everything out there as it was. The perfect disclaimer. Girl's a genius. She gets coverage. I get more. Notoriety and the Good Samaritan, not to mention the tax benefits on the donations and the insurance on those works that don't make it back. I mean … fuck!'

He was applauding himself.

Toni shook her head. 'Silly thing here is, Chris, I think you've underestimated the girl you took the picture of.'

'Really? I know *you* have.'

'Arvin almost died the other night.'

He pushed himself up against his desk. 'What, the Asian?'

'Our colleague.'

'So, what's that got to do with her or me?'

'You're an ass, Chris. You've let your ego and your bank balance get in the way of something good. What's worse is that you've invited someone to the table who's here to fuck us all.'

He got up and walked toward her, though not close enough that he needed to look up at her.

'Get out. You're done,' he spat.

'No, Chris, I'm not. You are.'

Toni dropped a shoulder, brought her fist hard across her chest and drove it into his face. It crumpled, and he dropped quickly to the floor. He was out cold. She grabbed the photo from his desk, stepped over him and headed for the stairs.

Trixie was at the bottom of them, her phone at the ready. 'What are you doing, Toni? Is that one of Chris's? Is he … Chris!' she shouted. 'Chris! Should I call–'

Toni grabbed her head and thrust it into the wall, denting the plaster.

Trixie lay sprawled across the floor, unconscious. Toni locked the door from the inside, closed it, stepped outside into light rain and disappeared down the street.

6 2 .

Hadley was sitting on the couch when Toni walked through the door. Arvin was opposite him, looking drawn but composed. She could see strapping around his right shoulder. She was still sweating despite the cold walk from the gallery.

'Toni, are you okay?' Hadley asked, getting to his feet.

'I've been better.'

She grabbed water from the vending machine, ripped the top off and took a deep drink.

'Let's just say we're done with Chris,' she said, wiping water away from her lips.

'Why? What happened?' asked Hadley.

'This picture is what happened,' she said, handing it to him.

He flipped it over and stared at the girl in the picture. 'Is that our journalist?'

'That's her. Jo Reid.'

Arvin was up, taking an edge of the frame and spinning it toward him.

'That's her alright, though it's not how I would have pictured her.'

'Tell me about Chris. Why have we lost him?' Hadley asked.

'Simple, really. He orchestrated the whole thing, as you thought he had. Publicity, tax benefits, insurance and fucking stupidity. What we didn't know is that he's done it all with her.'

'What makes you think that?'

Toni sighed. 'She's the girl I slept with the night of the robbery.'

'What?' said Hadley.

She didn't bother repeating herself.

'Her name is Kat,' said Arvin. He got to his feet and pressed himself against a wall.

It was his turn to be stared at.

'She's the reason I ended up in hospital. I approached her at the *Globe and Mail*. Her blogs were too pointed, they involved us all. I was convinced there was more to it. I tried following her, she lost me when she burst out of a shed door on a motorbike. Despite my best efforts she's since disappeared. She's targeted us all through our clients. She's done a piece on Chris, interviewed Leroy, and she drove Jordan to his suicide attempt through her last article. The only person she seems to have left alone is Christie. Though her drug scare at her last show seemed a little too close for comfort, given everything else that's going on.'

Hadley took a closer a look at the picture. 'She was there. She slapped Christie across the face as we left the building. She had blonde hair, but I recognize her. Christie called her a model or something. She's been to Christie's place.' He sat back down, holding the picture, his knuckles red and white on its frame. 'Shit,' he added. 'It's definitely her. We need to speak to Paul.'

'Why didn't you tell us all of this earlier?' Toni said, staring at Arvin. 'Or were you too fucked up to care?'

'C'mon, Toni. We're all a little–' Hadley began.

She kept going. 'I mean, what the fuck are we dealing with here?'

Arvin ignored her.

'Okay,' said Hadley, getting to his feet. 'Let's just remain calm. For some reason we're being targeted. Arvin – you said she was the reason you ended up in hospital. Why?'

Arvin took a deep breath, walked toward the boxing ring and sat on a corner of it.

'I lied to you all. And for that I'm sorry. I am a user. I smoke heroine or opium, depending on what I can get my hands on. I've done this for a long time, but in my mind, it's never affected me.'

Toni grunted.

'I take small, measurable doses. It's an escape, a mechanism to forget. Recently, with everything that's gone on, it has taken me a little sideways.'

'The drug tests? I can't understand how you could–'

'If you'd moved to blood, Hadley, I would have been outed. I'm afraid pissing into a cup isn't that hard to beat these days.'

Hadley didn't say anything.

Toni did, however. 'So your idea of control is almost dying in hospital?'

Arvin crossed his arms. 'What I ordered and what I got wasn't the same thing. I went back to the drug dealer who sold to me. He told me as much, and her name, before I killed him.'

'I don't care what you ordered, you … what the fuck!' said Toni. 'You killed him?'

'He knew things about me, taunted me with them. I didn't mean to … I just lost it.' Arvin was on his feet and pacing. 'She's the journalist. Kat looked into each of us. His death is on her and I plan to ask her why.'

'You're done, Arvin,' said Hadley. 'You realize that, don't you? Killing someone isn't something I can tolerate.'

Arvin nodded. 'I'm sorry, Hadley, truly I am. My intention wasn't to … to do what I did. There are things – personal things – that have affected me. They continue to and I snapped. I'm leaving as soon as this is done, but not before.'

'Are you … are we exposed in any way?' asked Hadley.

Arvin shook his head.

Toni chewed her lip. 'I can't forgive you for that, Arvin. You're not who I thought you were.' She hung her head, before eventually lifting it and staring at him. 'Who the fuck is it then? Why is she targeting us? Can anyone shed any light on how the hell we've gotten here?'

'That might sit with me,' said Paul from the door.

He was dressed in an awful gray and white, stained, checkered suit that bunched awkwardly on his shoulders. The buttons were loose on his front and he was red in the face.

'Paul?' said Hadley. 'What are you are doing here? I thought you were being processed?'

'That's another story.'

'We don't want you here, shithead!' said Toni, standing.

Hadley held her back. 'Why does it sit with you, Paul?'

Before he could answer, Paul was hit hard over the head with a white and blue aluminum baseball bat, wielded by a tall, lean man dressed head to toe in black. The Blue Jays logo was emblazoned on the bat's handle.

'Sorry Paul, though if you're going to attack, do it with favourable numbers.'

The most recognizable thing about Andrew Faris was his teeth – large, oversized, crooked things. And he was in the habit of smiling. Three men with guns walked into the gym on either side of him.

'What are you doing here, Faris?' asked Hadley.

'Hadley. You well?' He had a high-pitched voice that seemed out of kilter with his height.

Hadley blanked him.

Faris kept going. 'Your girl here owes me a lot of money. I've been polite. Been patient, though now … things have gone beyond where they should have. I sent a team over and they've come back to me injured and empty handed. And you were a part of that, as I understand it. Is that true, Hadley?'

'If by sending people over, you mean tying up one of my employees and attempting to rape her in her home, then yes, I stopped it. As any colleague or friend would.'

Faris looked sideways at one of his team members, whose face was still bruised, then turned back. 'She owes me money, Hadley, and I haven't seen any of it.'

'Did Paul give you her address?' he asked.

'Does it matter?'

'It does to me, Andrew. Because unlike you, I look after my own.'

'For what it's worth,' he said, looking at Paul slumped around his feet, 'yeah, he did.'

'Then why hit him over the head? Sounds like he did you a favor.'

Faris stared at Paul, now cradling his bleeding head in his cupped hands.

'Let's just say I was pleased to see him go when he decided to move on. Enough of the bullshit, Hadley. Have you got my money, Toni?'

She was rigid. 'Mr. Faris … Andrew, please. I'm ashamed of where this has gotten. Please leave my friends out of this. I'll pay you back … I promise.'

'How? Through another round of losses at my casino? Enough already, Toni. Strip the place, gents. Start with the small office at the back, cash deposit boxes, whatever you can find. You two, keep a trained gun on our friends here. Chances are they'll–'

But Faris was falling to the floor before he could finish, Paul's arms wrapped around his legs. He grunted as he fell. Paul was on top of him, a gun withdrawn from a leg holster and pressed firmly to Faris's head.

'Get back or he's done!' Paul shouted, blood running down his face.

Three guns were pointed in his direction. He smiled anyway. 'I'm closer, boys. If you want your next pay check, it'd be best if you lowered your gear to the floor and kicked them to my colleagues here.'

'Don't listen to him,' said Faris. 'Get the girl.'

'As much as she pisses me off, do that and your boss's head will be decorating these walls,' said Paul.

The first of the three lowered his gun. Faris was almost choking as Paul tightened his grip around his neck and pushed the gun into the side of his head.

The second man fired. The bullet thudded into Faris's right shoulder. Faris screamed, which gave them all pause.

Hadley was over the couch and laying into the third man before he could react. Arvin threw himself at the second guy, his foot connecting with the side of his head as he crumpled to the floor. Toni held the weapon the first one had placed on the floor.

'Now listen to me, Andrew,' said Hadley.

Paul let him go. Color returned to his cheeks. His shoulder was lopsided and he was whimpering on the floor.

Hadley stood over him. 'This charade of yours is done. This photo I'm holding belongs to Toni. It's one of Chris Finch's – you may have read about them. They've been donated across the city to various charities. If you can lift your sorry ass off this floor, walk out that door, leave her alone and never come back, you can take it with you. You'll be ahead. Am I clear?'

'This is bullshit, Hadley,' he replied. 'She owes me close to a quarter.'

Hadley got up, walked into his office. A minute later he was back, carrying a paper bag.

'This photo and a hundred large should cover it. Her debt will be repaid. Agreed?'

'Hadley ... don't,' said Toni.

Faris nodded. 'I've been shot. What am I supposed to say?'

'This is a big city. I don't want to see you again.'

Faris got to his feet slowly. 'And you won't. Though I don't want that bitch anywhere near my place,' he said, staring at Toni, cradling his injured side.

'Toni?' Hadley asked.

'Yes, okay,' she replied, her head down.

'There it is then. Paul, Arvin, empty the guns and hand them over.'

Cartridges fell to the floor and guns were returned.

'Now go.'

One of Faris' team took the picture, another the brown bag of cash and they followed him out the door. They didn't look back.

6 3 .

Paul lay on his back with the gun held loosely at his side, staring at the ceiling. He was bleeding from his face. The gray and white checkered suit had torn at the shoulders and was now bunched and crumpled beneath him.

Toni was first there, jumping the couch and kicking him hard in the ribs.

'Fuck! You bitch. Christ,' he said, clutching his side.

She stood over him, face livid, body shaking. 'I should kill you. Just stomp on that already ugly face of yours.'

'I'm sorry Toni … I am … I didn't know what he would–'

'Do? You mean send people over to rob and rape me? You sure that wasn't your request?'

He sat up, shaking his head, his right palm raised. 'Look, I know … we've had some disagreements, though it wasn't–'

'*Disagreements?* Is that what you want to call this?' Her face screwed itself up.

Hadley was on her, grabbing both wrists and pulling her away from him. She tried to shake him off, but he held her tight and walked her toward the back of the room.

'We don't have time for this,' he said. 'I don't agree with what's gone down, but there seems to be a lot more at stake than your personal feud. Agreed?' He walked to the middle of the room. 'Get up, Paul.'

Paul brushed himself off and got to his feet.

'You said this mess sits with you. I recognize her from the station. It's her that identified you, isn't it? The girl you were screaming at. Why?'

Paul raised a hand to his chin and covered his mouth before sighing through it. 'We have some history,' he said.

'Well don't keep us in suspense, we need to hear it,' said Arvin.

Paul took his time. He fetched a coke from the vending machine and sat down.

'I first met Kat Mathias at an institution. She couldn't have been more than sixteen or seventeen. I was a little older, though not by much. I didn't know anything about her, beyond the fact that she'd wound up in the juvie center. It was mostly for wayward kids. The majority of them had arrived via foster care, burglary or other small crimes. She was smart, cute, and just had a way about her. I was told she'd been in there for a few years, but didn't know much else about her. We liked each other.'

'Here we go,' said Toni.

Paul ignored her. 'At the time she was with some girl,' he said, staring at Toni, 'but she thought better of it and became friendly with me.'

'We don't have time for this, Paul. Give us the highlights, please,' said Hadley.

'Okay, alright,' he said, raising his hands. 'She was due for release when she turned eighteen.'

'Really? So you were hitting on kids way back then?' said Toni.

'I was only slightly older, thanks bitch.' Paul finished his drink, threw the can at the bin and missed. 'Before she was released she was attacked. Beaten and raped severely by some of the other girls. I was told, through the grapevine, that it was because of her attention toward me. I liked her. I was gutted with what went down. I lost my job, contact was cut and I was pushed out of there. It was a long time before she reappeared. I didn't recognize her when she did. She'd changed her hair, she was taller, and was just … different. I was bouncing at a club she walked into. We got to know each other, reconnected, and she moved in.'

Toni spat on the floor.

'I was an idiot back then,' said Paul, waiting for somebody to reply. No one did. 'I took her for granted. I was young … stupid and just unsure of what I … what I wanted. She fell pregnant. That complicated everything. I didn't know what to do. I mean I … I just wasn't ready. You know?'

The room remained silent, their eyes focused on his.

'At some point, I lost it. We fought. A lot. The last fight ended badly. She was hurt, upset. She chose to abort.'

'She chose? Or did you choose for her?' said Toni, staring bullets at him. 'You hurt her, didn't you? You fucker.'

He shook his head. 'I didn't agree with it. But she was done with me. I never saw her again. At least not until that ill-fated concert, and then again yesterday.'

'I don't believe you,' said Toni, pushing herself off a wall. 'You fucked her over when she needed you most.' She stood in front of him. 'And now, because of your absolute … stupidity, here we are.'

'Why do you think she was raped in juvie?' asked Hadley, getting up and pacing the room. 'I mean, the reaction to her getting involved with someone seems a little over the top, don't you think? You mentioned a girl. Someone she was with before you met her. Who was she?'

Paul looked thrown. He rubbed his bleeding and battered face. 'I don't know. Just another face in a desperate crowd is all.'

'Was the relationship serious? Did you hear anything? Did she look capable of doing something like that?'

'I don't really remember. Like I said, she was just another face in–'

'Think, Paul! What did the other girl look like? Is there anything you remember about her? Anything she did, might have said. Someone who knew her besides Kat?'

'I can't think. I mean, there's nothing I can remember. I don't know.'

He was rubbing his head, wiping the blood from his face with his forearm. 'There was something.'

'Yes,' said Hadley, stopping in the center of the room.

'She wore a yellow dress.'

'What?'

'Yeah. Kat wore a yellow dress. She wore it all the time. Her girlfriend, at least I think it was the girl, made it for her.'

'Fuck,' said Hadley.

They all turned to look at him. He never swore.

'Now that I think about it, she always wore these blunt scissors … on a chain around her neck. She–'

Hadley was running for the door before any of the others had even started to move.

6 4 .

I'm dressed in black once more. Wearing the obligatory shade of darkness those peddling fashion in color request we do. And that's okay. It suits me. I don't want or need to be seen. At least, not until I choose to be.

I sweep the floors, cap pulled down tight as I move from one side of the catwalk to the other. It's the usual chaos. Chaos she'd enjoy. It'll be the risk, that sense of not knowing, of her seeing everything teeter on the brink of disaster, before she decides to rein it in. It's power, you see. That sense of control, of deciding, manipulating the future to suit her.

She did it to me. I'm here to do it to her. To shape my own destiny. To push aside her own prediction of the future and turn it into mine. I can see her on the back room floor, through the long black curtains. She's wearing a pale yellow dress. I'll admit, it gives me pause. To see her move in a color I remember, something we shared, and for a split second I become her, watching me move in a dress, to have eyes as large as she must once have had for me.

But was what I did worth what I got? To turn everything on its head and punish … no, almost end an already sorry life? I don't think so.

The curtain closes and I'm in darkness. She's gone, as she left me before.

— ✖ —

I left with a packed lunch, money, and a contact at a small rural paper. I'd told Madam Rai of my love for the written word. She'd called a friend. I had somewhere to go. But as I left the safety of her house, I knew in my heart the clouds of a masked past were already gathering.

I'd fought it. Kept my head down. But the pull of the city and the frustration of knowing they were there was too strong. It had been years, and I'd carved out a normal life, but the faces of my past kept creeping in. There would be no future without erasing the past. I took a job at the *Globe and Mail*, settled into an apartment, waited, and watched.

It was almost a year before I saw her. I didn't know her name, but I recognized her at the bar he'd first found her in. She was still beautiful, there was no doubt about that. She had long blonde hair and wore three flowers in it. Was she still with him?

I needed to know if I had it in me. If I could go through with the thoughts that wouldn't leave me. What started as a drink soon turned into something else. She was a free spirit, much lighter than me, though most are. Her hands were gentle, lovely. It should have been hard to hate her, but it wasn't. These lovely, gentle hands had done what they'd done to me – to him.

We lay there in her small bed beside an open window next to the street. Rain bucketed down outside. Dark streets glistened beneath the streetlights we could see from where we were secreted. Their soft glow reached us, turning my pale skin translucent.

I flinched as her finger found the ridge of the scar across the flat of my tummy. 'What happened here?' she asked, her eyes studying my face.

'You,' I replied, without looking at her.

'Sorry?' she said, moving in closer, a frown spreading across her face.

I ripped a small reading lamp from a socket on the wall and swung it hard into the side of her face. She screamed as I struck her with it again, this time using its square metal base. I heard the crunch of her jaw dislocating, then a sucking sound as blood congealed in her throat. I could feel her hot tears, felt her body shaking as I reached for one of those beautiful soft hands, and broke it.

I dressed quickly and stepped out into the dark of the street as a fresh wave of water fell from the heavens. I walked to a nearby tree and vomited into a gutter beside it. She hadn't deserved that, but I'd needed it. The past had become the present once more.

— ✖ —

Now they move beneath me from my position in the rafters. I've seen the running sheet, she'll close the show, so I have plenty of time. From up here I can see the idiots that Chris organized to rob him. They're looking after her, and I have to ask myself, will Hadley and his colleagues show?

Shouldn't Hadley be here already? Paul's dumb, but I saw the recognition in his face. That angry fire I'd expect from anyone who knows he's been tricked. Trapped. He'll have called him from the cell he's been left to rot in. Hadley will connect the dots and realization will hit home. He's too smart not to know. I know him and I'd expect, by now, he'll know me. What I needed to do is done. I'm ready.

But first, she and I need to talk.

There she goes, walking down the hall ten minutes before her set, on time. I follow her, quietly. She's heading for the washrooms. I can see her undoing the top of her clutch, running fingers gently through its contents to make sure what she needs is still there.

The oversized door is in front of us. She marches toward it, not looking back. You'd think she would have learnt. She hasn't. Which is fortunate. She doesn't see me at first, as she turns to close the door. I'm standing there with a gun now trained on her forehead. Then she does, and her eyes go to my gun. They widen, and I kick the door. It hits her hard in the mouth.

'Ahh … fuuuccck!'

Blood begins to gush through her teeth, two of which are now jagged and broken. She does her best to catch the fragments in her cupped hands. Blood runs through her fingers, down the front of her pale yellow dress and onto the floor.

'What the fuuuu–'

I silence her with a gloved hand and close the door behind us.

'Do you know who I am?' I whisper, pressing the gun to the right side of her head. I remove my cap and present myself under the washroom light.

She's staring at me through the pain. I can see it dawning on her, pupils dilating, wide black circles that strain to capture as much of the face before her as they allow.

'Don't fuck with me, Frankie. Or should I call you Christie now?'

I press the gun harder against her skin; it bunches. She chokes, coughing and nodding at the same time. She pulls away from the gun, shaking her head from side to side, her lips already swollen. 'Ka … Kat. You're Kat,' she says spitting more blood into her hands.

'You're right, honey,' I say, smiling. 'Miss me?'

'I … I–'

'What? Didn't ever think we'd be doing this?'

Her face changes, crumbles on itself, bottom lip trembling.

'Where did you think I'd go? Let me guess. Nowhere.'

I pull the gun away from her head so I can look at her.

'Do you know what hurt the most? It wasn't you leaving … though you did. What hurt more was having you stay.'

Despite the bloody mess that is her mouth, she manages to look puzzled.

'What? You didn't think I saw you there? Watching me on the floor as one girl after another raped me? Tore and shredded the dress you made for me? And for what, Christie? What did you hope to gain? Teenage revenge? An enemy?'

She stands still, head hanging, saying nothing.

'Well you succeeded. Take the coke out.'

'Wh … wha?' she replies.

'You heard me. The cocaine in your clutch. Take it out. Rack up a line.'

She doesn't want to.

'That's what you came in here for, right? Your girls are heading out shortly, best you get things underway.' I cock the trigger and point the end of the gun toward her face.

She lifts her clutch over the thin glass shelf below the mirror. 'I have money. You … you can–'

'Rack it up!'

Christie jumps, her clutch falling to the floor. She's sobbing now, mascara running down her face. She drops to a knee, picks up the things that have fallen out and withdraws a bag of coke. Its contents spill onto the glass, forming a small pyramid of powder speckled with droplets of blood.

'Do it!' I scream.

She looks hesitant.

'Fucking do it … or die.'

She pulls a single note out of a jacket pocket and rolls it with blood-covered fingers. She's shaking badly now. She presses a bill to a nostril, leans in to the uncut powder and inhales. I force her to go again.

'Do you know why I'm here?'

'T-to kill me?'

'Do you think I shouldn't?'

She tries to bite her bottom lip, which I appreciate. She's trembling and finding it hard to focus. She pulls away from me.

'Give me the scissors.'

She's shaking harder now as she bends her neck forward. The chain falls over it and she hands me the necklace.

'Did you fuck him?'

'Wha? I'm not shhure I unnersta–'

'Paul. The boy from juvie? The one you sacrificed me for?'

'Tha … tha was your choishh. Noh mine.'

Clearly the coke has kicked in.

'Are you fucking serious? I did nothing more than kiss him.'

'An whah? You thinc tha planss … noh the fuckn futcha we 'ad planss for, was woorth it?'

'Did you recognize him?'

'Who? Paul? Ish he–

'He works for Hadley.'

'He'ssh noh–'

'Yeah. He is.'

She's still. As much as the coke allows her to be. 'So … yurff targoded Hadley? Thish whole shing, whash appened here ish … ish … for me?'

I just nod, then whip the gun hard into her head, knocking her unconscious.

I've parked a trolley in front of the door. Inside it are black covers used to hide the things you're supposed to remove unseen. I open the door gently, check the hallway, lift Christie over one shoulder and drop her into it, then cover her.

6 5 .

'Hi, Hadley, it's me,' said Christie's voice message.

Her voice was loud and clear, but he could hear the uncertainty coming through the dashboard of his truck as he drove. The time said he'd received it four hours ago. His phone had been switched off as he dealt with one calamity after another. He hadn't realized her next show was scheduled for tonight. He checked the time on his dash, weaved his way through traffic as she continued.

'I was hoping … but I haven't heard from you, so I'm guessing you're not available. I can't lie. It's a shame as I thought you were back … back to look after me.'

He could hear the steady sound of an engine in the background. She was in her car, no doubt en route to the venue. He could hear a window being lowered, the sound of a lighter and her inhaling. She did that to calm herself; she didn't smoke that often. He could tell she was pissed.

She'd called again less than an hour ago, this time to let him know she'd gone with an alternative. He stopped the message without listening to the end of it, and pushed his foot down on the throttle, roaring through traffic as quickly as he could, streetlights flashing overhead.

In no time at all he could see the lights of the center. He'd gone solo, though he knew the rest of team were behind him. He hadn't needed to say anything, they'd figure it out. He rushed to the valet service, threw keys at the closest worker and ran for the door.

The show was almost done. It wasn't until he saw Jonas that he thought the worst. Hadley scoured the room – there was no rationale to the way they were positioned.

'Where is she?' he asked.

'Back stage,' said Jonas. 'Don't, Hadley,' he said, placing a hand on Hadley's chest. 'We've got it under control.'

Hadley looked down at Jonas, who placed his good hand over the handle of a gun. It was tucked into a shoulder strap almost hidden by the bandages of his broken arm.

'The team's in there and they have the floor covered,' said Jonas.

'So where is she?'

'She ducked into the washrooms.'

'For what? How long ago?'

Jonas shrugged his shoulders. 'That's not my business. A few minutes ago.'

'You're a fucking idiot. Your business is exactly what it is. Which one?'

'Don't be a dick, Hadley. Whatever you think you can do isn't required. We're under control. The floor is covered.'

'I'm not here to doubt, Jonas. I mean no disrespect. Where is she?'

Jonas stared through him. 'She's in there,' he said, pointing down the hall at a distant gray door with a silhouette of a woman on it. It was partially open.

'Are you sure?' Hadley could tell that he wasn't.

He ran for the door, pushed it open. There was no one inside. On a glass shelf there were telltale signs of coke and traces of bloodied fingerprints, and more blood was splashed on the back of the door. There was pool of it on the floor.

His search was interrupted by the loud call of a horn. They were being summoned for the final walk. He recognized it as something Christie would do. He ran to the side of the stage – nothing. He surveyed the arena, but there was no sign of her. Everything was wrong.

Her models appeared in sequence, stretching out in the rainbow colors he'd seen several months ago as the lights overhead dimmed.

'And your final designer, the one and only ... Christie Fallon!' boomed the announcer over the PA system.

One by one the models filed out to rapturous applause, a picture of calm, of order, though Hadley knew better. He pushed past staff to the left of the stage, ignoring the catwalk. He ran toward the back rooms, passing the curtains that masked it all from the audience out front.

'Where's Emily?'

It was chaos out back. Staff were panicking, the models were being talked down, there was no sign of Christie. He didn't recognize any of the faces.

'Emily, Christie's assistant. Is she here? Emily? Emily!'

'Shhh,' said a staff member in black to his right. 'They'll hear you out front.'

Emily appeared. 'Hadley?'

'Where's Christie?' he asked.

'No idea. Though her timing couldn't be worse. I need to–'

But he was gone, running from one side of the stage to the other, pulling aside curtains, searching back rooms, checking the washroom doors for a sign, speaking to staff – anything to discover where she was.

She'd be dressed in black. The girl, Kat. Her only way in would have been as staff. His head was reeling, there were more than a hundred of them in the building. There was no time.

Hadley remembered her slapping Christie at her last event. She'd left as a model. Was she out there now? Dressed as one? Or would she be media? With a press pass, camera at the ready? For what?

Something she'd done. Something she'd want to see. His head hurt as he spun from one thought to the next.

He saw Arvin coming through a door near the entrance, Toni close behind him, and Paul arguing with Jonas at the door. He waved at them, spun his fingers in the air, directing them to split up and move quickly.

They followed his order. It would happen before the end of her set, he knew it. He watched the models come and go, moving from one outfit to the next. Time was ticking, they were almost done. Sweat ran freely down the sides of his temples and down the small of his back

Then they were marching out as a unit, the final parade of all her work. His heart was pounding, he was helpless, left without a clue, with nothing.

Then he looked up.

6 6.

Applause rang out as the models took to the stage one final time. Cameras pushed the darkness from every corner of the room as they pulsed like strobe lights on either side of the runway.

Long legs stretched in the tallest of heels as the staff and music called them into their final positions. A crescendo of noise told everyone that Christie had once again delivered the goods.

Christie woke. Her head pounded and her jaw ached. She was confused about where she was, what she was doing. She tried to bring her hand to her head, but couldn't move it. It was tied to something, stretched out and fastened. She managed to turn her head, only slightly, but enough to realize things weren't as they should be.

Her stomach flipped. She was up high in the roof, suspended above the crowd, the catwalk, above everything. Cameras sparked and flashed below her. How had she gotten here? Then panic set in. She tried to scream, but she was gagged, her mouth full of what felt like a soft cloth, with tape over it. She could barely breathe. She shook her head, tried to pull free, searched the rest of her body, saw the blood on her yellow dress, grunted with the effort before it all came crashing in.

It had been her. The girl in the white latex suit. The one she had teased and fucked, who had laughed and antagonized her. Who had written about her. It had been Kat, her old friend. The girl she'd hurt so many years ago. How hadn't she known? She'd been wasted. Though she'd looked nothing like the girl Christie had known. She'd been nonchalant about who she used.

Christie's nostrils flared as she tried to get fresh air into her lungs.

'Hurts, doesn't it?' said Kat, squatting on a platform opposite her.

Christie turned her head the other way. Kat was dressed in black, a cap pulled down tight, her eyes bright underneath.

She tried to speak, could only make a strangled sound.

'Don't bother trying to talk. Actions speak louder than words, right? And you've said plenty, honey.'

Kat crossed to her, keeping a low profile as she moved, placing her face inches from Christie's.

'This has been a long time coming, Christie. You almost ruined me. Left me in pieces behind you. I was broken. I mean, what kind of friend … no, what kind of lover, leaves a seventeen-year-old girl on a floor to be raped by fucking savages? And for what? A kiss?' Kat spat on the floor. 'The thought of you – of ending you – helped pull me together. And here I am, whole.'

Christie made a muffled sound.

'Do you know why I slept with you? Pretended to be your little plaything? I wanted to know if you'd recognize me. Well, you didn't. More importantly, I wanted to know if you were still the arrogant, heartless bitch I remembered.' Kat looked directly at her.

Christie turned away as tears filled her eyes, the pain of knowing, of remembering what she'd done. Of who she'd become. Knowing it was all too late.

'Needless to say, the conclusion I came to brought us together. It wasn't easy getting you up here,' she said, surveying the crowd below. 'It'll be much easier getting you down.'

Christie's eyes were wide. She began thrashing, though couldn't break free. She was tied to a long steel rod.

'Don't worry, lover. They'll know it's your collection.'

Kat bent over and kissed her wet cheeks.

Hadley thought he saw movement deep within the roof. He was in survival mode. Nothing made sense. Christie would die if he couldn't figure it out. That much he was confident of.

He was oblivious to the crowd around him. He focused on an area in the roof and nothing else. He saw it again. Not much more than a shadow. The stage lights were facing down, though the sidelights in the roof were picking up the movement behind them.

He ran past the audience watching the end of Christie's set. He was almost at the back wall when he looked up again and saw her leg poking out from the rafters, a bit of her yellow dress wrapped around it. She was attached to something. Hadley ran his eyes down the wall; there were ropes and pulleys cinched to the side of it. She was strapped to some sort of gurney that had gotten her up there.

Christie was hovering above the center of the stage. One pulley led to another, and now he understood what Kat was doing. He felt his whole body shaking. He turned to look through the curtains as the applause continued, the models standing sideways, facing the back of the runway, waiting for the designer to show her face.

The media and the huge audience behind them waited for Christie to make her appearance. Each model stood still, in promotion mode, their lips stretched across perfect teeth as they waited for her arrival.

Hadley ran toward the pulleys, but they were already spinning. He looked up in disbelief as Christie fell gracefully from the roof in a sweeping arc, her right arm held out to the crowd via a steel rod, as if receiving the adulation. He could hear her screaming through a gag as she swung past him; saw the terror in her eyes as she plummeted toward the stage, a cable wrapped around her waist. It tightened, and sliced through her lower body.

Smiles disappeared as Christie swung down through the black curtains toward the crowd, blood gushing from the fissure in her abdomen, spraying the faces of the models underneath her.

Applause gave way to screaming, and cameras burst to life as photographers thought of the front page instead of fashion. The audience rose as one to its feet, stampeding toward the exit.

Christie's head flopped to one side as her eyes closed. The arcs began to slow as the trail of blood below her thickened.

Hadley stood underneath her. He caught a heel, then a foot, and gently stopped her moving. He pulled her down, reached up and undid the straps, ignoring the cameras that flashed around him. He released her broken body and cradled her gently to the floor, tears streamed down his face.

'Christie? Christie, honey?' he said, holding her chin.

He shook her. But she was gone.

Toni, Paul and Arvin surrounded him, blocking the cameras.

'Hadley?' said Toni. 'Hadley. I'm sorry. What happened? What can we do?'

He was still shaking as his head rose.

'She's here … Kat. Get the fucking girl,' he said, without looking up.

6 7 .

Arvin worked his way through the crowd. He watched Toni and Paul run for opposite sides of the building. Hadley was on the floor holding what was left of Christie. He was surrounded by medics, but they were already covering her body and attempting to prise him away from her.

Arvin stood still, stopped himself amid the chaos. There was plenty of it. Tears ran down faces. People were running, others were stationary, shocked at what had happened. Several were screaming, hiding their faces, trying to understand what they'd seen.

Arvin breathed deeply, forcing himself to a quiet calm. He knew this venue, he'd been here before. What would he do if he was her? She'd be dressed as staff, in black. She'd been in the roof; she'd needed to hide, and dark clothes would keep her in shadow. Had she come down after Christie had fallen? Everyone had been focused on Christie, though Arvin knew Kat wouldn't have been. Her job was done the moment she let Christie go. She would have heard the result.

Arvin searched the roof of the arena and the struts beneath, for any sign of movement. There was nothing. He ran toward the back of the stage, through the cluster of models pushing the other way. He took a back door and stairs to a landing above the floor. Now he had a clear view of the room, unobstructed by the activity below him. He searched the roof again; he could see the cables that held the gurney above him. He traced them to the pulleys on the walls. They were slack.

He saw a large square duct several feet above the platform Christie had fallen from. The gray mesh casing was on, but one of the corners hadn't been fastened properly. It tapped the wall gently as air poured through it.

Arvin pictured the large pipes connected to the east side of the building. He climbed down and began running for the side door.

Kat scrambled through the steel duct, breathing heavily as she pulled herself along. She'd left her platform the second she'd let Christie go. The look in Christie's eyes as she fell had been more than enough, though it hadn't stopped Kat from looking back at the mess below before she eased herself into the duct and pulled the casing shut.

She'd seen Arvin standing in the middle of the arena, before he turned and looked up, then ran toward the back of the room. She'd been right to move. She heard the reaction from the floor. She couldn't help but smile through tears as she slid through the air duct, crab-like, determined to get to the vents on the other side.

She'd seen Paul out there – he must have escaped, but the damage was done. He'd end up back inside, anyway.

Just get out, Kat, into the fresh air. Leave this place. You've done what you set out to do.

She could hear sirens in the distance. Good. The more chaos the better. Another sixty feet and she'd be on her way. It was cold in the duct as air was forced through it from the giant turbines connecting the outside world to this one. She wasn't going all the way. There was a storage room beside the vents inside the building, just to the left of the exit.

Light appeared through the mesh to the side of the duct she was in. The whirring of the turbines was louder now. Kat pushed the mesh away from the wall. She worked her way through it and gently lowered herself to the floor.

She adjusted her cap and patted herself down. She pressed the side of her head to the door. The corridor outside sounded quiet enough;

all she could hear was the steady drone of the turbines beyond the service door. The exit was only thirty feet away. Kat pulled the service door open and stepped out. No one to the right. She swung her head the other way. Arvin was standing in front of the exit to her left, his gun arm extended directly at her.

'You must be Kat,' he said.

'I don't know what you're talking about,' she replied, walking toward him. 'There was a problem with the air vents. I–'

'You should know he's dead.'

Arvin had no choice other than to stall her. He had no back up. He was still weak from the drugs and the wound he'd received in the attack.

'Who?'

'Your tall friend, the drug dealer. The one you asked to poison me.'

'Really, Arvin? You think you'd be standing here if I'd wanted you dead?' She took a step toward him, her arms out.

In one motion she raised a hand, reached behind her head and threw her cap at him, before sliding across the floor trying to sweep his leg. He was quick enough to jump. Then she was on her feet, pushing off one wall and spinning at him with a round house kick that found its mark in the center of his back, slamming him into the wall as his gun emptied itself into it, then fell to the ground.

She was fast. Arvin braced himself. Her stance told him she was practiced. Kat lunged forward, leading with her right fist, which flew past his face. Her left connected with it before he could think to turn. Arvin's head rocked sideways, but he managed to bring his elbow back around to hit her hard in the side of her chest. He heard air rush from her lungs.

He pushed forward, bringing a knee up hard into her stomach. She turned, and it collided with her hip as she spun. She kept going, avoiding his follow through, bringing two hands down hard on the back of his neck. He fell to the floor.

Kat stood over him. 'You should know that I liked you, Arvin. I'm sorry it came to this, though she got what she deserved. Stay out of it.'

Arvin looked up, only to see the side of her foot rushing toward his head. And he was gone.

Kat ran for the eastern exit, pulled open the door to fresh air and stepped out into the night. She felt relief – before Paul's fist slammed into her face. She hit the ground hard, stunned. Then she was being lifted and dumped into something, felt a soft cloth against her face. There was the sharp smell of chloroform. She fell into darkness.

'Hadley? It's Paul. I'm heading for the front exit, think I've got a tail on her. Will keep you posted. Over.'

Paul pushed his trolley to the far side of the parking lot, where he'd left his truck. The lights in the far corner had been busted out, so it was hidden in shadow. He wrapped the cloth around her, checked behind him then quickly dumped her into the open rear door of the cab.

He started up his truck and pulled out into a side street. A line of blue and red lights filtered into the far side of parking lot, sirens screaming as they surrounded the building. Paul allowed himself to smile as he pulled on to the highway and lost himself in a sea of lights.

68.

'Hadley?'

'Go on, Paul,' Hadley responded.

Toni listened to their voices on her RT, checked her location. She was in the eastern corridor of the arena. She'd seen Arvin heading this way, and when he hadn't reappeared, had crossed the floor to find him.

She turned the corner and saw him lying on the ground beside the door. She checked his pulse – it was strong and he was breathing, so she pushed on toward the door.

She opened it in time to see Paul pulling out of a side exit two hundred feet away, his truck's tires squealing. In spite of what had just happened, the motherfucker had lied to them. He had Kat, she was sure of it.

Toni turned back toward the door and spotted a motorbike beside it. A black helmet was resting on a handlebar and the keys were in the ignition.

She recalled Arvin mentioning their girl had lost him on a bike. Looked like she'd been planning on a quick getaway. Toni grabbed the helmet, straddled the seat, switched her RT to a private line and called Hadley.

'Just seen Paul pulling out of the eastern exit, pretty sure he's got her. I'm on a bike and in pursuit. Over.'

'Bastard. Don't lose him, Toni. Keep your phone on … I'll track you. I'll be following.'

She pulled the helmet on, keyed the ignition and the bike roared to life. She spun the back wheel round and headed for the exit. She turned the corner just as the police drove into the parking lot.

Paul checked his rearview. There were lights in every lane, everything seemed normal. He didn't have far to go. The chloroform would keep her asleep until they got there. He checked the silhouette of her body in the back of the cab. It was still. He smiled to himself, silently applauding his earlier decision to circle to the back of the arena and park not far from where he'd spotted her bike.

Had he been the only one listening when Arvin had talked about her riding a motorbike?

He'd left the arena and had made for the exit at the back of it. He heard them fighting from behind the door. Arvin was still weak. If it opened, it had to be her. And he'd been there to take her out.

He activated his hands-free screen, and Jordan's name sprung up.

'Yeah, Hammer?'

'Hey, Jords. Good news, man. I've got her.'

'Got who?' He sounded like he'd been asleep.

'The girl, buddy. The girl who almost killed you.'

Still nothing.

'The one who cut your fucking wrists!'

'What the fuck? Holy shit! Is she … alive?'

'Yes she is.'

'Right. Okay.'

'I need the money though, buddy. Cash, no checks, no fucking transfers and shit. Cash, okay? All of it. We clear?'

'I'm not sure I can raise that kind of coin–'

'Fuck off, Jordan! I'll need it. The whole one-twenty-five. I'm leaving town as soon as I hand her over. I need to know you're good for it or she's gone.'

'Yeah, alright. Bring her in.'

'I'll be there in twenty.'

Paul wound his way north of the city up Bathurst before taking a side route towards Jordan's York Mills-Windfields estate. He focused on the road, occasionally flicking his eyes to the rearview, seeing nothing behind him but distant light on the horizon. So far so good.

Toni could see his taillights in the distance. His truck rode high so he was easy to spot. The night air was brisk; she wasn't dressed for it, but loved being back on a bike. It had been years. She'd forgotten how much she missed it.

Her jacket was slightly open at the neck, the cool air wrapping itself around her. A bright half moon shed its light between tall leafless trees. Toni dropped a gear and took a sharp left to follow him off the main road. She killed the headlight. She steered the bike into the center of the road until her eyes adjusted to the darkness, thoughts racing through her head.

What was Paul up to? This whole thing made no sense.

Christie was dead – she'd been an A-grade bitch. Toni had never liked her.

Kat had planned this retribution, acted on her need for revenge. Was it extreme? Of course it was. Though what would Toni have done if Christie had organized a raping party for her? She'd have killed her.

The girl's a psychopath.

Is she really?

So what had Paul done? What wasn't he telling them?

Toni rode past one oversized gate and on to the next. They were heading for Jordan's place. She'd been there before, when he'd been placed under house arrest for an incident in Illinois. Hadley had posted them all on shifts to supplement Paul's own detail until it had blown over.

The guy was a pig, just like his bodyguard. They deserved each other. Her team didn't need this bullshit, though. The whole fucking thing was a mess.

She pulled up, killed the engine and walked the bike further in before stashing it in the trees to one side of the drive. She left the keys in the ignition and the helmet on a handle, taking note from the bike's owner.

Fortress-like gates were closed to the street. The house was enormous. It was a low-lying single-level complex nestled between two giant lawn mounds that hid most of it from view.

Toni walked round the back to the southern side, where she remembered there was a shed butted up against the wall. It was overhung by a tree, which they'd been forced to cut back when Jordan was under house arrest. That had been years ago, before his star had faded.

If she was nimble enough, she could climb the tree and jump across onto the shed roof.

She made it, climbed down and worked her way along the boundary, searching the dark, staying clear of the cameras and sensors.

The rock wall through the central part of the house was lit up on one side. A large rectangular pool glowed through the oversized glass doors leading to the back.

Toni worked her way closer in then lay flat on one of the grassy mounds, from where she could see inside the house. She watched as Paul carried Kat, slung over his shoulder, wrapped in gray cloth. He followed Jordan into the lounge and dropped her, sack-like, onto a large couch. Toni scrambled to a side door and slipped inside.

'You got it?' asked Paul.

'Yeah, it's here,' replied Jordan. 'Though first I want some answers. How do I know it's her?'

Paul ripped the cloth off her body.

Jordan exhaled.

'Wake her up.'

6 9 .

Paul held smelling salts under Kat's nose and she stirred, then opened her eyes. The lights were low and her head hurt. She tried to push herself up, but couldn't. Her hands were tied to her feet. She grunted.

'Do you remember me?' Jordan asked.

Kat's eyes were wide; she shook her head. She spotted Paul, which sparked a breathing frenzy through the gag silencing her.

'So you know this guy?' said Jordan.

She ignored them.

'Take off the gag, Hammer.'

Jordan held his wrists out to her. The scars were red, twisted, puckered and angry. Kat searched his face, the ageing rocker with serene blue eyes. For all his wealth and fame, he looked lost.

'You want to tell me why you did this?' asked Jordan.

'I don't know what you mean,' Kat replied.

'Don't lie to me, bitch! It was you I fucked that night, wasn't it?'

'Who would know?'

He slapped her hard across the face. Blood ran from a corner of her lip.

'Why did you cut me?' His face was screwed up as he spoke, his cheeks flushed. 'I don't know what you fed me, but I know you didn't want me dead, otherwise you wouldn't have called the cops. So let's call it a statement. Why bother?'

'Why don't you ask him?' she said, staring at Paul.

Jordan turned to look at Paul, then turned back. 'I'm asking you.'

Kat lowered her eyes. Jordan grabbed her face, squeezed her cheeks white. 'I'm going to ask you again. Why did you cut me?'

'I don't know. I saw your last show and thought you needed saving.'

Jordan punched her hard in the stomach; breath rushed out of her lungs. She fell from the couch to the floor, gasping. Air found its way back in and she began to laugh, lightly at first then a deep resonant laughter that filled the room.

'You think this is funny?' asked Jordan, pacing the floor. 'Give me a gun, Hammer.'

'Listen, Jords. This chick is fucked in the head.'

'Give me a fucking gun!' he screamed.

Paul stood his ground. 'Where's the money? I told you I'd bring her to you in exchange for the money.'

'The blue and white bag by the door,' said Jordan, without taking his eyes off her.

Paul crossed the floor and grabbed it, tore open the zip and bounced the bundles of cash around inside it.

'Thanks, Jords,' he said, handing him a gun. 'This is clean, just remove your prints when you're done. I need to get going.'

'What was she talking about, Hammer?' Jordan asked, turning to face him, the gun hanging loosely in his hand. 'Do you know this girl?'

'Like I said, she's a psychopath. Why else would she fuck, cut and leave you, then call it in, man? Can't you see what we're dealing with here?'

Jordan took a step back. 'Wait. How do you know her, Hammer? Is she here because of you?'

Paul held his hands out. 'Jords ... listen buddy. This girl, she's ... she's a fucking manipulator, man! Do you get that? She's a journalist. She ... she crawls into your head, wreaks havoc, takes the shit she needs and then she fucks you with it! I'm done with her, man. I've got to go.' He turned toward the door.

'You're not done, Paul,' he said, swinging the gun around in Paul's direction. 'I need to know what this is all about.'

Paul reached for the door anyway, only to be confronted by Toni with her gun arm extended.

'Why don't you tell him?' said Toni, her piece trained squarely at Paul's face, walking him back in.

'Who the fuck is this?' said Jordan. 'Wait. She works with you, doesn't she?'

Paul sighed from the doorway. 'What are you doing here, Toni?' he spat.

'Just following your lying ass from a crime scene. I see you've kidnapped our key suspect. That's helpful.'

'Toni—'

'I'm done listening to you, Paul.'

'What the fuck is going on here?' yelled Jordan.

'I need you to put down the gun, Jordan,' said Toni.

He lowered it to Kat's head and took a step closer. 'I don't see why I should. This thing almost killed me.'

Toni could see Kat tied up on the couch, bleeding and breathing heavily.

'Jordan, I'm asking you to drop the gun. Just put it down and let her speak.'

'Don't listen to her, Jords,' said Paul.

Jordan looked hesitant. 'This is bullshit,' he said, stepping backwards.

'Drop the bag on the floor and sit on the couch, Paul.'

Paul didn't move. His dark eyes were focused on Toni's face.

'Sit the fuck down, Paul, or I'll just pull the trigger. Your face could use it.'

'Fuck you, Rodriguez,' he replied.

The bag fell to the floor and he took his seat.

'Jordan, I know you've been hurt by this girl. We all have. But I need to you put the gun down and take a seat so we can figure this out. Can you do that for me?'

He stood still for while, nodded, then placed the gun on a coffee table and sat down.

'It's Kat, isn't it?' asked Toni, her gun still pointing at Paul's head.

Kat nodded, but avoided looking at her.

'We know each other, don't we?' asked Toni. 'Why don't you tell us what's going on here? What's your connection with Paul?'

Kat said nothing.

'Come on, honey. Christie's dead.'

'What the fuck! Christie … as in Christie Fallon?' said Jordan.

Toni kept going. 'That's what you wanted, right? Well, if this shithead over here has his way, you'll be gone as well. What did he do to you?'

Kat surveyed the room. 'Can you at least undo the ropes between my hands and legs?'

Toni pulled a knife from her boot and cut the rope linking the two together, leaving her wrists and feet tied.

Kat spat blood onto the floor. She surveyed the room and the three faces staring back at her.

'Get her some water, Jordan,' said Toni.

Jordan got up and came back with a bottle of water, which he threw to her before retaking his seat.

Kat opened the lid and sipped before speaking. 'I met him at an institution I was being held in. At the time I was in a relationship with a girl.'

'Christie,' offered Toni.

'Frankie, as I knew her, but yes,' Kat replied, staring into space. 'Paul arrived; he wasn't much older than me.' She looked up at him. 'He was cute, naive about all of us, though gentle and fun.'

'Are you sure this is the same guy?' Toni said, waving her gun at Paul.

Kat stared at him, studied his face. 'He used to be. Time changes us all, I guess. I was foolish to think he'd be the same person.'

'He told us what happened to you when he was forced out. What

Christie did to you. So I understand why you retaliated, though I don't condone it.'

'What would you have done, Toni?'

'I couldn't say.'

'I don't think you realize what I've been through. Imagine if you'd come from a severely broken home. Christ, one of my parents killed the other with a broken dinner plate when I was nine years old!' Tears we're running freely down her cheeks now. 'I mean, what do you think it's like to be shifted from one family to another? To see the disappointment in everyone's faces when nothing works? To be locked up for a good portion of your life?' She wiped the tears from her face with the rope holding her wrists. 'I was left on a concrete floor, having been beaten and raped by girls you don't ever want to meet. I know you better than you think, Toni. You'd have killed her too.'

'You and I slept together. You targeted my employer, my colleagues, all of us – for what?'

Kat sighed, her shoulders sagged. 'A little attention, I guess. His, mostly.'

'And what? You discovered that Christie worked with us and hey presto, time to bring it all down, other clients included, right?'

She smiled. 'The world works in mysterious ways.'

'What did he do to you?' asked Toni.

'He was no better than the rest of them. He beat me. He took a life from me.' Tears pooled in her eyes as she spoke. 'This guy,' she said, raising her tied hands toward him, 'who I pinned so much hope on, turned me into my mother. And that was something I couldn't accept.'

'This is fucking bullshit,' said Paul from the back of the room. 'I don't need to listen to this.'

'What do you mean he took a life from you?' said Toni.

'I was pregnant. Only nine weeks along, though all was good. Then we argued. We fought, and he made a decision. He threw me down the stairs. Not happy with me being broken at the bottom of them, he followed me down, then kicked me in the stomach, killing the life inside of me. Then he left me there. I woke in a small clinic days later. I barely remembered getting there. I had a broken leg, a broken arm and fingers, as well as a broken soul,' she said, staring at him.

'So why drag us into all of this? Why not just kill the pair of them and walk away?'

'The fact that you worked with him, only to discover Christie was a client, made me hate you all. It made me want to make an example of both of them. She loved the stage, I thought it best she died on it. As for this guy, I wanted more for him. I hoped he'd be locked up for–'

A cushion knocked Toni off her feet, a heavy, thick, patterned thing that crashed into the side of her head, taking her to the ground. She got to her feet and scrambled for her gun.

Paul was up, reaching for his own sidearm before she heard the sound of a window smashing and looked over to see an outdoor chair tumbling through it. The chair collided with Paul, and was followed by a bloodied figure.

Hadley was on top of him, Paul scrambling for anything he could find to fend him off. Hadley's fists collided with his face. What was left of Paul's suit split down the back as he tried to hold Hadley's arms.

Jordan was on his feet, scrambling for the gun, before Toni tackled him to the floor.

Kat slid off the couch and along the ground. She picked up a large glass shard and began working it furiously between her hands. The first rope unraveled and she began working on her feet.

Toni had Jordan in a headlock. He tried to roll his body around and on top of her, turning bright red with the effort, but got nowhere as Toni's lock held.

Paul was out from underneath Hadley, his face slick with blood. They held each other by the collar. Paul reached back, ripped the leg off a wooden drinks stand and brought it hard across the back of Hadley's head. Decanters and glasses shattered as Hadley joined them on the floor.

Paul took a knife from his boot, stepped above Hadley and stood over him. Toni was scrambling for the gun before Kat drove herself into Paul. The pair fell through the broken window and into the pool.

Hadley crawled back to his feet, before Toni and Jordan followed him outside. They watched as the pool bubbled, tendrils of blood rising and blooming before Paul and Kat surfaced, Paul's arm around her neck and the knife under her chin.

Toni's gun was aimed carefully at them.

'Let me end it, Toni,' Paul screamed. 'All I ever did was fight back, that was it. This bitch is a liar and a killer! She's ruined us all. I'm fucked anyway, she's seen to that!'

'He's the liar, Toni,' said Kat, her head barely above the water. 'He doesn't care about anyone but himself. He's only here for money. Kill us both if you have to.'

Toni moved her gun from one face to the next, ignoring the voices around her. She thought of her own life, her own family's struggles; the poverty and oppression they had lived under. She saw Paul's mouth moving, watched the knife in his hand. She searched Kat's face, her pale skin and dark eyes. She thought of the body bag Christie lay under, then pulled the trigger.

E P O L O G U E
— N O T E   T O   S E L F

I want to talk about the future and how we choose to see it. For the longest time I've been a prisoner looking back. Someone trapped in history. In things I haven't been able to let go of, for whatever reason. And believe me when I say, there are a lot of them.

I've come from a tough upbringing. Things really didn't go my way. I think of the much-lauded Nature versus Nurture debate, of its contributors in Freud, Jung and Galton. You know the study, where psychologists have argued you're made up of who you were born to, versus how or what you were taught as you grew.

I'm its worse case study. What happens when you're born into an ugly family and then, after you've left it, grow up in an ugly environment? Bad things, you'd think. Here's where I nod slowly.

Yet, here I am. Writing to you, in what I hope is a thoughtful, carefully laid out piece. I'm not sure how you'll get to read this, though chances are you've read about me. I acknowledge, even the ugliest of killers, rapists and the poorest of thieves have managed to put pen to paper and have successfully tricked their readers, who may or may not become suitors, into thinking they're nice people. I promise you two things: that's not what I'm trying to do here; and I know that I'm good. Promise.

What does a future look like to you? Are you a fan of the unknown? A planner or more of a take-whatever-comes kind of personality? There's merit in both, though I'd have to say I probably fall into the latter. To a point. There are things I have planned for, things I have done. Some, in all honesty, I haven't been proud of (see earlier note), though none have given me a clear view on how I might tackle a future. Who knows what lies around the corner?

Take Antoni Gaudi, the great Spanish architect who helped shape and transform the city of Barcelona with his Parc Guell, his masked balconies, his rooftops and his giant melted-wax cathedral that is Sagrada Familia, with its tall, cone-like spires, still being built to this day. He knew he wouldn't see their completion, though a trolley car ensured he didn't see much of his vision at all.

There are consequences of looking ahead, just as there are consequences of not. Maybe I've always been scared of the future? Of being forever guilty of living in the now, unwilling to plan for anything beyond an immediate goal.

Well, I'm seated on a plane hurtling toward some kind of a future, heading for a country I've never been to before. In fact, this is my first flight to anywhere. My partner sits next to me. She's not what I thought she'd be. She's shared the place I grew up in, but was born and bred in a country much further south. We've traded stories. Mine has been ugly, though hers has been nowhere near a picnic. Either way she's here and I'm thankful for it. Thankful for someone with the capacity to look past an ugly present with a thought to creating a better future.

Right now we have no plan. We have money, thanks J.F. Thank you, Hadley, you are one of the nicest men I've ever known and I'm thankful for it. Sorry, Arvin, but I'm sure the extremes I've pushed you to might lead to a rethink of what you want and need from this life. I wish you all the best.

We have some semblance of direction and a willingness – no, a need – to be together. This is about creating distance, putting the past where it belongs, behind us.

There's a coastline below me. Turquoise waters with caramel sands. I don't know what to expect. We crossed mountainous terrain, a crumpled blanket of land lightly covered in patches of snow stubbornly refusing to give in to a change of season.

I thought about crashing. Our plane hurtling toward a rocky outcrop that would sweep the undercarriage out from beneath us, leaving a battered tube of steel that would drive itself into a wall of rock, crushing almost everyone.

I said, almost. We're seated at the back. Miraculous survivors, a duo removed from all civilisation, presumed dead, left alone to fend for ourselves, to look after each other, isolated from the rest of the world. Or something close to that. Am I nervous about where I'm going? Of course. Though for first time in my life, it feels like a good thing. My mind and my eyes are open to a future.

REVIEWS

Thank you for taking the time to read *The Security*.
I hope you enjoyed it. It's tough to get noticed,
so if you loved it, let other readers know by leaving
a review on either Amazon or Goodreads.
I really appreciate it.

ACKNOWLEDGEMENTS

I want to start with you. Thank you for taking the time to purchase this book and to read it. There are plenty of writers out there to choose from, so I appreciate you finding me. There are several people I would like to thank, Janet Hutchinson – for her wisdom in structure and sage advice around making a good book, great. To Sue Copsey, my wonderful editor and local confidant. To my wife Lou; my daughters Zambezi and Coco; to the wonderful calm presence that was our pet Labrador - Vader, who left us as I finished this.

AUTHOR BIO

Scott Butler's first home was on an air-force base in
Blenheim, New Zealand. His love of books came from
the birthday gift his father continues to give him
every year. Scott works in advertising. He writes novels,
short stories and blogs about original ideas he wants to share.
If you enjoyed this book, take a look at an earlier work
with *Drive*. Or, for other regular short stories and blogs,
subscribe to his website: *scottbutler.co.nz*

https://twitter.com/blackinkdreams/
https://www.facebook.com/thewrittenwordinink/
https://www.instagram.com/scottbutlernz/

www.ingramcontent.com/pod-product-compliance
Lightning Source LLC
Chambersburg PA
CBHW021232060726
47590CB00005B/1732